The Roommates

Rachel Sargeant grew up in Lincolnshire. She spent several years living in Germany where she taught English and she now lives in Gloucestershire with her husband and children. She is a previous winner of *Writing Magazine*'s Crime Short Story competition, and her writing has appeared in *My Weekly*. She has published three novels and her most recent, *The Perfect Neighbours*, became a top ten Kindle bestseller.

 @RachelSargeant3
www.rachelsargeant.co.uk

Also by Rachel Sargeant

The Perfect Neighbours
The Good Teacher

RACHEL SARGEANT

THE ROOM MATES

HarperCollins*Publishers*

HarperCollins*Publishers* Ltd
1 London Bridge Street,
London SE1 9GF

www.harpercollins.co.uk

First published by HarperCollins*Publishers* 2019
2

ISBN: 978-0-00-833189-4 (PB)

Set in Minion by Palimpsest Book Production Ltd,
Falkirk, Stirlingshire

Printed and bound in the UK by CPI Group (UK) Ltd, Croydon CR0 4YY

MIX
Paper from
responsible sources
FSC™ C007454

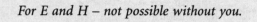

For E and H – not possible without you.

THREE YEARS AGO

A car horn blares and instinct makes her jump back. Male driver, early thirties. Mouth open in an oath as he speeds past, skidding on the bridge's frosty tarmac. She can't be bothered to gesture after him. Defiance gone.

Clutching her elbows for warmth, she makes it to the opposite side. Her jacket's not much of a coat these days. Zip bust from straining. The barrier along the side of the bridge is tall – nearly her height – but she peers between its vertical railings. The river below looks benign. No boats are out in mid-winter to ruffle its grey-green surface. A few dog walkers and cyclists brave the promenade. The café's open but the air's too bitter even for smokers to sit outside.

Wind picks up, making her stumble. For a moment she longs for the warmth of the bonfire under the bridge where the others will be. A few cans and a bit of weed. Where's the harm? But she can't go there because of Danno. Can't bear to see her betrayal reflected in his eyes. To see how her lies have destroyed him.

With her back against the barrier, sheltering from the worst of the weather, she squats and watches the traffic. When a passing lorry causes the bridge to judder, a change of plan flits through her mind. It might be quicker, more certain. But she can't do that to a driver. She's damaged enough people. People she loves. Her eyes smart. She stands up.

Searching for places to climb, she walks close to the barrier and spots possible toeholds – welded joints on some of the metal posts that are fixed into the ground at regular intervals There's a lull in the traffic and she hears her heartbeat. Loud. A shiver passes through her. Can she do this? What else is there? No one wants her, can't blame Mum and Jade.

In one swift movement, she grips two railings, wedges the side of her foot on a bolt and hauls herself up. An icy blast hits her head and neck. When she looks down, the river looms in and out of focus. Her head spins so much, she's sure she'll over-balance. Determination deserts her and the dizziness makes her afraid. Her hands clench the top rail and she ignores how much the cold metal burns.

As she stares down at the water, Leo's face flashes across her mind. This isn't because of Danno – or Mum or Jade. Most of all she's failed Leo. Her breathing slows and the unsteadiness fades. Her doubts begin to disappear. She levers herself higher.

No more pain, no more loss, no more hurting those who care – used to care. The burden lifts. Limbs and belly light for the first time in months. All over. She smiles. Places a knee on the top of the barrier. One final breath.

"Amber!" A voice shrieks along the bridge before the wind swallows it whole.

PRESENT DAY

Chapter 1

Sunday 25 September

Imogen

"You should have gone to a Russell Group university." Imo's mother makes her pronouncement after ten minutes of stop-start traffic inside the campus. She's got her brave face on, pretending to be forthright and normal.

Imo shrinks into the back seat and casts an anxious glance outside, but there's no change in the faces of the students walking past. They haven't heard the insult despite the open car windows. Wide-eyed and chatting, they stream on, like Glasto, but without the mud and wellies. It's been warm all month. Imo was sunbathing in the garden yesterday, trying to suppress her gut-wrenching nervousness about today. So much is riding on it. Her chance to escape the life of grief and guilt that she and her family haunt.

What does her mother mean anyway? What difference does a university league table make to the traffic jam? Has she forgotten the free-for-all to get into Freddie's uni four years ago? But Imo remembers her mother wasn't there. Dad and Imo took Freddie.

That same day Mum drove Sophia to Nottingham. Imo holds back a sigh; they were ordinary then.

A girl in a bright pink T-shirt steps up to her father's window. "Welcome to the Abbey." She hands him a hessian bag with *Abbey Student Union* printed on the side in the same pink as the T-shirt.

Imo's belly flutters. It's happening. She's become part of the exclusive club of students who call it the Abbey despite it saying University of Abbeythorpe on the website. She leans forward, snatches the bag from her dad and looks inside. Leaflets on the Abbi Bar and Takeaway, the Student Welfare Service, and Avoiding STDs; a freshers' wristband and a packet of condoms. She quickly clutches the bag on her lap. If her dad had seen inside, he'd have turned the car around, despite being in one-way traffic. And Imo would have understood. Risk weighs differently in this family.

The car park is behind a line of bushes on the right side of the road. They park and debate whether to take the luggage with them. Freddie advises leaving it until they know where Imo's room is. Imo backs his suggestion; anything to avoid her old Groovy Chick duvet being paraded through reception. Her mum made her bring it, saying that uni tumble driers might damage her new one of the New York skyline. Imo didn't want that one either. It was a birthday present and she intends to leave everything about that day behind. She'll never be able to look back on turning eighteen with anything but ache and horror.

A large vehicle chugs into the car park. A boy in a high-vis jacket walks ahead and marshals it lengthways across four parking spaces. It's an ancient ice-cream van painted sky blue, *Cloud's Coffee* in bold purple lettering above the serving hatch. A thickset woman, with hair the same shade of blue as the van, climbs out the driver's side. She pulls her seat forward and a girl jumps down. Taller and slimmer than the mother, and tidier too; her hair is short and blonde.

"Take this, Phoenix." A man in the passenger seat passes her a holdall. Imo can see where she gets her looks from. Father and daughter are blessed with cheekbones. Not many people could carry off a name like Phoenix, but this girl can. She exudes athletic star quality.

Imo's family follows the stream of people towards the main accommodation reception. Sweat seeps into her hoodie but she can't take it off despite the late summer heat. Even though she got it at the British Heart Foundation shop, it's a Jack Wills. And first impressions count. She spent two hours on Thursday planning her arrival outfit. Like her mother, she can play at normal.

They pass other students and their parents coming out of the building, clutching white envelopes, presumably containing the keys to their home for the next ten months. On the open day last year, Imo walked into this wood-panelled foyer, giggling with other Year Twelves on a trip from her school. Was that the last time she laughed and meant it? Not the fake chuckle she gives these days when her family play real-life charades. She swallows hard.

The hall echoes with the chatter of dozens of families. More students in pink T-shirts usher them into three lines. Imo's family stand in the left-hand queue. Imo shifts from foot to foot, unable to stop her legs from wobbling. Wishing her parents weren't with her. Hoping nobody will recognize them.

She swivels her head to look at the white-washed pillars behind the long reception counter. They're adorned with posters advertising the *Freshers' Welcome Party*. The line moves swiftly and soon Imo is in possession of her envelope, with instructions to turn right out of the building, enter the annexe at the back and take the stairs to the first floor. Scared of heights since Inspector Hare's visit shook her family rigid – since she saw the broken body and imagined the fall – she'd asked for a ground-floor room when she filled in the accommodation form. At least they haven't put her at the top of a tower block. It's been months since she climbed higher than the second storey in any building, even though it's an irrational fear. Inspector Hare had got it wrong again.

On the steps outside, right in the way of other families coming in and out, her parents stop for another debate about fetching the luggage. A Mini Convertible sweeps into the crisscross box of the no-parking zone in front of them. A high-heeled black sandal steps out of the driver's side. The sandal strap coils along a slender ankle. When the driver stands up, the strap disappears under the hem of black palazzo trousers. The young woman shakes her head and thick, dark curls cascade over her bare shoulders. She's wearing a white broderie anglaise blouse. A gypsy top, Imo's grandma would call it, but there's nothing rustic about its wearer.

"Mid-blue," Imo's dad says. "That's the colour I'd go for too if I ever got one."

Imo and her mother share a smile. Only her dad could see a beautiful woman and show more interest in her car.

A sudden prickling feeling tells Imo that she is being watched. It's a familiar sense, one she has struggled with regularly over the past few months. Freddie has too – even worse for him. She swallows down a knot of fear and forces herself to look at the crowd. Students and parents rush past in the heat, not looking her way. She tells herself that it's just her imagination. That nobody's recognized her.

Then she freezes. A tall, hooded man is standing in shadow under a tree on the opposite side of the street and smoking a cigarette. Dressed all in black, too old to be a student but clearly not a parent. But it's not Imo he's staring at; he's watching the beautiful woman's every move. His eyes follow her as she turns to lock her car. A shiver runs down Imo's spine.

When the man sees Imo looking, she drops her gaze to her envelope, hands trembling. Wariness of strangers is another product of the last few months, and this one looks like a stalker.

The young woman puts her keys in her handbag and walks past Imo into the reception, leaving a waft of expensive perfume in the air. When Imo looks back across the street, the man isn't there.

Chapter 2

Imogen

"Smile," her dad says, as he sticks out his backside to bring Imo into his viewfinder. "Let's have one for the album." His turn to play-act normal. But Imo's face is pale. Her mind still fixed on the man outside, on the way his gaze followed the woman through the crowd. Is that how *it* happened before?

"Imogen, are you all right?" her mum says, concern in her eyes.

"Fine, still a bit car sick." Imo smiles weakly and sits down on the bed, hugging her knees to her chest. At least her family didn't see him. She lets the sound of her parents bickering stop her mind from racing.

"Mind where you put your feet, Rob," Mum squawks, pointing at a pile of clothes on the floor.

"I didn't touch them."

"You were about to."

Imo bares her teeth. It's like Christmas. Everyone's got up early and they're all in one room. Arguing. A tremor passes through her. They won't next Christmas. Some things are worse than arguing.

The room is small: single bed, desk, slim wardrobe, grey carpet tiles, door to an en suite. Surprisingly modern after the imposing reception hall. When they unlocked the flat, Imo noticed other doors in the long hallway. She shudders at the thought of her flatmates appearing now and recognizing her family.

"Mum, are you nearly ready to go?" she says hopefully.

But her mother is still unpacking and doesn't reply. With an armful of shampoos and conditioners, Imo goes into the tiny bathroom. The sink – half the size of their basins at home – is fitted close to the loo and there's no bathroom cabinet.

"I wish we'd had room in the car for a toiletries stand." Imo calls. "I bet that girl in the big van brought one."

"And a cornetto maker," Freddie pipes up.

Dad laughs and Imo walks back into the room. But a shadow falls over her mum's face and she turns towards the window, arms wrapped around her body.

Pretending not to notice, Dad empties the last cardboard box. "Where do you want your German vocab book?"

"Underneath my pillow." Imo tries to smile but her heart's not in it. Her backchat is coming out on autopilot, her hand shaking with nerves. She saw other students on the stairs, making the trek to her floor and beyond. Confident, sharing a joke with each other. Why is it only her that doesn't know what the hell she's doing?

Dad joins Mum by the window. "She's got a gorgeous view of the hills," he says.

"It's grass," Mum says, her normal mood a memory.

"And south facing. This will be a sunny room."

Imo's belly flutters again, unnerved for a reason she can't define.

"Right." Dad sighs and turns from the window, wearing his bravest face. "I suppose we'd better leave you to it." He gives her a hug. "Keep in touch. Have a brilliant first term." He hugs her tighter. "And stay safe."

Freddie pats her back. "Good luck with the audition, Sis."

Oh God, she hoped he'd forgotten. He found out from the website that the uni will be putting on *Jesus Christ Superstar* in December. The auditions are this week.

"You will go, won't you?"

"I haven't been to a dance class for a while." It's been seven months, as he knows – as they all know. She feels the heat of her family's attention on her. "I might not have time."

"Course you will, love," Dad says. "University isn't all about work."

"It's hardly about work at all." Freddie grins, but then grows serious. "Promise you'll audition."

Dad strokes her arm. "It would do you good."

Mum stays at the window, rubbing her elbow like she always does when she wants to bail out of a conversation but still listen in. Like she does when Inspector Hare visits. Freddie and Dad keep their well-meaning eyes on Imo and she feels the room closing in.

"Okay, I promise." It's worth lying to see the relief on their faces.

She sits back on the bed and watches them line up in the small space by the door. Any second now her world of eighteen and a half years will quit with them. Her throat is hard.

Dad and Freddie give her a goodbye peck and head out into the stairwell. When they've gone, Mum sits beside her. "I notice you didn't bring the lamp Grandma gave you."

"I forgot." Another birthday gift she needs to shed. Everything from that day is toxic.

Mum places her hands on Imo's shoulders and looks her in the eye. "You don't have to do this. I'm not making you." Most decisions are impossible for Mum these days, but she was quick to agree that Imo should take up her uni place.

Imo tries to wriggle free, but her grip is firm. "I want to be here." Would it have been different if she hadn't already accepted the offer before the world tilted?

Mum lets go. "If there's anything …" She turns away to rub her eye. "Ring me, day or night. Just ring."

"Of course." Imo forces a bright smile.

"And you've got your personal alarm?"

"Always."

"Show me."

Imo hesitates, but only for a moment, knowing her mother won't leave until she's seen the tiny, red-topped canister. Imo retrieves it from her coat pocket and holds it out.

"Keep it with your phone," her mother says. "You need both at all times."

She watches until Imo has shoehorned it into a front pocket of her jeans. They hug, her mother holding her tighter than feels comfortable. Then she grasps her wrist.

"And never come home on your own on the train. We'll come and get you."

Chapter 3

Phoenix

Three of them are in the kitchen drinking Phoenix's instant coffee. Her mug has *Elexo Engineering Solutions* in turquoise lettering on the side – a freebie she picked up from a science and technology careers fair. The peroxide blonde – Amber? – waves her Amnesty International mug in the air. Phoenix isn't sure whether she means to brandish it, but she moves her hands a lot when she speaks.

The third girl – Phoenix has forgotten her name – sips out of Polish pottery. Expensive. Like the Mini Convertible she swept up in. Phoenix has kicked off her trainers to pad around the kitchen in woolly socks; this girl is in classy sandals.

When are they going to sit down instead of acting like it's a cocktail party? Phoenix has the urge to move from the cooking area to the easy chairs in the dining end of the kitchen. She shifts her weight and listens to Amber.

"I'm doing Theatre Studies. I'll probably go into directing and writing." Amber's bangles and friendship bracelets cascade down her wrist as she drags a hand through her bleached crop. "We need more women in pivotal roles. Smash through the glass ceiling of the existing patriarchy."

The rich girl suppresses a yawn. Ignoring Amber, she looks at Phoenix. "Where are you from?"

Phoenix hesitates. She's worked out her backstory but toys with the truth. These girls are her flatmates. Why pretend? Why: because the rich girl might judge and find her wanting. But before she can decide how much to say, Amber's off and running with her own answer.

"I'm from Chadcombe in Surrey. My dad works for a top accountancy firm in Town. That's London Town. We call it Town."

The rich girl's face doesn't move, but Phoenix smiles. Amber must be a Home Counties kid, away from home for the first time. Wholesome, but naïve. Doe eyes in kohl and sweetheart mouth behind purple lipstick. Perhaps she'll work hard and do her parents proud. Yet Phoenix wonders about her; something desperate in the rapid way she speaks.

Another girl steps into the kitchen.

"Hi, welcome." Amber turns to greet her. "What's your name?" She steps forward and hugs her, holding her half-drunk coffee behind the girl's back.

"Imogen … Imo." The girl swallows. Despite hunching her shoulders inside her Jack Wills sweatshirt and looking down, she's striking. Her blonde hair looks natural like Phoenix's own, but this girl can grow it long. It's well on the way to her waist and she wears it loose.

Amber steers her in front of the others as if she's the hostess. "This is Imogen, but we can say Imo. I'm Amber and this is Phoenix, named after the actor."

Phoenix winces. Why do people always assume that about her name? Phoenix is the mythical bird that rises from the ashes. Fire – that's why her parents chose it. Almost an obsession. She winces again as she remembers watching one of their obsessions turn deadly.

Imogen holds out her arms for a light hug and Phoenix understands why she wears her hair over her face: her cheeks are raging with acne. She looks anxious and there are dark shadows under her eyes.

"I think I saw you in the car park, getting out of a blue ice-cream van," Imo says.

Phoenix smiles nervously, wondering how many others noticed it.

"I saw a big van as I drove in," the rich girl says. "Are your parents caterers?"

Phoenix hesitates. "That's right," she lies.

Amber completes the introductions for Imo. "And this is Tegan. Have I got that right? A Welsh name?"

Tegan – so that's the rich girl's name and explains her mellifluous accent – doesn't step forward but waits for Imo to reach her. Even in her designer sandals, Tegan's the shortest of the four of them, but there's something ten-feet-tall about her. Phoenix doesn't expect to be having many kitchen chats with her after today. Their social circles won't intersect.

"What are you studying?" Amber asks Imo.

"German and Business."

"I can't do languages. Except BSL – British Sign Language – which I learnt in a day." Amber leans in close to the newcomer. "But I know Epic Theatre. You must have heard about that if you're doing German."

"A little …" Imo pauses and gives a weak smile.

Phoenix feels for her. It must be daunting that someone knows more about her subject than she does.

"In Year Twelve, I acted in a Swiss play." Imo's hands are clenched by her sides and she sounds nervous. "About an old woman seeking revenge on the man who got her in trouble when they were teenagers. Is that the sort of thing?"

For a moment Amber hesitates, a flicker of something behind her eyes. Then she shrieks, "That's it. What was the set like?" In her eagerness to talk drama with Imo, she steps in front of Tegan.

"What are you studying, Phoenix?" Tegan asks in a voice loud enough to make Amber move aside.

"Mechanical Engineering."

"Interesting," replies Tegan, sounding like she thinks it's anything but.

Amber runs with the conversation again. "We'll try to keep the drama talk to a minimum, won't we, Imo?" She links arms with the girl she's known for all of five minutes.

Tegan puts her Polish mug on the kitchen top. "I'm into the arts if they make money. Business is my thing."

"So are you studying Business like me?" Imo asks.

"For the moment," Tegan replies. "I left school a year ago and I've been building my product range since then." She bends down to the handbag at her feet and takes out a pouch. In a deft movement, she reconfigures it as a bomber jacket and puts it over her shoulders. Her dark hair is stunning against the ice pink. "Ideal to keep the rain off on a night out and it fits in your bag or …" she lays it on the kitchen top, folds in the sleeves and draws the sides together in previously unseen zips "… have it as the handbag itself."

"You're selling these?" Amber takes hold of the newly formed holdall.

"Fourteen ninety-nine, because of the craftsmanship. But I'm offering them on campus for ten pounds, two for eighteen."

Amber pauses for a moment, turns the bag over in her hands. "I'll get my purse."

Imo follows her out. Tegan looks at Phoenix expectantly.

Phoenix makes her best poker face. What craftsmanship? These plastic macs are most likely churned out in a Third-World sweatshop. She weighs up her options. Choose your battles. She's going to be sharing a flat with this girl. Why make it awkward? She pulls a tenner from her jeans pocket.

"Thank you so much," Tegan says. But the brightness is false. Phoenix knows conceit when she hears it. Tegan's used to getting what she wants. Phoenix's dad, Sonny, thinks university is a holding pen between bouts of real life. Tegan the businesswoman might be the kind of student he'd admire.

"What made you choose the Abbey?" Phoenix asks.

"This was as far away from home as possible on a tank of petrol." Tegan snorts. "What about you?"

The truth? Her head's full of designs for show equipment innovations, some worth patenting. Mech Eng is the way she's going to stay in the world she knows, doing what she's good at but without the risks. She shrugs. "Same as you, I suppose."

The other girls come back with their money. Amber's still holding Imo's arm. Firm friends already.

"What do you all think of this flat?" Amber asks. "I could do with more wardrobe space."

Imo and Tegan agree. Again Phoenix stays silent. Until she moved in with Carla and Antonio, her desk converted to her bed.

"So do you think it's just the four of us in this flat?" Amber points at each of them. "Let's see if I can remember: Imo doing German and Business, Tegan Business, Phoenix Engineering. And me Theatre Studies."

"There are five rooms." Tegan unfolds her demonstration holdall and restores it as a pouch to her handbag. "There must be one more person."

"I wonder if they'll get here in time for pre-s," Amber says.

Phoenix gives her a puzzled frown. If Preez is part of the university registration process, she's never heard of it.

"Preez?" Imo asks, beating her to the question.

"Don't you know? Everyone knows *that*." Amber laughs, clutching her chest theatrically as if it's the funniest thing she's heard. She straightens up when she sees their blank expressions. "Pre-s means pre-drinks. You go to someone's flat to get tanked before you go out. There are some *amazing* clubs around here, but drinks in clubs are so expensive. Pre-s are at Ivor's tonight, downstairs in Flat 7."

"Which clubs?" Tegan jumps in. She pauses to admire the confusion on Amber's face. "If it's pre-drinks in Flat 7, where are you going afterwards?"

"Umm … Not tonight," Amber bites her lip. "I'm staying here."

"Well aren't you the raver. Off the rails already," Tegan jokes.

But Amber looks away, a flash of anxiety crossing her face.

Amber

As the others continue to chat about themselves, Amber moves to the kitchen window to conceal the heat in her face. She gnaws her thumbnail. Despite putting on what she thought was a full-on performance, one of her new flatmates has found her out, seen through her. Why did posh-girl Tegan embarrass her, even after she bought one of her stupid jackets?

What about the others? Phoenix is a bit of an unknown – could go either way. Hopefully she won't throw her lot in with Tegan. Two mean girls. It'd be a long year and she might not be able to keep up the pretence. Imo seems nice. Reminds Amber of Verity, kind but dopey. In Vee's case, it was the weed, in Imo's it looks natural. She's not that dumb, though. Amber nearly lost it when she talked about the play, but thinks she hid it well.

Amber thinks about the other girl she met when they were queuing for keys at reception – Lauren – and wishes she was sharing with her. That could be a real friendship. Amber swallows, blinks away a dangerous thought and concentrates on safer ground. They're both doing Theatre Studies – even though Lauren is joint honours with another subject – and, like Amber, she has a unique sense of style. She hopes they'll be put in the same drama workshop group.

Behind her, Tegan's voice is strident as she recounts her five-year business plan. What to do about her? Try harder to fit in?

After everything that happened at home – the way Mum and Jade ended up despising her – Amber must become a different version of herself. *A better one.* Still a liar, but lies are her only currency. They'll just be better lies.

Her belly clamps as her thoughts stray again. She grips the side of the sink and feels the heat drain from her face. Whenever she thinks of that time too much, her belly relives it. People might call it her mind playing tricks, but if they'd done what she had, they'd feel it too. Guilt and punishment, all in her gut.

Using her hand as a scoop, she takes a drink from the cold tap. When the ache subsides, she gazes out of the window, giving herself time to look calm before turning to her flatmates. By craning her neck she can see the end of the main campus road and watches a few vehicles cruise by. A black car turns into their avenue and crawls past, the driver peering up at the hall of residence. Something about him makes her pause. He must turn around out of eyeshot, because he reappears and parks on the opposite kerb.

At this distance, it's hard to make out his features, but she sees him lift binoculars to his eyes and focus on her window. Amber bends over the sink, her heart thumping. By the time she looks up again, his car is moving off. She shudders. A pervert? Stalker, after an eyeful of teenage flesh? But if she alerts the others, they might think she's imagined it. Not as bad as Mum and Jade not believing her, but not the start she wants. Without saying anything, she watches the car drive away.

Chapter 4

Phoenix

Phoenix rinses the mugs the others have left in the sink, sensing it's a sign of things to come. If they'd have lived like she did, they'd wash up as they go. But she can't imagine posh-girl Tegan clearing up after herself. And Amber? She belted out of the kitchen like she'd seen a ghost. Maybe she can work on Imo. Get her on cleaning duty by Reading Week.

Back in her room she finishes her unpacking, only her posters still to do. The magnolia-painted breeze block walls are speckled with Blu Tack from previous occupants. Pinching together a decent clump, she affixes her favourite poster, smoothing the edges. The intensity of the orange and black image almost heats her fingertips. Magnificent. *A long time ago.*

She forgot to ask what time the flat party gets going, but it becomes apparent when the floor begins to pulsate. Ivor, below in Flat 7, must be letting rip with his speakers because his mummy isn't there to tell him to turn it down. Pathetic. She changes her T-shirt and combs her hair.

There's a knock on her door. It's Amber, apparently over whatever spooked her in the kitchen. She's gone for full greasepaint.

Industrial quantities of eyeliner, attempting an edgy Amy Winehouse. She's clutching Malibu purchased from the Cost-cutter near the student union.

"Is there time for me to get something?" Phoenix asks as they go into the hallway.

"No need." Tegan comes out of her room, empty-handed. "There'll be plenty of booze."

After calling on Imo, they follow the throbbing bass downstairs to the open front door of Flat 7 and squeeze into the crowded hallway. The layout is the same as their flat, so they head to the kitchen. The music is a couple of decibels lower here, and they can hear each other if they shout. Bottles of various alcoholic potions occupy the work surfaces. Amber finds a stack of paper cups and sloshes out four measures of Malibu. After adding a dash of cola, she and Imo knock theirs back. Never a fan of rum, Phoenix pretends to sip hers.

Tegan leaves hers untouched. "Business first." She heads into the hall.

From the kitchen doorway, Phoenix watches a sandy-haired boy lunge in for a hug. Tegan endures it stiffly and pats his back. It must be Ivor and she's keeping him sweet. Phoenix's assessment seems to be confirmed when he nods and lets her move through the guests in the hallway, parting them from their student loans in exchange for her folding jackets. Against the din, she perfects her sales pitch in mime. Still wearing the same clothes as earlier – palazzo pants and white top – she's the best-dressed student here, even with the additional accessory of a money pouch strapped round her hips.

A few lads drift past Phoenix into the kitchen. She follows and swaps her drink for a can of beer. Amber and Imo still hover over the Malibu. The boys swarm round Imogen like flies on an elephant turd. Hers is tart with a tan look: leopard print mini-skirt, long-sleeved, lacy crop top. Acne hidden under layers of foundation.

Amber moves in, eyeing the boys. She's more covered up than Imo but not in a good way. Baggy black linen pants, white cotton top, working men's boots. If Phoenix screws up her eyes it's rich-girl Tegan's wardrobe. Screws them up tight.

"Genuine Romany." Amber knocks back her drink and holds out the seam of her trousers. "Belonged to my grandmother. I'm from an old gypsy family."

Phoenix chokes on her beer. If Amber's a Romany, then Tegan's jackets are handmade in Chelsea.

A box of pizza makes its way between hands. Amber takes a slice, turns it over and sucks it. "I like the sauce, but I'm gluten free." She passes the rest of the box to Imo and sways in time to a new tune that drills pneumatically out of the speakers in the hall.

A boy that Phoenix recognizes from the Engineering open day takes a couple of four-packs of Strongbow Dark Fruit out of the fridge. He smiles when he sees her. "Come and sit with us. We've found somewhere quiet," he shouts.

She follows him down the hall to the furthest-away bedroom. Two boys and a girl sit on the bed. They hand her a cider and she shuts the door. The walls vibrate but at least they can talk. She and the boy from the open day sit on the floor. The other boys are doing Engineering too and the girl is a chemist.

When the cider runs out, Phoenix says she'll get more and goes back to the kitchen. The music's still full blast, banging its rhythm into her throat. There's no sign of Tegan – probably moved on to another flat party to flog her jackets – but Imo and Amber are there. Imo's at the sink, no boys buzzing near her now. Phoenix smells the sick as she approaches. Imo's holding back her hair in one hand and leaning against the basin with the other. There's a ketchup-coloured streak on her sleeve.

Amber is dancing on the tiny floor with a couple of other girls and Ivor. The host grips his drink while swaying and twisting not quite on the beat. A tall man stands against the fridge, hood up, his eyes glinting under the fluorescent lights. He's older than the others and a gap has formed between him and the dancers. A postgrad loser, Phoenix thinks. When Ivor overbalances towards him, the man barges past.

"Sorry, mate," Ivor slurs, and gawps at his beer puddling on the floor.

But the man has gone.

Chapter 5

Monday 26 September

Imogen

An explosion in her sleep illuminates one of her what-if night-mares: mouldy walls, a shrivelled body hunched over bent knees, cold floor. Imo thrashes against her sheets, curls foetal, trying not to hear the tortured whimpers in her dream. Fighting for breath. Pressure on her chest, crushing, crushing …

She sits upright in bed, skin clammy, pillow damp. Blood pounding in her trembling limbs. It takes several moments to register she's awake. Unsteady on her feet, she reaches the bathroom and vomits into the toilet.

She returns to bed, still feeling dreadful, only vaguely aware that someone is walking beside her, holding her arm. Their grip firm.

***

Light burns through her eyelids and her head throbs. The pain gets worse when she flicks open her eyes. Sun streams in through the gap in the curtain where it's hanging off the rail. Her mother tried to fix it and told Imo to report the fault. She won't, though; the idea of maintenance people coming into her room ties her in knots.

When she turns over, she sees her arm, still in the lacy top she wore the previous evening. There's a white, bobbly mark smeared on the sleeve. A flash of recollection: Amber dabbing it with wet loo paper. Imo sniffs the tissue residue and retches. It still stinks of puke.

She recalls handing her room key to Phoenix when she couldn't get it in the lock. Phoenix led her in and laid her on the bed. A plastic bowl appeared from somewhere.

Imo checks the floor. The bowl's still there, mercifully empty. But the motion of leaning over makes her guts squirm and she coughs bile into it. A long slither of creamy saliva hangs from her mouth and she rubs her face on the pillow.

Never again.

But it was a good night. Normal. The Imo from *before*. She pads her hand over her bedside locker and finds her phone. Yep, five friend requests, all from boys. As she deletes them, there's a flutter of panic in her chest. What if she bumps into them on campus? It's not like Tinder where she can flirt and forget – thirty-two Super Likes and no intention of meeting any of them. These requests are from boys nearby. They mustn't find out her Facebook profile is empty. She unfriended everyone except her sister, Sophia.

Still she did all right last night, didn't she? Talked, cracked jokes, faked the odd laugh? Another wave of nausea rolls through her gullet and she spits more bile into the bowl. A flashback: she puked in the night. After a nightmare. She can't remember the dream now but it was probably the recurring one about the cellar. The slime-covered walls, the shape on the floor with its bone-thin limbs. She shivers despite the sweaty cocoon of her duvet.

Amber must have cleaned the bowl. No, Phoenix took her to the loo. That's right, isn't it? Both have short blonde hair, but Amber's has a temporary look that doesn't quite work with her skin tone, and Phoenix stands a good few inches taller. Yes, Phoenix sorted out her puking. Then sometime later Amber told Phoenix she'd take over.

Amber: "Imo and I are good friends."

Phoenix: "You've just met."

Amber: "In this life, maybe."

Imo can't remember Phoenix's reply. After she'd gone, Amber kept talking.

"I never sleep well … It's not just Dad; I can't see Leo." Sitting on the end of Imo's bed. "What if …?" Pacing the room. "I should be there …" Tugging the curtain that won't shut. "Why can't I put things right …?"

Imo sits up. Everything rocks. She's never had a head fug like this before. So bad her memories of Amber's words must be hallucinations. Her own disturbing dreams have got bound up with the drunken ramblings of her new flatmate. It must be the booze. If she stays sober, it won't happen again. A price worth paying. University is supposed to be a new start, without the nightmares.

She peels off her top and supposes it will have to go in the bin as she doesn't know how to work the washing machines. A mild panic hits her: when did she take her skirt off? Hopes to hell she wasn't so drunk she did a striptease.

The phone pings with another text from her mum. How many is that? Since February, she's averaged ten a day, but now that Imo's away from home, her mother has upped her anxious bombardment. She doesn't read it. If she thinks of home, she'll buckle.

Mercifully, the skirt is a dead leopard on the floor in front of the loo. Her throat craves water. Head swimming, she turns on the taps, but the cold water runs tepid. She can't drink it like that.

She sends a new text: Loving it here. I'll call later. In some ways it would be easier if Mum phoned her, but, by some unmentioned pact, they agreed months ago that Mum would only ring if there was a sighting. Or worse.

Phoenix

Phoenix is in the kitchen, making a coffee.

"Want one?" she asks when Imo creeps in looking like death in a dressing gown.

Imo shakes her head, takes a mug off the draining board and fills it with tap water. When she leans against the sink, Phoenix is pretty sure it's the only thing keeping her upright. Not surprising after the skinful she sank and brought up again. Does Imo remember her bad dream? Phoenix hopes not. She remembers listening to Imo's moans. How Imo thrashed under the covers, twisting and yelling. She'd wanted to stay with her, but Amber insisted on doing her shift. Hopefully Imo's also forgotten Amber's creepy words of comfort. Phoenix shivers as she remembers the desperate look in Amber's eyes. God knows what else she said after Phoenix left.

She moves a hot-water bottle off an easy chair in the dining area and suggests Imo sits down. The vinyl upholstery makes a *fut* sound when Imo lands.

"What's that?" She points to the drink on the coffee table, flinching at the smell.

"Hangover remedy," Phoenix explains. "Amber left it there for me. Tastes like candle wax." She's never tasted candle wax, but she knows it would be like this.

"Where is Amber?" Imo yawns.

"Must have gone back to bed, said her leg was hurting."

When Phoenix got up, she'd been surprised to find Amber stretched across a chair and the coffee table, hugging a hot-water bottle. When she saw Phoenix, she pressed it against her knee. Phoenix offered to make an ice pack for her leg, but Amber declined.

Imo leans over to the table and sniffs the waxy drink. "Have you even got a hangover? I didn't see you drinking."

"Cider. My mouth's like a Portaloo."

Imo holds her head. "I'm going to lie down."

"Haven't you got a library induction session?" Phoenix asks. She passed Tegan on her way out, looking fine in designer jeans and another broderie anglaise top. "Tegan mentioned a library talk for Business students."

"I'm totally dead." Imo puts down her cup and lurches out of the kitchen.

Chapter 6

Tegan

Tegan's app directs her from her parking space in front of the geography tower to the university library. It looks like a giant greenhouse, several storeys of tinted glass. She makes small talk with other Business students who are waiting for the doors to open. It's an investment; no time to pitch to them now, but her saleswoman's instinct tells her to schmooze.

Amber, one of her three blonde flatmates, walks past with a group of weird-looking students – duffle coats, combats, tie-dyed scarves that look as if they've been in an autopsy. Tegan waves. It might pay to be neighbourly. But Amber looks away, ignoring her. Bloody cheek. Tegan catches the tail end of a story she's telling the gaggle around her.

"… Cumberbatch is great to work with."

Tegan looks at the ground and shakes her head.

After a few minutes, a man in an un-ironed shirt, with a beard to match, appears inside the library entrance and releases the glass doors. He holds up his hands. "If you're expecting an induction, it's in Lecture Room 2."

"Are you sure, mate – *library* induction?" one of the boys asks.

But the man goes back indoors. No one knows where the lecture room is and they drift off in different directions. Tegan and a few others search but find only Lecture Room 1 in the Business Studies block, with no sign of another lecture theatre.

"Stuff it," Tegan mutters and returns to her car. She's not that bothered anyway about using the library. When her business takes off, she'll pay someone to do her research. She opens the roof of the car and gazes up at the geography tower. All the parking spaces are designated disabled but hers is the only car here. Where to now? The first Business Studies lecture isn't until tomorrow. There's time for a drive around the town centre to see if any of the independent shops will stock her jackets.

Her fists clench as a thought makes her shiver. She'll show *him*. People make it big in business all the time through hard graft and a good idea. She'll be a success without her father's tainted help.

Something glints at a third-floor window. The glare from the sun is too bright for her to see what it is. Maybe someone's looking out, and so what if they are? They're hardly going to slap her with a parking fine from up there.

Light glimmers again. It's bloody binoculars. Some doddery old perv of a geography professor is spying on the campus, gawping at fresher totty from his ivory tower. Her fingers form a V. She points them at the window, making clear she's eyeballed him. The figure steps out of sight but is too fleet of foot for an ancient academic. Tegan grows cold and notices that her hands are shaking on the steering wheel.

Suddenly her passenger door opens and Amber gets in, disturbing the air with cheap, fruity scent. "Take me to the flat."

"Try asking nicely before you scare the crap out of me." Tegan's heart races, thoughts of the watcher still rattling.

Tears streak Amber's face and clumps of mascara look set to dive off her lashes. "Social anxiety," she gasps. "Sometimes crowds get too much for me and my leg's hurting." She pants, rhythmically, as if she's going to hyperventilate.

"That must make it hard during a show." Tegan's heartbeat has calmed, and settled on sarcasm.

The panting stops and Amber stares at her. "Show?"

"On stage, with you being a drama student. Acting all the time." Acting right now, if Tegan's any judge.

Amber breathes out. "I'm more of a director, behind the scenes. I have to keep my anxieties under control."

Tegan starts the engine. *Cumberbatch my eye.*

As she pulls away she glances up at the tower once more. And catches a glimpse of a tall shadow at the window. A face stares down at her. And her hands shake again.

Chapter 7

Amber

The fragrance in the car is subtle but expensive. Half like its wearer – Tegan's definitely on the pricey side but there's nothing subtle about her silent disapproval. The more Amber sees of her, the more she resembles her sister, Jade. Not only her dark hair and freckles, but also her stance. Straight back, manicured nails on the steering wheel, hard eyes.

No doubt the last thing Tegan wants is Amber occupying her passenger seat, but Amber had no choice. Couldn't walk another step after the shock she's just had. It was only the trick of the light, but she had turned and fled, barged people out of her way, panic rising in her throat, stomach crippling in pain.

Why doesn't she just tell Tegan a version of the truth instead of faking the stuff with her knee? She told Imo when they were drunk – sort of told her – so why not Tegan? Or Phoenix? She seems okay so far, better than expected. Not a deep thinker, into engineering and … Amber leans on the window as she scrolls her memory. What else does Phoenix do? Something sporty if her physique is anything to go by.

Amber bites the inside of her cheek. Maybe she should ask

her flatmates questions and listen to the answers, instead of masking her secrets with babble. Instead of play-acting the part of an intellectual liberal so others will feel too intimidated to enquire about her background. A stupid role to pick as she only scraped into this university with a plea of extenuating circumstances. All lies. There were reasons for her poor A level results, but not the ones she gave.

Taking a deep breath, she continues with the disguise she's been perfecting since she arrived. "Shall we go to the canteen?" she asks enthusiastically. "We can have a proper chat."

"What, now?" Tegan glances at the clock on her dashboard.

"Early lunch. Please, I'd like to."

Silence and Amber thinks she sounded too pleading. That's always been her downfall. Begging gets you nowhere. *On her knees, clinging, sobbing, screeching …*

"If you're paying," Tegan says. She pulls into the kerb and reverses up a side road. They turn around and park in the loading bay behind the kitchens.

"Shouldn't you …?" Amber starts, but changes her mind. She hates it when people run her life; she won't tell Tegan where to park.

The canteen queue moves slowly. Students everywhere. Remembering who she thought she saw, her belly tugs, as if she's being pummelled from the inside, and she keeps glancing over her shoulder. Suddenly she's back *there*, in the moment. *In the hours.* Hurting. As a substitute for doubling over, she rubs her knee. Channels her ache into her leg. No one must see the truth. She straightens up, ignoring the funny look Tegan gives her.

As they wait, most people gaze at the TV monitors around the walls with Lady Gaga videos on repeat. Tegan uses the time to check her sales figures on her phone.

"It's like Hogwarts." Amber scans the busy dining hall. Tables the length of railway lines. "Where are we going to sit?"

"With Slytherin," Tegan sneers.

After they've loaded their plates and poured a couple of coffees, Tegan leads the way to the clean end of a table beyond a group of older students gathered round a tablet. Postgrads probably.

Amber makes another attempt at conversation. "Are you going to the Freshers' Fair? I'd like to join the drama club, if they have one, and maybe take up a new hobby of some kind. University is a chance for new beginnings."

Tegan rolls her eyes. "Next you'll be saying we're on a journey."

"Sorry." Amber blushes into her salad and chips.

Tegan sighs. "I suppose I could look for a business enterprise group."

Amber can't think how to reply and feels uncomfortable again. Nothing in common with this girl. She shivers. Nothing in common with anyone. Her gullet heaves at the memory of what she did.

She puts down her fork and tells another lie. "I can't eat this. I'm allergic to tomatoes. It's the alpha solanine."

Tegan rolls her eyes again. "Is alpha whatsit not present in upside-down pizza then?" She waits for Amber to look at her. "Remember the party in Flat 7? You tucked in good and proper."

Amber hunches her shoulders and returns to picking tomato slices out of her salad. Found out again.

"By the way," she says eventually, in another try at faking it. "I forgot to mention they've moved into the last room in our flat."

"They?" Tegan asks. "Is it a couple?"

Amber shakes her head, puts on her persona. "One individual. I designate all humans as they; gender is a social construct."

"Okay," Tegan says slowly. "For those of us who are less enlightened, can you give me a clue which bits of they's anatomy dangle?"

Amber struggles to keep a straight face. "The less enlightened would call them male."

"A guy?" Tegan says, laughing.

"I think he, they, is from Thailand," Amber says between chuckles.

Tegan's laughter freezes. "Thailand?" Her knuckles whiten as she grips the edge of the table.

"They don't speak English so I couldn't find out their name. Don't suppose you speak any Thai?"

"No."

The force of the word silences Amber. The good-humoured conversation has evaporated as inexplicably as it materialized. She burns her mouth as she hurries to finish her drink.

"Thanks for the lift." She stands up and heads out of the hall. Trying to befriend Tegan was a mistake. Imo is a better friend – and Lauren, the girl she bumped into on arrivals day. That's a friendship Amber hopes to cultivate.

Chapter 8

Tuesday 27 September

Imogen

Moonlight finds the gap in Imo's curtain, but the room passes for dark. No thudding bass invading through the floor from another flat, no doors slamming, no traffic outside. But it's the quiet of dread not peace. When she lies awake at home, every car she hears is the police with news, or Sophia coming home without her keys. In this silent space, her brain won't switch off, spooling through the what-if scenarios of what might have happened and the white-hot anger of why it happened to them.

Still feeling rough from the Sunday night's drinking, her throat's killing her. The soreness in her mouth will be a cough by morning. Getting sick can be added to her other failure: so hungover she turned up late to the library and couldn't find the induction talk. She walked past rolling stacks of journals, bays of textbooks, miles of computer screens. No one to ask. Sweat beading on her brow, she forced herself to take the lift to the upper library floors. Tried not to think about the broken body, how it must have fallen through the air, how it must have landed. No sign of a talk when she peered in, although she didn't complete a full sweep; too scared of seeing the drop out of a window.

Pulling the duvet up, she turns over. Tomorrow will be no better. The Business Studies introduction clashes with the German welcome talk. Two lectures will be missed in as many days. She's unravelling, not good enough for uni, can't manage like the others. Maybe it's too soon. But would another year make her stop seeing kidnappers behind every parked car? Stalkers under the trees outside her window? Will the familiar face she seeks have become so much less familiar that she'll no longer search? And will that what-if nightmare of the dark and the cellar have faded?

She looks at the red-canister alarm on her bedside table and imagines the disappointment vying with relief on her mother's face when she drops out. On the days when her mother still functions, she works as a nurse. The first thing she does when she gets home, after she's checked for messages from Inspector Hare, is read the obituaries in the evening paper, to see which former patients have died. "That didn't take long," she says. She'll say the same when Imo quits.

An idea about the timetable clash tomorrow comes to her, something her mum – the old version of Mum – might suggest. She fires off a text to Tegan, asking her to collect the handouts from the Business Studies talk. Lies back on her pillow, feeling lighter in her chest. Things will work out. Her first problem solved on her own. She's a student now, not a school kid.

Ten minutes later she's still awake. Her throat hurts and coughing threatens no matter how she turns her body.

There's a knock at the door. She freezes. Tegan come to tell her off for texting her at this hour?

"Imo, it's me." Amber's voice. "I need painkillers."

Imo unlocks the door and Amber stumbles in, doubled over. She falls on Imo's bed and clutches the pillow to her stomach. Her short, bleached hair has crinkled, no doubt suffering the dual effects of bed head and natural wave. She wears fluffy grey slippers and a tartan dressing gown. Without the make-up and weird quilt coat she wore yesterday, she looks younger, vulnerable. Imo lets out a gasp; she reminds her of Sophia.

"What is it?" Amber asks.

"I might have a paracetamol in my purse." Imo recovers and reaches for her bag, feeling light-headed at the comparison she's made.

"I'm allergic to those. There's an all-night petrol garage outside campus." Amber sits up, wrapping the edges of the Groovy Chick duvet over her legs. "They'll sell ibuprofen. Our taxi will be here in three minutes."

Imo suppresses a sigh, no desire to go out in the night and irked that Amber has given her no choice. But Amber's anguished face makes her feel guilty, especially as Amber stayed with her when she was throwing up the night before.

"Let's wait here for the driver's text." Amber curls up. "I can't stand for long."

After the taxi arrives, it takes them an age to get outside. Amber stops several times on the stairs to hug her belly. Imo pictures the meter ticking.

The driver, a young guy with thick, black curls, pulls a face when she tells him their destination, no doubt disappointed at the meagre fare. They travel in silence, Imo shivering in her jacket and jeans. She should have put on a sweatshirt. The faint smell of alcohol in the back of the taxi makes her nauseous and she looks out of the window to settle her stomach. The campus is deserted. A few lights on in the other halls, but no one out walking – or staggering – and no other cars. Eerily quiet. Imo imagines someone watching them drive past, someone lurking outside the flats waiting for their chance. She thinks of Sophia running for her life through dark streets.

Even out on the main road, they are alone. When they reach the floodlit forecourt of the filling station she notices Amber's grey face, screwed up in a wince of pain. She tells her to wait in the taxi while she gets the tablets.

"Three packets, please," Amber says softly. "I'll pay you back."

But when Imo gets to the counter, the woman won't sell her three boxes of ibuprofen. "Maximum of two per customer. It's the law."

Back in the taxi, Amber takes the tablets and swallows four down without water. "People should be allowed to buy as much medication as they need, for whatever reason. If I want to commit suicide, it's my business."

Imo stares at her and feels colour draw from her cheeks.

Amber doesn't seem to notice. She folds her arms, a cold gleam in her eyes, not doubled over any more. "I won't, though. Not today. Suicides are determined people. You would be surprised. When it comes to it, most of us find we don't have the guts."

Imo's chest palpitates against the seatbelt.

But Amber's mood switches and the cloud passes. She seems restored within seconds of taking the medication. Leans forward to ask the driver his name. "Do you give a discount for frequent travellers? We're interested in finding a reliable firm."

The driver warms to the theme. "You call me, Hamid Cars. I'll look after you. Better than Uber, better than College, or A Cabs." He rubs his hand through his thick hair. "The thing with College Cars is they're a rip-off. Five pounds for this, five pounds for that."

He pulls up at their hall of residence. "That's eight pounds fifty, please," he says.

Still shaking from what Amber said, Imo struggles to get the money out of her purse. Amber goes back to her room, promising to refund her for the tablets. She doesn't mention the taxi fare.

Back in bed, Imo doesn't sleep. Suicide has always been one of the what-if explanations her family considered. For the rest of the night, it's firmly lodged as a certainty.

Chapter 9

Imogen

The academic block is modern, built in red brick in the last twenty years. Most of the buildings are at least five storeys high. Imo gives silent thanks that she knows the languages department lecture theatre is on the ground floor.

Dozens of students saunter towards the buildings, chatting noisily in small groups, not an anxious face among them. In the distance she thinks she sees Amber, arms linked with a girl who looks like a Goth. Imo's thoughts rush at the sight of her loose black clothing, reminiscent of the graduation gown in the photo that flooded social media. Something positive her family could do in the first few days, but now Imo hates the image.

Sunshine has brushed aside the gloomy start that greeted her when she left the flat. The beech trees beside the path cast big shadows over the beds of marigolds. Autumn now. How soon will the leaves shrivel and spin unanchored through the air, heading downwards? *Falling.* Bile rises to Imo's throat at an unwelcome memory of the mortuary, but she forces it down.

Hood up, earphones in, she walks on, pretending to listen to music. Missed one lecture already and missing another now. Tegan hasn't replied to her text, so probably won't take notes in Business Studies.

A few girls dot around the middle of the lecture theatre and a line of lads sprawls at the back. There's a brief pause in their conversation as Imo enters. She goes to the far end of the front row next to the wall. If the lecturer stands where the computer is, she'll be out of his eyeshot. As she switches off her phone, a text from Tegan flashes up: Yeah no probs. Imo smiles to herself; Business lecture notes sorted.

The trace of the smile lingers when the Goth girl she thought she saw with Amber sits on the other end of her row. The girl doesn't smile back. Imo puts in her silent earphones again. To think she's wasted her best face on a crow.

Confident, laughing voices fill up the seats behind her. The crow shuffles towards Imo to let more girls into their row. Imo's relieved when she takes a place three seats away. But peeved too: why doesn't she want to sit with her?

Eventually a woman appears at the computer. Slim and wrinkled. Long, lank hair but no hint of grey. Red kilt, orange tights, flat brown ankle boots. She launches into German. Imo loses the thread after: *My name is Dr Wyatt.*

The lecturer switches to English. "I want you to come up here one at a time and introduce yourselves. Two minutes max and don't tell us what you got in your A levels. No one cares. Who's going first?"

One of the lads from the back row strides to the front. His German is fluent. Two minutes, three minutes, four. Imo thinks his grammar is dodgy, but he's using vocabulary she doesn't know.

By the end of the lesson, Imo's decided she loves this boy, David. Because he talked so long and also insists on asking the subsequent speakers questions, there isn't time for Imo's row to present.

Dr Wyatt puts a reading list on the screen. "These are the links to the articles you need to study for next time."

Imo's copying them down when the crow girl leans across. "They're on the intranet. You don't need to do that." Imo puts down her pen, feeling stupid.

"Right," Dr Wyatt says. "You're free to get to all those freshers' parties that my lecture has inconvenienced. Can I have the register back?"

The students look at each other. Some edge up the central aisle towards the door.

"No one leaves until I get the register."

They look back at the rows, searching, until crow girl points at Imo. The register is lying next to her pencil case. Only six names on it. It was passed to her and she didn't notice. Red-faced, hand trembling, she signs her name and gives it to the row behind. Crow girl gives a sympathetic smile but can't hide the sneer in her eyes.

Chapter 10

Phoenix

He's wearing lilac. The trousers are denim and the tunic is heavy-duty cotton. Not as tall as her, but solid, box-shaped. Bull-necked. He fills the doorway and doesn't invite her in.

"I thought I'd better come and say hello as we're flatmates." Phoenix wishes she'd asked Amber to do the introductions. "I'm Phoenix." It comes out as an apology. "What's your name?" She tries putting a won't-take-no-for-an-answer tone into her question.

It sort of works. He mutters something, growls it really. *Riku?*

She smiles and tries out the basic Thai she picked up when her family did a season in Bangkok years ago, but he tilts his head to the side in apparent bafflement. She tries hello in Mandarin and Japanese. Nothing. He must be from somewhere she's never heard of. Depressing, as she thought she knew the world pretty well. From the doorway she sees a small rucksack and a sketchpad. Something familiar hanging on the wall gives her hope for common ground, and she nearly breaks her cover story, but his unsmiling face stops her in time.

"Well, nice to meet you, Riku," she says backing away. She

intended to invite him to the Freshers' Fair. But even with her best linguistic gymnastics, she doubts she'd make him understand and he'd probably decline anyway.

On the way to her room, she scoops up the post from the doormat. Pizza delivery leaflets, taxi fliers and electoral registration letters for previous occupants. She cleared one heap of junk mail yesterday. No one else bothered and the pile was already spreading along the hallway. Another domestic duty that's going to fall to her.

In need of a friendly face, she knocks on Imo's door. Hears movement inside but has to knock again before Imo appears, red-eyed.

"I can't get onto the intranet and I've got a German assignment to do by tomorrow. Why is it always me?" Imo blinks hard, suppressing tears.

"They can't have set you work in Freshers' Week. It's bound to be optional."

"There's nothing optional about Dr Wyatt." She goes back to the bed and picks up her laptop. "I'm going to get kicked off the course in the first week."

"Do you want me to try?" Phoenix takes the laptop, but no matter which icon she presses, a *no server* message appears on the screen. "I don't think it's your fault. The uni's system is down."

"Great," Imo says, swallowing a sob. There are dark circles under her eyes, and her cheeks and chin are a plague of acne.

"Have you eaten?" Phoenix offers her mother's preferred salve to tearful children. "Come with us to the Freshers' Fair. You can get free snacks there. The intranet might be up by the time you get back."

Imo makes a big sigh and wipes her eyes on her sweatshirt cuff. "I'll come along, but I'm not joining anything."

They get a shock when they call on Amber. Turquoise kimono and red bobbed wig. Her make-up is a tone lighter than usual and her lipstick matches her hair. Perhaps she's hoping for a Geisha Girl Society.

Imo whips out her phone. "Let me take a photo."

"The car's in the main car park," Tegan says, coming out of her room and checking her handbag for her keys. She sees Amber's wig. "You look like an Edam cheese."

Amber scowls and suggests they walk as the fair is in the other direction and it's a beautiful afternoon.

"Is your ankle better?" Phoenix asks.

"Fine thanks." She flexes her foot.

Phoenix smiles. Wasn't it supposed to be her knee that was hurting?

The walk turns out to be a good idea. Crowds of freshers head the same way. The mood suits the sunny weather.

"Where are you from, Tegan?" Amber asks. She looks at her flatmate while they walk, as if she's making a supreme effort to listen to the answer. The uncharitable part of Phoenix can't help thinking it's an act.

"Cardiff."

Phoenix has been to Cardiff but doesn't say. She was christened at Mermaid Quay in the tent by a local vicar. The baptism is supposed to bring the whole family health and happiness. She stiffens as she walks. Tell that to Cloud.

"Where's your home town?" Amber asks, turning her intense expression on Phoenix.

She shrugs. "Born in Shrewsbury." The planned two-week stopover stretched to six when Cloud went into labour early en route from Carlisle to Gloucester. "My parents work all over."

"Cloud's Coffee. I remember your parents' amazing van," Imo says. She looks at Tegan. "What do your parents do?"

"My mother shops."

Amber and Imo laugh, but Phoenix isn't sure Tegan meant it as a joke. Her face doesn't move.

"And your dad?" Imo asks.

"We're here." Tegan ignores the question and jogs up the steps to take the Great Hall door from a boy who's holding it open.

Last time Phoenix was here, it was kitted out with display boards and smiling lecturers on an open day, eager to hook potential students. They mostly spoke to her parents. Today there's no one over thirty years old in the room and it's laid out with brightly decorated stalls and tables. Freshers throng inside the entrance, not knowing where to start.

Taking charge of their group, Amber leads them to the row of stalls on the far left. "It looks like these are political societies," she says. "We can walk down and back up the other side. No loitering by the Tories." She glances at Tegan, who narrows her eyes.

Amber strikes up a conversation with a punk girl from a campaigning charity. They look set to put the world to rights for several minutes so the others move on. Imo seems to be hunching her shoulders, looking around surreptitiously.

Amber meets them at the Conservation Volunteers stand and sees Tegan browsing the literature. "You're not going to join, are you? I can't imagine you in wellies."

"Why not," Tegan says. "Someone's got to protect nature from land-grabbing scumbags. And I like the idea of hacking down deadwood and pulling up unwanted growth."

The other girls exchange a glance, wondering what deadwood Tegan has in mind.

As they pass the languages aisle, Phoenix stops to say: "Hello, how are you?" in Bulgarian to a pretty woman in national costume. It's the limit to what she learnt after their season in Plovdiv, but it earns her a biscuit that tastes like a pretzel. She follows the others to the performing arts area. Imo declares that she'll have enough on with her coursework and doesn't sign up for any groups. Phoenix and Tegan leave their names with the Bhangra society and help themselves to onion bhajis.

They can't drag Amber away from the Drama Society stall

even though other people are waiting to speak to the stallholder.

Something prickles along Phoenix's spine, the sensation that someone's watching her. She scans the room. A tall figure in a black hoodie stands with a group of students, waiting to sign up for the Film Society. His brooding body language is oddly familiar. It's the man from Ivor's kitchen in Flat 7. He's probably harmless – a mature student, uncomfortable among the kids – but she feels sweat begin to seep through her T-shirt. He glances over at them again and she realizes it must be Imo that's caught his attention. He's a man after all.

Imo and Tegan wander on and she catches them up. When she looks back over her shoulder, she can't see the man. She breathes with relief.

When she inadvertently makes eye contact with the boy on the chess stall, she feels obliged to go over. "I used to play a bit with my uncle," she tells him. "Quite enjoyed it."

The boy gives a tight smile. "We have three levels of membership: beginners, recreational and tournament. But to be on the tournament team, you must, *must* practise."

"How many hours a week do you play?" Tegan asks, taking his leaflet from Phoenix.

"A minimum of fifteen hours a week."

"Babe magnet," Tegan mutters sarcastically as they walk away. When Tegan sees the Society for Deaf Students, she points at Amber who's finally left the Drama stall. "Get her to practise the sign language she says she learnt in a day." There's a smirk on her face as she carries on down the aisle.

But, when Amber reaches Phoenix and Imo, she stops dead. The little colour visible under her pale make-up fades. For a moment her features are frozen and she stares ahead of her, as if she has seen a ghost. Phoenix moves closer, ready to catch her if she faints. Is it a melodrama brought on by being caught out in a lie?

Amber's shiny eyes dart the length of the stalls and she tugs the fringe of her wig, her chest rising and falling. "I'll wait outside," she gasps.

Before Phoenix can reassure her that they don't really expect her to know British Sign Language, she's started weaving through the crowds towards the exit.

"Do you think we should go after her?" Imo asks.

Phoenix has had enough of Amber's crises and wants to see the rest of the fair. "If she chooses to flounce out, that's up to her."

"I know but …" Imo tails off.

Tegan comes back to them. "What's he looking at?" she says through gritted teeth. Phoenix follows her gaze. Across the room by a staircase, Riku, their new flatmate, is staring at the exit.

"He must have the hots for Amber. She went out that way," Imo suggests.

They watch as Riku, still looking at a group of girls by the main door, goes up the stairs to the balcony.

"Creep," Tegan mutters. Then she plumps her hair, making it look even thicker. "I'm off to find the sports societies."

Before Phoenix can follow, she once again realizes someone is watching. Turning around quickly, she sees a girl with striking blue eyes looking at them. She feels herself blush.

"She's got sweets. Come on," Imo says, noticing the girl and apparently forgetting her concern for Amber.

When the girl presses wristbands and lollies into their hands, Phoenix's wristband slips to the floor. She sees the inscription as she bends down to pick it up: *Abbey LGBTQ*. Her face on fire, she stands up and finds that Imo has moved on.

"I've got to … my friend's over there," Phoenix tells the girl, not catching her headlamp eyes. She hurries away.

Imo is near the Parents' Group stall, the last one in the aisle. A dark-haired woman – at early thirties, probably the oldest person in the room bar the creepy man in the hoodie – is talking to a young couple in front of her desk. A little girl with a curly mop of auburn hair sits under it, engrossed in a sticker book.

"We can advise on antenatal classes and, thinking ahead, there's a crèche for when the little one is six months old," one woman says.

The man nods and puts an arm across his pregnant partner's shoulder.

"Do come along to our barbecue on Saturday. Let me get you a leaflet." As the older woman reaches behind her, the little girl clamps her arms round her legs. The woman scoops her up and presses a leaflet into the pregnant woman's hands. "You're about to take the most magical and precious journey of your life."

Phoenix smirks at Imo. The woman sounds like one of those middle-class earth mothers they interview on Radio 4 when someone's been banned from breastfeeding in a Jacuzzi.

"Don't think this stall's for me," Imo whispers, turning away. "I have enough trouble looking after myself. I'd never cope with a kid as well."

The final aisle is given over to sports societies. Two guys, muscling through their T-shirts, home in on Imo's pert backside. Tegan's at the far end, sauntering towards them. She flicks her hair, obviously loving her own slice of attention.

After Phoenix has signed up for archery and Tegan's taken a leaflet for tennis, they work their way to the exit through the crowds of freshers still arriving. Phoenix wonders which ailment Amber will greet them with when they find her outside.

The steps and forecourt in front of the Great Hall are busy with students, but Amber isn't one of them.

"She could have waited," Tegan says, setting off for the flat.

"Hang on," Imo calls. "Let's check round the back. There might be benches."

Tegan follows Imo and Phoenix. "Doubt Amber will be on one. Bound to be allergic to wood."

There's only a small car park on the far side of the Great Hall.

With her phone to her ear, Imo spends ages walking back and forth and peering in car windows. When she seems satisfied Amber hasn't taken refuge there, she strides back to the forecourt. Phoenix and Tegan rush to keep up.

Shaking her head, Imo puts her phone away. "She's switched off her mobile."

"Don't sound so worried," Tegan says. "We don't need sniffer dogs just yet."

Imo wheels round, eyes narrow. "Don't joke about something like that," she snarls.

Tegan backs away.

"They have search dogs for a reason." Imo's voice is tight and preachy. "Some families rely on them …"

"Okay, I get it," Tegan says, still moving backwards. "Lighten up." Her sandal catches something on the tarmac that makes a metallic jingle.

"What's that?" Imo asks, squatting by Tegan's feet, her sudden anger apparently forgotten. "A bangle." She holds up a silver bracelet. "Amber's, for sure. I remember her wearing it."

"Come on, Imogen. How can you tell?" Tegan says.

Imo shrugs and pockets the bangle. "I'll keep it until we see her." Her voice tails off and she looks nervously around the crowd. Her hands clench into fists.

Chapter 11

Imogen

Why did Amber run off like that? Did something trigger a panic attack? Imo swallows. That was one of the what-if scenarios Inspector Hare suggested for Sophia: panic leading to amnesia.

Her phone rings. Freddie. She snatches it off her bedside locker, heart thumping. He never rings. Never. *It must be news.*

But that's not why he's called.

"Don't forget the audition is on Thursday."

"I'm not going," she says as her pulse returns to normal.

"You promised."

"I'm already behind and it's only the first week." She tries to keep her unhappiness out of her voice. "The computers don't work so I can't do my German. How can I keep up with everyone else if I'm in a show?"

"Do what you do best."

A stone settles in her stomach. What is her best? The same as his. Trying to hold everything together. Their parents don't need more distress.

"Are you still there?" There's an intake of breath down the phone. Is he thinking the same thing? "I meant flirting and dancing. You're good at them." He chuckles. Imo can tell it's forced; he's trying to laugh away other thoughts.

"How's flirting going to help me with German post-war politics?" She plays along with a forced chuckle of her own.

"You'll find a way."

After he rings off she scans the notes she made in the lecture. All she copied down was the first link and one article title before the crow girl told her to stop writing. She won't make that mistake again, she'll write the bloody lot down. But that won't help her with tomorrow's seminar.

Do what you do best. There is something she could try. It's crazy, but maybe. She opens her Tinder app.

***

Finally climbing into bed at 3 a.m., she hopes she's done enough to keep Dr Wyatt happy. The responses have been coming in dribs and drabs. She's spent the evening and half the night learning them. They might be garbage – useless for Wyatt's seminar – but what choice does she have?

It's darker in the room tonight despite the broken curtain. But images of the day flood her mind. After the German lecture from hell in the morning, the fair was fun. Until Amber stormed off.

It was nice of Phoenix to call for her but she can't help feeling she was just being polite. Phoenix and Tegan are both out of her league. There's something old soul about Phoenix, and Tegan acts more like thirty than twenty. Is that down to having a gap year? Imo thought rich kids got wrapped in cotton wool and knew nothing of the real world. Where does Tegan get her streetwise cynicism?

Amber's more on her wavelength. She forgot to ask if she'll be auditioning on Thursday. Maybe if she can get Amber to go, she'll go too.

It could be her usual fatigue, but for some reason she feels calm. A difficult day is over and she's made a friend in Amber. Now she welcomes rest.

Sometime later, in her dream, she registers Amber sitting on her bed.

"You will come to get me, won't you?" Amber whispers.

Imo stumbles through her slumbering mind. Get her for what? She says she will, then the dream fades.

Chapter 12

Wednesday 28 September

Imogen

When the alarm doesn't go off, it's a miracle Imo manages to wake at all. Half an hour late and touch and go whether she'll make the German seminar. Her hoodie and jeans are by the bed. Yesterday's knickers will do, save on the handwashing.

She goes to the bathroom. After she pees, she washes her hands, pushes a flannel under her armpits and makes a monumental effort to brush her teeth. She doesn't plan on talking to anyone today; it's almost pointless caring about fresh breath.

Suddenly, remembering her dream about Amber, a prickle of doubt crosses her shoulders and she shivers. But there's no time to call on her flatmate, even though she hasn't seen her since the Freshers' Fair. She tells herself the dream meant nothing. Thinks again about her usual cellar nightmare. A what-if that even Inspector Hare doesn't like to mention.

After swigging from the cup by her bed, she leaves the flat and heads to the modern languages block. It's a sunny day – seaside bright and warm, maybe twenty degrees. More people are about than she'd hoped. In pairs and groups, confident, smiling, fitting in. Dr Wyatt's not the only evil academic who calls lectures in Freshers' Week. She sinks further into her hoodie and remembers she hasn't combed her hair. Who cares?

She tries to run but has to stop, coughing harshly. Out of her eye corner, she sees a man standing across the road at the end of the pathway. The memory of the tall man smoking under the tree on arrivals day makes her sprint-walk past a group of boys. Her eyes fix on the ground – dark tarmac, bare earth at the side. A gardener must have dug up the beds overnight. They were full of marigolds yesterday. University policy? Root out those about to fade? How long until they come for her?

The seminar room on the first floor has seating for twenty and she takes a seat round the horseshoe of desks. The chairs soon fill up and the crow girl from yesterday's lecture is forced to sit next to her. Is that a smile? No, she's sniffing. She can beggar off if she thinks Imo smells. Should have got here earlier and selected another seat.

Dr Wyatt comes in and launches into her bullet-fast German. Imo surprises herself by getting the gist.

"Let's have someone we didn't hear from yesterday." Dr Wyatt's eyes settle on Imo.

Her acne glows inside her hoodie and she desperately scrolls on her phone screen, looking for her notes, such as they are.

"Stand up," Wyatt says in German. "You don't need your phone."

From every angle of the room, eyes are on Imo. The lump in her throat is concrete. David gives her a thumbs-up. She takes a breath and launches into German.

***

"That was enlightening, wouldn't you say?" Dr Wyatt paces inside the horseshoe of desks at the end of the seminar, the flat soles of her boots slapping the floor. "Some of you did the reading I set, most of you didn't. But, I have to say, one or two of you went the extra mile." She looks at Imo. "Keep it up."

Imo is ten feet tall. As good as anyone. She's got her brother Freddie to thank for his throwaway comment. *Do what you do best.* Maybe he's right about the audition too.

"Fancy a coffee?" the crow girl asks as they leave. "There's a Starbucks downstairs."

Imo's cough starts hacking again, but she's too surprised to decline. She follows the girl's black cape to the ground-floor café.

They buy refreshments and perch on bar stools in the window. It's not Imo's preferred location – people walking past outside can see her – but it's doable; none of them know her family, know their story. As a kid she hated her common surname, now she's grateful for being Smith. At least she can remain anonymous despite everything that's been on TV.

The girl's name is Lauren. She tears apart her chocolate cookie. "Where did you get that stuff from? When the intranet came on last night, I read all the articles in the links Dr Wyatt gave us. Took me hours on Google Translate, but I don't remember half of what you said. Are you German?"

The tiny flame that's flickered inside Imo since the seminar glows brighter. "Do you really want to know?" She leans forward, the compliment having made her talkative. "I messaged all the German guys I've matched with on Tinder and asked their opinion. Then I learnt what they said by heart."

Lauren chokes on her biscuit. "How many guys was that?"

"I changed my Tinder Bio to: 'I'm looking for a guy who loves post-war German politics'. To be honest, not many knew what I was on about. Viktor and Markus were useful, though. They were strongly opinionated in different ways." She coughs again. It wrecks her chest.

The drink warms her. She can do normal things after all. Coffee with another student. Like everyone else. Even draw on

60

the flirty Imogen from *before* to help her out with coursework. Sometimes. It's not like she's trying to *be* that person again.

Lauren puts down her cup. "What have you tried on your skin? I've gone through the over-the-counter potions. I wanted to go hard core but I couldn't while I was …" She pauses and goes red. Imo notices her hand has started to shake. "I mean … when my mum wouldn't let me. She can't stop me now I'm here. Have you tried it?"

Imo wonders what Lauren almost let slip. She shakes her head. So it's got round to her acne. It's all anyone sees when they look at her. She glances at Lauren's face. Spots round her nose and chin. No big deal. Imo's had months of inflamed pustules on her cheeks, a face she hates and getting worse.

Lauren stares at her, waiting for an answer. Imo has no wish to prolong the conversation. What's the point? She's not going to be friends with this girl. Too much effort. Amber's the only person she's met at Abbeythorpe with whom she feels remotely comfortable. Amber does all the talking and has even more neuroses than she does. She thinks of the bangle lying abandoned on the tarmac, of the look of terror in Amber's eyes as she left the fair, and wants to check she's okay. She decides to call in at the canteen in case she's gone there.

"I said I'd meet a friend for lunch," she says and finishes her coffee.

Lauren looks at her phone. "A bit late, isn't it?"

Imo stands up and sends Amber a text.

"Enjoy your research," Lauren calls out as Imo leaves. She must think she's looking at Tinder.

***

Amber doesn't reply to Imo's text and she's not in the canteen or her room. When Imo follows the sound of Radio 1 to the kitchen, she finds Phoenix and Tegan tucking into beans on toast.

"Have you seen Amber?"

Phoenix looks up. "She might've gone back to the Freshers' Fair. It's on all week." She returns her attention to her plate. "Probably bending that drama rep's ear."

"But you haven't actually *seen* her?"

Tegan waves her fork. "You know you're not her mummy."

Imo wants to ignore the insult but feels her face reddening. "I had this weird dream about her," she blurts out.

Tegan opens her mouth but Phoenix knocks her wrist to silence her.

"I'm sure she's fine," she says kindly.

Tegan puts her finished plate in the sink. "Is it just me or are you finding Amber a bit odd?"

Phoenix joins her at the sink. "She's all right most of the time, but I can't keep up with everything that's wrong with her."

A Nicki Minaj song comes on the radio and Tegan turns it up high. She sways in time to the beat, watching Phoenix wash up.

Their new flatmate suddenly appears in the doorway and makes them all jump.

"Hi, Riku," Imo says, when she's caught her breath. "Have you seen Amber?"

Face dark and thunderous, he heads past her to the radio. A moment later the music volume drops. Tegan's eyes carve daggers into his head, but he doesn't notice. Returns to his room, without uttering a word.

"You only had to ask if you wanted it turned down," she calls out.

Phoenix dries her hands on a tea towel. "Let it go, Tegan. It was a bit loud."

"Maybe you should have offered him some food," Imo says. "Make more of an effort to be friendly."

"I tried offering him coffee," Phoenix says, "but he didn't answer the door."

Imo heads into the hallway. "Maybe that's what Amber's doing: not answering. I need to knock louder."

Phoenix follows and grabs her shoulders, steers her back into the kitchen. "Relax, Imo, I knocked on her door and listened at it for ages. She's not there. Let me make the three of us a coffee."

"Not there?" Imo feels a tickle of unease, a familiar feeling of loss. A sense that someone is missing. "But she *has to* be."

Chapter 13

Tegan

Tegan lays out her stock samples on the kitchen table. She knows they won't survive a night's clubbing – theft or beer spillage will get them – but she might get some advance sales before that happens. A cough seizes her throat and she covers her mouth. They've all got coughs. When Amber reappears, she's bound to claim she's dying of consumption.

She watches Phoenix dry the mugs on the draining board and put them in a cupboard. Tegan can't work her out. The girl has the looks and briskness of a tomboy so where does the regimented domesticity come from? Not boarding school – she lacks the polish of any of Tegan's school friends; it's more like she grew up in the army.

They hear a knock somewhere down the hall and find Imo trying Amber's door again.

"This can't be right." Imo's words sound slurred, and it's not just because of her cold; she's already holding a WKD. "Where is she? Why hasn't she answered my texts?" She knocks again and wobbles on her heels. After another minute, she totters back to her room.

Phoenix says she'll get a fresh tea towel from hers. Alone in the kitchen, Tegan hears a sound behind her.

"Christ!" She jumps. Riku's in the doorway. "You shouldn't creep up on people. What do you want?" she snaps.

He stares, cocking his head.

"Well, say something," she demands and immediately knows she's conceded the high ground. If someone threatens by not speaking, you have to give them silent menace back. Shout and you've lost. Her dad's dictum. She tries to recover her position with a face-off, her brown eyes into his.

Eyes still locked on hers, Riku backs out of the kitchen. For a moment Tegan's insides quake. She curses herself for feeling rattled.

Imo comes back a few minutes later, holding out her mobile. "I've called Hamid. He'll be here in a tick to take us into town." Her mouth seems to struggle to work as she explains Hamid is the taxi driver Amber got to know when he took them to the all-night garage. "She got us a good rate."

Tegan can't believe Imo is doing the same Business course as she is. Hasn't she heard of market forces? Students are calling taxis every five minutes. Hamid and his mates can charge what they like.

But it turns out Imo has another motive for booking Hamid. On the short journey into town she quizzes him about Amber.

"She's got shortish hair – dyed blonde, wears unusual clothes."

"Sounds like most students."

"You picked us up on Monday night and drove to the petrol station. She had stomach ache."

There's a flicker of recognition on his face. "Eight pound fifty? I remember."

"Have you seen her since?" Sitting forward in the back seat between Tegan and Phoenix, she holds out photos of Amber on her phone, including the one she took before the fair.

"Sorry, love, can't look. I'm driving."

"Just a quick glance."

Tegan's impressed; with a drink inside her, Imo doesn't take no for an answer. But the driver says he hasn't seen Amber since that night – with or without her red wig.

"Are you sure? If she went anywhere by taxi this week, she'd have gone with you because of the discount," Imo says, leaning on Tegan.

Tegan shrugs her off and studies Hamid's expression in the rear-view mirror. He looks perplexed by the mention of a discount. As for knowing about Amber, it's doubtful he can distinguish one pissed student from another.

Imo gives up, shifts onto Phoenix's shoulder and closes her eyes.

Hamid, realizing the cross-examination is over, slips into driver-patter. "So anything you girls want to know about Abbeythorpe, you ask me. Anything."

"Okay, thanks," Phoenix says, adjusting the weight of Imo's head. "So where's the best nightlife?"

"Exactly," Hamid says. "Anything like that you wanna know, just ask me."

He pulls up on a taxi rank behind a black Mercedes. Tegan's chest tightens.

"Bloody amateurs," Hamid says, gesticulating. "Where's a traffic warden when you need one?"

Through the windscreen of the cab, Tegan makes out a shape in the driver's seat of the Merc. Skin tingling, she hangs back while Phoenix and Imo get out. Only after they've paid Hamid and headed towards the bouncer on the club door, does she scoot after them.

Chapter 14

Thursday 29 September

Imogen

She climbs in the shower, headache threatening. As she stands under the rushing water, her dreams flicker through her mind. *Get me, won't you?* Amber, again, her face merging with her sister Sophia's.

A memory from the club itches and she scrubs her body harder, feeling dirty. Buoyed by Jägerbombs, there had been a moment – maybe even ten minutes, as much as three tracks on the dance floor – when she'd forgotten her grief and enjoyed herself. Became the old Imogen – the one that went underage drinking with her mates, the higher her heels, the tighter her skirt. Then she saw him. At first she had thought it was just a trick of the light, her mind imagining things after a few too many drinks. But when she turned back for a second look, she had known for sure. It was him. The tall man standing across the dance floor. Hood up, watching her as he had done Tegan on arrivals day. Imo sensed his eyes rake over her body. He gave her a chilling smile.

Running to the ladies, she bumped her way through the crowd apologizing, spilling drinks. She made it to the loo in time to throw up. When she came out, Phoenix had an orange juice ready for her. Tegan – grim-faced – suggested they call it a night. Imo agreed. What must they have thought of her erratic behaviour?

Her phone rings as she's towelling dry. She lets it buzz, knowing it'll be Freddie without checking the screen. After he's rung off, she texts him: I'm going, okay. The audition is today. She can't remember changing her mind, but she must have done. Why else has she got up for a shower and left out leggings and a long-sleeved T-shirt? Is she ready to live again?

Among the pizza delivery ads on the doormat lies a note for her from Royal Mail, telling her to collect a parcel from the student union building. How's she supposed to know where the post room is? It's probably spare hankies or a pillowcase from her mother.

There's a package addressed to Riku outside the flat. How come his parcels get delivered and she has to collect hers? She props it outside his door and doesn't knock. There's still no reply from Amber's room and she heads to the audition alone.

***

The auditions are in the theatre on the first floor of the student union. Three tiny backsides greet her when she rounds the corridor. Skinny girls in sports shorts and legwarmers using the bottom two steps of the staircase as a barre. Imo feels fat and unsupple. She has a coughing fit.

A chubby girl with purple hair and wearing the name tag *Doris* ushers her into a side room. "A word of advice," she says as she fixes a sticker with a number thirty-one onto Imo's chest. "Even if you're not sure of your words, keep singing."

It's a small room clearly used as a costume store. Rails of Elizabethan doublets hang alongside sparkly mini-dresses. Three girls, all wearing black Musical Theatre Society T-shirts, stare at her as she picks her way through the busy room looking for a seat.

"Over here," Lauren calls out and pats an empty plastic chair. She's wearing her black cape over her dance clothes. Imo joins her but the intimacy of their coffee together has gone and neither can think what to say. They sit in silence while others chat.

Lauren keeps looking anxiously at her watch.

"Could be ages yet," Imo suggests eventually.

"Hope not. I've got to get … go somewhere at twelve thirty." She goes slightly red and changes the subject. "A lot seem to have been in uni shows before. They must have come back early for the audition. Have you done any musicals?"

Imo shrugs. *In a different life.* "Once or twice. You?"

Lauren lists a few shows she did at school and says she's studying Theatre Studies as well as German.

Imo sits up. "My flatmate, Amber, does Theatre Studies. I thought she'd be here. Actually, I think you know her. I saw you with her before our first German lecture on Tuesday."

Lauren looks away. "Not me," she says quickly. "I don't know her."

Imo frowns, recalling when she walked across campus and spotted Amber linking arms with a girl in a black cape. It must have been Lauren.

"I could have sworn it was you. Are you sure?"

"Yep," she snaps, then adds: "There was a girl called Amber who didn't turn up to the Theatre Studies Meet and Greet last night. They read out all the names and she was the only one missing."

Unease seeps across Imo's shoulders, but before she has time to ask anything else, Doris appears and tells her the panel is ready.

"Don't be nervous," she says as she shows her the way onto the stage. "Break a leg."

There is an audition panel of six at the front of an auditorium. All name-badged: Theo, Alice, Rusty ...

Theo speaks before she can read the other names and asks her to sing. With heat rushing through her face, Imo waits for the introduction. Her voice is hoarse from coughing and she inwardly winces at how off-key she sounds, but she makes it to the end of the song. Theo thanks her with a blank expression and says they'll see her later at the dance audition.

She doesn't have to wait long. Doris calls twenty girls, including Imo, onto the stage. Imo hasn't danced properly for months and isn't sure her limbs still can. Not since Sophia disappeared. Tears prick her eyes but she blinks them away as Alice from the selection panel takes them through a warm-up. Surprised to find that jogging on the spot lightens her mood, Imo leaps into star jumps and shifts easily into stretches.

By the time they start the corner exercises, it's the old version of herself that launches into spot turns and split leaps.

"Give it more," Alice calls out from the wings.

Imo dances on, unencumbered by the baggage of the last seven months. Her steps are light, her body toned. She soaks up the panel's attention. They can look and judge as much as they like. They don't know her story.

The panel applauds when the routine finishes.

"Good job, ladies," Alice says. "We'll let you know."

Imo leaves the stage glowing with energy. She gets her things but on her way downstairs she glimpses a man on the landing. An eerie coldness settles and she fears it's him again. The tall man. She hurries outside. Is this what Sophia felt when she disappeared, that a man was following her? Did she see him everywhere she went until one day he came for her?

The early autumn sun warms her and she banishes her stupid thoughts. Today is a good day, normal. Her walk is brisk and new, as if she's using her legs for the first time after a long hibernation. She can do this. Learn to compartmentalize. Sorrow in one box, a new life of university and dance and friends in others. The world can still turn with Imo enjoying the ride.

When her phone goes she's sure it's Amber, responding to her latest message. She will be able to stop worrying. But it's a cold call. Student Life Insurance. *I'm Jordan. How you doing? How much do you love your family? Do you want them to have something after you've gone?* The call blasts open the lid Imo thought she'd gently closed. What made her think she'd be able to forget her loss? She tries to force the phone back into her jeans, but it slides from her trembling fingers and lands against the kerb.

The lights are still working and the screen appears undamaged. She picks it up and walks on. The phone has survived but her happy pace is a thing of the past. Pulling her hoodie over her hair, she trudges along the path that leads to the student halls. She detects someone approaching behind her. The footsteps are slow and lolloping, long casual strides. Imo keeps walking but moves to the side of the pavement to let them pass.

But no one hurries by. She senses that the figure has slowed their pace to match hers. Feeling uncomfortable, she dawdles so they'll have no choice but to overtake.

A shadow passes her right shoulder. A tall, rangy figure in a black hoodie saunters past. Heart thundering, Imo stands stock still. The man must sense she's stopped moving because he turns his head. Imo drops her gaze to the ground to avoid eye contact. Her neck feels damp with sweat and she wonders what the hell to do. Turn and run? With those long legs of his, he'd catch her in no time. Was this what it was like for Sophia? Did she brazen it out and walk on? This path's deserted and hidden from the road. No witnesses. Even if she'd brought her personal alarm like she promised her mother, who would hear? Her hand is shaking as she grips her phone. Call Tegan and ask her to meet her in the car? Even if she could persuade her stroppy flatmate to do the favour, it could take her ages to arrive.

A giggle rings out on the path ahead. The sweetest sound Imo has ever heard. Coming towards her, fifty yards in front, is a couple, holding hands.

Imo waves, runs towards them without looking back. "Where've you been? I've been waiting ages," she shouts. When she reaches them she whispers: "Can I walk with you, *please*?"

The boy gets it, eyeing the hooded figure on the path. "Are you okay?"

"He's creeping me out, that's all." Imo tries to sound casual, even though her pulse is racing.

"Stick with us," the girl says and moves aside to let Imo walk between the two of them.

They set off, breathing heavily. When they look up, the tall man is no longer on the path.

"I'll be okay now," Imo says. "Thanks." She leaves the couple at a run and hares towards the hall of residence, jumping at every noise in the bushes. When a bird flies off a branch, she almost cries out. Thankfully more students appear on the path and her heartbeat calms.

Finally she sees the no parking zone and the steps of the hall's main reception and decides to enter that way. It's more visible than going around the back and through to her block. Breathless from her run, she summons one last burst of energy up the steps. Panting, at the top, she pauses and looks behind her. Across the road, exactly where he stood on arrivals day, the tall man leans against the horse chestnut tree, smoking.

Chapter 15

Phoenix

Phoenix surveys the dead baked bean cans, squished teabags and crushed cheesy Wotsits on the draining board. She gets a whiff of old tomatoes and loads a box of pizza crusts into a bin bag.

Living in a caravan when she was younger meant she was used to keeping the tiny kitchenette spotless, but she's also done her fair share of industrial-strength cleaning. "This is a new dimension of mess," she says aloud.

Imo helps her with the bin bag. Phoenix can't work out whether she's in a massive sulk about tidying up, or something else is bothering her. Bad audition? She hasn't said a word since she got back.

Tegan walks in, wearing a pair of Marigold gloves.

"Finally," Phoenix says, not hiding her sarcasm.

Tegan holds an empty crisp packet at arm's length. "The uni should employ cleaners."

"I'd rather be in my mess than someone else's clean," Phoenix says.

"What the devil does that mean?"

"Nothing," Phoenix mutters. Pointless explaining; a girl like Tegan could never understand the concept of housework.

As if to prove her wrong, Tegan collects glasses and bottles and pours the contents down the sink. "No sign of Amber, though, is there? When's she going to do her share?"

"What if she can't help?" Imo says suddenly, letting go of the bin bag. "Have either of you seen her?"

Tegan shrugs and Phoenix shakes her head. She got no reply when she knocked on Amber's door earlier after she'd delivered another parcel to Riku, the third one since he moved in.

"What if someone's got her?" Imo's voice wavers.

"*Got* her? Where did that come from all of a sudden?" Tegan leans her back against the sink.

"I think there's a stalker on campus." Imo speaks in a rush, clenching her fists and pumping them in and out of her sweat-shirt sleeves. "A man followed me after my audition. I shook him off, but when I got here he was across the road. And it's not the first time I've seen him."

Phoenix's thoughts go straight to the figure at Ivor's party. "In his thirties, dark hoodie?"

"That's him," Imo exclaims. "Has he followed you, too?" She looks at Tegan. "I saw him watching you on arrivals day. Have you seen him?"

The colour drains from Tegan's face and she turns back to the glasses in the sink. "Must be a friend of Ivor's," she mutters weakly.

"I doubt it. Probably a gatecrasher." Phoenix remembers how he spilled Ivor's drink and didn't apologize. "I think he's a student, though. He was at the Freshers' Fair."

"My God." Imo sinks onto a chair. "That's the last time we saw Amber. What are we going to do?"

"Nothing." Tegan whips round, a flash of annoyance in her eye. "Phoenix has just told you he's a student, not a stalker."

"But he was down there, under a tree, smoking." Imo points out of the window.

"Where else is he supposed to bloody smoke? Why shouldn't he be outside? He probably lives here."

"But …"

"Enough, Imogen. You can't go around accusing people of stalking. You're being paranoid." Tegan waves a rubber-gloved finger. "This stops now." She turns back to the sink.

Not wanting to take sides, Phoenix picks up the bin bag and continues to fill it. Imo sits on a chair, looking as if she's trying not to cry. No one speaks. Eventually the silence is broken by the ripple of a text message on Imo's phone.

Chapter 16

Friday 30 September

Imogen

Thank you for auditioning for JC Superstar. Unfortunately, we cannot offer you a part. Show tickets available mid-November. Please get in touch if you can help with sales.

The same message was sent to her on email as well as text, but with the added bonus of a list of the successful actors. It's gone around Imo's mind so many times that she's learnt the cast list off by heart. The first name was Doris Evans as Mary Magdalene. The audition usher got the star part.

She had left the kitchen to read the text in her room. It's what she deserves. How could she have pranced around that stage like the Imogen from *before*? How could she forget, even for a second? Her head thumps and she needs caffeine. She heard Tegan and Phoenix return to their rooms a while ago so heads as quietly as she can to the kitchen.

The bloody kettle won't boil. She realizes the flex isn't switched on at the wall. Tegan's harsh words fill her head. Imo gets everything wrong. How could she mistake a mature student, standing outside his hall, for a stalker? She'd never have dreamed up something so outlandish a year ago. She was normal back then.

She pours her tea and some of the hot water misses the mug. She finds a stinky dishcloth on the draining board and mops the wet patch. Chucks the cloth in the bin and wishes she could climb in after it. When she's slopped enough water over her coffee granules, she heads out with her mug.

Amber's door is open and Imo stands stock still in the hallway. She has a moment of fury. She's been worried sick, left countless messages, made a fool of herself in front of her flatmates and now Amber's back without a word of apology. Intending to tell Amber exactly what she thinks of her, Imo marches up the hall.

But it's a male voice she hears coming from Amber's room. "We can let you have some cardboard boxes." The accent is local. "It doesn't all have to be out today. We can give you another week."

"That's kind of you." A female voice, older, strained. "I'll take what I can and pack the rest. My other daughter will collect it next week."

"Right you are, love. Let me just deliver these and I'll get you the boxes." The man steps into the hallway. He's in an Abbeythorpe maintenance team shirt and carrying three parcels. "Morning, love," he says cautiously to Imo.

She becomes aware of her short dressing gown and matted hair. He slips past her and knocks on Riku's door.

"Morning, sonny, I've got your mail."

Riku's door opens, two hands stretch out to take the parcels and the door closes again.

The man shrugs, says, "Bye, love," to Imo and leaves the flat, whistling.

Imo knocks on Amber's open door. A middle-aged woman sits on the bed, an open, empty suitcase at her feet. She looks up at Imo. "Are you Amber's flatmate? Come in, love. I'm her mum."

Imo looks at the suitcase. "Are you … Is she …?"

"She's already gone. Off travelling."

"When's she coming back?" Imo's voice rises, all fury forgotten. Amber's gone? Who's going to be her friend now? She silently admonishes herself for being selfish when Amber's missing her course. That matters more.

The woman shakes her head. "Her text said she'd changed her mind about uni. It wasn't for her." She gets up and peels a large poster from the wall and curls it around a roll of others already on the floor. "I thought this time she'd settled down." She sighs and rubs her hands through her mousy grey hair. "What's your name? Were you a friend?"

Her eyes rest on the dressing gown and it makes Imo feel filthy.

"I'm Imo. All four girls in this flat hit it off, but we're not on the same course. Except me and Tegan, we do Business." She shuts up. Why would Amber's mother care what her daughter's flatmates study? Her ex-flatmates. "When did she send the text?"

"I picked it up Tuesday evening when I checked my phone before the ten o'clock news. I tried phoning back but, whenever I try, her mobile's switched off. I expect she's got a new phone if she's gone abroad. It would cost too much to stay on a UK network."

Inside her dressing gown sleeves, Imo's arm hairs stand on end. She knows about switched-off mobiles, about calling the same number over and over again. About listening to an answer machine hundreds of times. She swallows. "Did you try the app when you got the text? The one that shows where the sender is. Amber might have downloaded it."

Amber's mum gets her phone out and passes it to Imo. "I wouldn't know about that, love. See what you think."

It's the same geriatric iPhone 4S as Imo's. After scrolling for a few seconds, Imo's sure that neither Amber nor her mum have the app. She speed-dials Amber's phone. She's been calling all week and she gets the recorded voice again, telling her the phone is switched off.

The person you are calling is unable to take your call …

The message clangs with terrible familiarity. Every day she calls Sophia's number and hears this same message. Same wording, same mechanical voice.

"Are you okay?" Amber's mum steps towards her, a worried look on her face.

"Sorry, it's just a bit of a shock, that's all. I didn't know she'd left." Imo sits down heavily on the bed. Calms her breathing, stares at the phone in her hand.

Without thinking, she sends a text to her own phone. It pings in her dressing gown pocket. For some reason she needs to have the woman's number. She passes the phone back. "I'm sorry she's gone. Amber's nice."

The woman looks straight at her. "Thank you." She stands up and hugs her. "Thank you for saying that."

Imo steps back, aware that she mustn't let her fears rub off on this woman. This isn't the same; Amber's got in touch and explained her absence. No need for the cancer of uncertainty to infect another family.

After saying goodbye, she returns to her room and lies on her bed. Eyes wide open, her whole face stiff with fatigue.

Chapter 17

Phoenix

At noon, Phoenix knocks on Imo's door, sure that she's awake. She heard her earlier in Amber's room.

Imo lets her in and heads quickly to her desk. Facebook is open on her laptop, a list of people named Smith fills the screen.

"Thought you only went on Tinder," Phoenix says.

Reddening, Imo slams it shut.

"Were they relatives? I couldn't help noticing the surname on those profiles."

"A hobby of mine, finding people with the same name as me. It's great fun." Imo gives a giggle. It sounds forced.

Phoenix smiles cautiously. What's going on? Imo can't have got over the audition rejection already. Her hair's still greasy and she's in that awful dressing gown. Still pissed off about something, for sure.

"Do you mind if I open your curtains?" Phoenix asks.

"It's too bright ... Okay, if you must." Imo scrunches her hair into a sloppy bun and tightens her belt.

Phoenix explains why she's come. "Tegan and I are going back to the Freshers' Fair and would like to take you with us. Seeing as you didn't get a part ..." She pauses, resets her tact-ometer. "Now you've got more time for hobbies, you could sign up for Bhangra. Tegan and I have joined. It should be a laugh. Maybe you'd like to come too. And Amber – now's she's back. I heard you talking to her."

But Imo looks away and explains it was Amber's mum in her room. "Amber's jacked in uni and gone travelling. I just don't get it."

"Already? I sussed the girl was a bit, you know, unstable, but I thought she'd give it more than a week."

"It's not even a week. She texted home on Tuesday saying she'd left. If only she'd told me her plans, I could have talked her out of it."

Phoenix looks at the laptop. "Have you tried her Facebook account? Or maybe some of the other Theatre Studies students are in touch with her. Come with us to the Freshers' Fair and we can ask around."

"Do you think anyone will remember her?" Imo looks past Phoenix, her eyes moving out into a squint. "Did you see her after we were at the fair together on Tuesday?"

Phoenix trawls her memory. Amber had had one of her funny wobbles and went outside the Great Hall. "I don't think so, even though I knocked on her door a few times. We can ask Tegan on the way. I'll call for you in twenty minutes. Does that give you time to shower and dress?"

Thankfully Imo ignores the clumsy hint, her mind still on Amber. "So neither of us saw her go." Her skin grows pale. "Apart from her bracelet by the side of the road, she left without a trace."

Chapter 18

Phoenix

Phoenix understands when Tegan offers to drive to the Freshers' Fair. She must have taken one look at Imo and decided the girl is fit to drop. The hollows under her dull eyes are deep and grey. She smells better than she did earlier, but showering hasn't extended to washing her hair. It hangs limply down her back. And yet she has surprising energy for discussing Amber. As they hunt for a parking space behind the Great Hall, she quizzes Tegan about the last time she saw their flatmate.

"Can't remember." Tegan stops speaking to make a three-point turn at the end of the tiny car park. "Not since the fair, I don't think." There's another pause as she crawls forward, checking for spaces. "That must be when she did a bunk." After she's reversed expertly into a narrow space between a Ford Ka and an old Nissan, she switches off the engine.

Imo continues: "I thought she was my friend. I thought she trusted me."

"Maybe she dropped us a hint that she was unhappy, but we didn't pick it up," Phoenix suggests as they walk round the building to the entrance. "Are you sure she didn't mention the idea of leaving when the two of you talked?"

Imo slows her pace and falls behind, a look of concentration on her face. "There might have been something, but I was too drunk to remember. It was that night when she looked after me. She seemed troubled, but I could have just imagined it."

Phoenix pushes open the Great Hall door. It's much quieter inside than when they were here on Tuesday. No more than a dozen freshers wandering round. As sad as a Christmas market in the drizzle. Phoenix wonders how they can keep the fair going for much longer, but remembers that it's Refreshers next week when the second years come back to party.

Imo strides off, asking loudly if anyone does Theatre Studies. A boy in a brown poncho says yeah, but shakes his head when he sees the image of Amber on Imo's phone. No one else comes forward.

"I knew this wouldn't work," she says, coming back to Phoenix and Tegan. "I talked to a Theatre Studies girl yesterday who thinks Amber didn't turn up to the first department meeting. If that's the case, none of the drama students will know who she is." She squints into the middle distance, her expression unreadable.

Phoenix takes her arm, hoping to distract her. "Let's get you signed up for Bhangra. We can ask about Amber after that."

They head to the aisle with the dance societies, but Imo stops after a few paces. "Something happened here to upset Amber. We need to find out why she left."

Tegan folds her arms. "To be fair, Imo, lots of things upset Amber. I only knew her for two days and I already had to avoid talking about gender and tomatoes."

Imo turns to Phoenix. "Will you help?"

Phoenix sighs. It's not what she had in mind, but maybe it's best to let her make her enquiries and get it out of her system.

She goes with Imo as she holds out her phone to show the stall-holders on the political stands the picture of Amber in the red wig. One or two remember her outfit but nothing more. The punk girl from the human rights charity smiles when she sees the photo and recounts the gist of their debate. But she offers no clue where she might have gone.

It's the same story on the Drama Society stall. The boy shakes his head. "Shame, I really think she might have persuaded us to try Epic Theatre."

The beautiful Indian girl on the Bhangra stall remembers them and offers her tray of bhajis. Phoenix smiles and takes one. She explains that they've brought Imo along so that she can join, but Imo holds out Amber's photo on her phone. When the girl shrugs and says she hasn't seen her, Imo thanks her and moves straight on to the next stand. Phoenix throws up her arms and apologizes.

"Why didn't you sign?" Tegan hisses when she reaches Imo.

"In a minute," Imo says. She presses her phone. "I've sent you Amber's picture. If all three of us ask at the stalls, it won't take long."

Tegan gets out her phone. "I came to university to become the next Alan Sugar, not Sherlock." She heads for the chess stand.

Phoenix watches Imo go to the student from the Deaf Society. He looks at her phone screen and shakes his head. Phoenix wonders if she should go after Tegan; she's bound to be terror-izing the poor chess boy. But she realizes that the girl at the LGBTQ stand is looking at her. The one who was on duty last time they came. Black hair and blue, blue eyes.

After a breath, Phoenix approaches her. The young woman takes Phoenix's phone and studies Amber's Geisha Girl picture. "Is she Trans?"

Phoenix swallows a laugh. That was one of the few things Amber hadn't claimed. "Not as far as I know."

The girl rubs her chin. Neat nails. Long slim fingers. "You

know, I think I do remember her. She was standing just over there, staring this way. Was she thinking of coming out?"

Phoenix feels herself blush. "Who knows?" She gives what she hopes is a casual shrug. "She never said."

The girl places the phone back in Phoenix's hand and closes her fingers over it. "I'm sorry she left before we got a chance to speak. But come back if you want to ask me anything else. I'm Keren by the way."

Phoenix can't hold her gaze and tells the floor her name.

"Any luck?" Imo asks behind her.

Phoenix takes herself away from the stallholder, grateful for Imo's interruption.

The last stall in the aisle is the Parents' Group. Imo approaches the same dark-haired woman who was manning it on Tuesday. There's no sign of her little girl today. The woman smiles politely.

"Did you see this student here a few days ago?" Imo shows her the phone.

The woman's eyes stay on the image, apparently studying the red wig and white make-up. Then she looks up, shaking her head. "Sorry. I don't remember her."

Imo moves close to the woman's desk, invading her space almost. "Are you sure? It would have been on Tuesday."

The woman moves her leaflets so they are in a pile between her and Imo. "The Parents' Group doesn't get many takers in Freshers' Week. We're just here to speak to the odd mature student who's a parent. I tell them about the uni crèche and the family barbecue we've got next Saturday lunchtime. But I don't know why we bother for so few people. Posters around campus would be more effective." Her eyes move over Imo's left shoulder. "I went off rota around four o'clock on Tuesday. Perhaps your friend came after that?"

Imo shows the woman another photo, of the four of them in the kitchen on the first day. "That's what she usually looks like."

But the woman scarcely glances at it, shaking her head again.

Imo doesn't budge and holds out the bangle they found outside after their last visit to the fair. "Perhaps you saw a girl wearing this?"

The woman screws up her face, as if she wants to say something patronizing, but instead lets out a sigh. "I'm afraid not. Should I?"

"It's all we've got left of her." Imo pushes the bangle over her knuckles and watches it slide down her wrist.

Phoenix ushers Imo away before she declares the bangle a sacred relic. She gives the woman what she hopes is a conspiratorial smile: *Kids, eh?* and picks up a leaflet for the family barbeque. "I'll spread the word."

Imo needs the loo and Phoenix goes with her. They pass Riku on the stairs. He has his back to them, forearms over the banister. Imo says hello but he doesn't hear, or so he pretends.

When they come down, he's still there, staring intently at the fair below.

They retrace their steps, scouring the room for Tegan on their way. Phoenix is relieved she's not still with the boy from the chess club. Like a child who pulls legs off an insect, Tegan might have taken similar pleasure with her very own chess pawn. When Phoenix spots her in the sport clubs' aisle, they go to fetch her.

"Something happened to Amber before we got this far," Imo tells her. "These sportspeople have nothing to do with her decision to walk off. Let's go back to the flat. This was a waste of time."

"We should still ask, you never know." Tegan makes eye contact with a clean-shaven student in a Raging Bull polo shirt. Reluctantly she peels away when Imo heads to the exit.

Phoenix taps the family barbecue leaflet against her lips, mulling over what she's observed. At least two people acting weird. Maybe something, maybe nothing.

Chapter 19

Imogen

The lecturer's parting shot at the end of the Business Culture lecture is to thank them for attending the optional Saturday session. The word optional causes the students around Imo to squawk, some even dropping *Fuck offs* under their breath. Tegan's eyes become heat-seeking missiles trained on the man's smug mouth. But he shrugs off the protest, as if he instigates it every year and lives for the moment.

When they get out of the lecture, Imo suggests to Tegan they hang around outside the academic block. "We can show Amber's photo to anyone who walks past."

"You've got five minutes. I've wasted enough of my Saturday already." Tegan speeds along the corridor. "So what if people do remember her? That doesn't mean they'll know where she is."

"Thanks, Tegan. I appreciate it." Five minutes is better than nothing. There were plenty of new students walking about the campus on Tuesday. Someone must have seen Amber when she came out of the Freshers' Fair. Did she say anything? Which way did she go? Was she with another student? A cold shadow crosses Imo. All the parallels with her own family flood her thoughts. But she dismisses them, forcing a lid on her imagination.

She steps ahead of Tegan and reaches the exit. "Perhaps we can ask around the halls when we get back. It won't take long to cover our block."

Tegan sighs noisily. "If she managed to leave without *us* noticing, I doubt our neighbours will have seen her. Besides, Phoenix has already asked around. No takers."

"What? When did she do that?" Imo looks closely at Tegan. Is it a lie to fob her off?

"After we got back from the fair yesterday. She was in a mood weird enough to match one of Amber's. Said she wanted to see if anyone in the block had seen her. I'm not going to that fair again in case I get possessed as well."

Imo feels a rush of excitement. If Phoenix took the trouble to knock on doors, she must be anxious about Amber. Maybe Imo hasn't got it wrong.

Tegan walks away so Imo calls after her. "You said I could have five minutes."

To her surprise Tegan comes back. She scrolls through her phone and finds the image of Amber in her kimono and wig. "They'll think I'm a pimp if I tout this about."

Two boys, turning into the Business Centre, falter when they hear the word pimp. Tegan brandishes her phone at them. "Think you can afford that, do you?"

But her sneer vanishes and her eyes freeze on something over Imo's shoulder. A car crawls past and the driver leans over the passenger seat for a better look. Imo's insides lurch when she recognizes the driver, still with his hood up, wearing sunglasses even though it isn't sunny.

"I'm leaving." Tegan's voice is hard as she sets off to her car.

Imo catches her up. Safety in numbers, even though the man has driven off. "That was him. That creepy older student. Maybe he has something to do with Amber. I know you said he can't be a stalker, but why do I keep seeing him everywhere?"

"Fuck should I know," Tegan snaps.

They travel in silence, Tegan's white hands gripping the wheel.

Back at the flat, Imo toys with asking round the block whether anyone saw Amber with the stalker. But she doesn't know which neighbours Phoenix has already spoken to and she isn't in her room to ask. Imo goes on Facebook for much of the afternoon, checking periodically if Amber has signed in. She hasn't. Nor has Sophia. And she hasn't set up a new profile in her name. Imo lies on her bed, her mind in turmoil. *Get me, won't you?* Thoughts of Amber make her shiver. History repeating itself. The answer phone message rings through her mind: *The person you are calling is unable to take your call …*

Imo tosses and turns, wishes she could take her batteries out and sleep. Maybe take them out permanently and welcome oblivion.

Chapter 20

Sunday 2 October

Imogen

It's gone noon, and it's hot and bright in bed. Imo gets up. Silence. Phoenix has pushed a note under the door to say she has archery club. Tegan will have gone off with the Conservation Volunteers to annihilate rhododendrons. As the intranet is working again, Imo has no excuse for not getting on with the reading links that Dr Wyatt gave them in the last seminar. It's about the Third Gender and Imo doubts anyone on Tinder will be able to help. Amber would have plenty to say on the topic. But she's not here.

Something shifts in her belly and her muscles tense. Is a person any less lost if they send a text before dropping off the face of the earth? Amber's mother has accepted it and, although she sounded disappointed, didn't seem surprised. But she wasn't with Amber in her first two days at uni. Didn't see her confidence, excitement. A bit fond of histrionics, maybe, but not about to throw in the towel before the first lecture.

Imo can't leave it, but who can she tell? The police? And

say what? If they took her seriously, they'd question Amber's family.

She shivers, recalling that first phone call her dad made. The first of many. Three in the morning. Her eighteenth birthday. She was back from the clubs and at the kitchen table, trying to conceal the double vodkas in her speech. But her parents didn't notice. Their eyes wide, faces white. Mum listening as Dad spoke. In her drunken state, Imo didn't know at first who he was calling; she could only hear his side of the conversation. But it wasn't long before the tone of his voice and the look in his eyes hit home. And she understood.

"Doesn't live here, but was expected hours ago."

"Nottingham."

"That's right, a master's student."

"There wasn't a row."

"Not on medication, no."

"Hasn't left a note, not with us."

"Facebook? ... We'll check."

"Never, nothing like this before."

No, Imo shivers. She won't do that to Amber's mother without good reason. Maybe years of Amber's flights of fancy have exhausted the woman. No energy left to fear the worst. Why should Imo start a police rollercoaster, when the only direction is down through gloom, confusion and disbelief?

Surely Amber notified someone in the university hierarchy that she was giving up the course. Perhaps she had to fill in a form stating her reasons for leaving and her future plans. Imo's no way of accessing that, but the student reps might know.

She gets her laptop and sits on the bed. The University of Abbeythorpe website has a section on Student Welfare Services. A head-and-shoulders shot of a girl, with a shiny smile in one of the official pink T-shirts; welfare rep for first year undergraduates. Imo clicks the link and makes an appointment for 11 a.m. the next day.

Too exhausted for her German reading, she lies on the bed and sends her mother an upbeat text. Mum's done well so far today; fewer than ten texts – one or two with family trivia – not all urgent advice for keeping safe. Imo presses send, leaving out her concerns about Amber. The last thing her mother needs is another lost girl.

When Daisy Was Twenty Months Old

Tummy full of Mummy's egg and soldiers, Daisy sits contently in her car seat in the back, breathing in the tang of Mummy's peppermints. They sing songs and Mummy chuckles in that happy, pretty voice of hers.

Mummy sings: "This is the way we wash our ..."

"Fay." *Daisy wipes her cheeks with her fists.*

"This is the way we comb our hair."

"Comb a hair." *Daisy points her fingertips down the sides of her head.*

"Clever girl." *Mummy laughs.* "You can say more than all the other babies." *She pops another mint in her mouth.*

Why is Mummy talking when Daisy wants singing? "Again," *she demands.*

"Sorry, sweetie. Where was I ...? This is the way we brush our teeth."

Daisy smiles and gets ready to sing.

Suddenly, the car brakes and Daisy's head knocks against the side of the seat. Everything inside her body stops, and she can't move. Then the hurting bursts across her forehead and into her hair. She starts to howl.

Mummy turns round, eyes thin and face red. "Shhhhhh. Not now. Be quiet."

Through blurry tears, Daisy can see flashing lights and men in hats on the road ahead. "Don't make a noise," *Mummy says. She sounds angry and there's a look in her eyes that Daisy has never seen before. Mummy turns the car another way, before the men in hats reach them. Her face is all dark and scary. The car speeds up. Mummy's jaw is tight and she keeps looking out of the back window.*

"This is the way we put on our clothes ..." *Mummy sings, but her voice sounds gritty and she keeps repeating the same line. Her forehead is shiny with sweat and Daisy doesn't feel like joining in.*

The agony in Daisy's head and the effort of not screaming force her to close her eyes. For ages and ages, until Mummy has stopped singing and there are no sounds except the fast engine and Mummy's noisy breathing. Even when she senses the car finally stop, Daisy keeps them shut, only looking up when she feels herself lifted and pressed against Mummy's soft, quilted jacket.

"What is it, sweetie? Tell Mummy."

Daisy bursts into fresh crying. "Bump a head," she sobs.

"Where, sweetie? How did you bump it?" She holds Daisy's chin and scans her forehead. "There's nothing to see."

"Car," Daisy says, pain still fizzing across her skull.

Mummy rocks and shooshes, all the while patting across Daisy's hair. "Naughty car."

Pain throbs again and Daisy rears away from Mummy's chest in a new wave of howls.

"Shall Mummy kiss it better?"

Solemnly Daisy leans forward to receive Mummy's special magic. Tired out from crying, she relaxes as Mummy settles her in her car seat.

"No one hurts my baby. No one," Mummy mutters as they get back in the car and drive on. "They won't find us."

Chapter 21

Monday 3 October

Imogen

The Accountancy lecturer changes his figures on the interactive whiteboard, nodding gratefully to the nerd kid at the other end of Imo's row who reads out his answers. Imo feels for the man, worries how his confidence has dissolved so completely within twenty minutes of their first lecture. The class's attention wavered the second time the nerd piped up with a correction. Now, with the nerd's third intervention, they chat openly, ignoring the lecturer. Tegan plays on her phone.

Poor guy. He's younger than most lecturers and looks like he might actually give a damn. He's vaguely familiar too. A mad idea that he was at the nightclub last week makes Imo squirm. God, she hopes not; she made enough of a fool of herself in front of her flatmates without a lecturer having a ring-side seat.

She makes a point of concentrating, taking notes as he talks through the balance sheet. She's the only one listening, so he seems to address the lecture directly to her. She tries to look intellectual and silently prays he won't ask her a question. She suppresses several yawns. After a day in bed, sleep didn't come through the long night.

The nerd's hand shoots up again and the lecturer has to erase more figures. Imo studies him. Early forties, maybe. Wispy hair and a suit that looks as if it's made of wood. What's gone wrong for him? Why isn't he a hotshot accountant? He's not even a proper academic. The ones with PhDs waste no time in affixing "Dr" to the start of their name, but he introduced himself as plain Sean Hennessey. Has life not quite worked out? Imo feels a wave of affinity.

She's chosen the seat nearest the door for a quick getaway but feels bad when she slips out ten minutes early for the welfare interview. Hopes Sean Hennessey won't take the loss of his one attentive student to heart. She vows to read some chapters from the accountancy textbook before the next lecture, or at least buy it.

She's left it a bit late and has to run. The Student Welfare Services is on the ground floor of her hall of residence, next to the reception area where she picked up her keys on the first day. She knocks on the open office door and steps inside, hot and thirsty. Two students sit over computers at desks facing each other. One is a mixed-race guy in a sleeveless shirt and blue trousers. He smiles.

The other student is the shiny-smiled white girl from the website photo. Imo's forgotten her name, even though she read it last night.

"Imogen? Would you like to come through?" She brings her to a room at the back of the office and invites her to take a seat on one of the sofas. She sits down on the other one and picks up the iPad that's on the seat.

"Can you explain why you've come to see me?" Straight down to business, no preamble. Don't uni reps go on empathy courses?

"I'm worried about my flatmate. No one has seen her since Tuesday afternoon."

The rep nods expansively but her blank expression doesn't change. "So where do you think she is?"

Imo squirms under the girl's intense gaze. The blinds billow slightly; the window is open behind them. Family-sized bottles of Fanta line the wall beside a filing cabinet. Imo's mouth is so dry she has trouble swallowing.

"Imogen?"

"Her mother thinks she's gone travelling, but Amber seemed happy here to me."

The girl – is she ever going to introduce herself? – opens the iPad. "Has her mum told the university officially? What's her name?"

Imo shrugs. What's her mother's name got to do with it? She's starting to wish she hadn't come. Maybe she could call back when it's just the other student here. He might be more help.

"You don't know your flatmate's name?" The girl's face is still passive, but she can't keep incredulity out of her voice.

Imo realizes the misunderstanding. "Amber," she says confidently but feels stupid again because she doesn't know Amber's surname.

The girl asks for the address of their flat and looks them up on her screen. "Amber Murphy, Room 2, Flat 17. Yes, I've got her. It says here she quit her course on the twenty-seventh of September."

"But why?" Imo perches forward on the sofa. "Why did she leave?"

The girl doesn't reply for a moment. She reads something on her screen and scrolls down. Then she puts the device aside and rests her hands on her lap. "Have you made other friends?"

"Me? Of course." Tegan, Phoenix, Lauren, Riku. Friends right? The Fanta bottles stare at her and she can feel her lips cracking.

"Good. So you've got people to talk to?" The girl's gaze is intense again.

Imo bites her tongue. Someone to talk to, isn't that what this shiny girl is here for?

"What are you doing for fun?" the rep asks.

The question crushes Imo as she realizes what this welfare rep sees. A spotty girl with greasy hair and in Saturday's sweatshirt, clinging to the transient friendship of someone who chose to leave. She stands up. "I've got a lecture."

The girl stays seated, a smile on her lips. "Are you getting enough sleep? It's a problem for freshers, all those party nights." She laughs like a granny.

Imo gives a tight smile back. What could she tell her: people like her mostly don't sleep?

The rep reaches out and taps Imo's arm. "Don't worry about Amber. It's confidential so I can't say what, but there's more information in the file." She moves her hand to the iPad. "It's not surprising she left university. We see it every year. The best thing you can do is forget about it and enjoy yourself."

When she escorts Imo through the front office, the male student doesn't look up from his computer. Imo has a panicked feeling that he's heard every word.

"Try making a plan of what you're doing at each hour of the day. Time for work, for fun, eat, sleep, that sort of thing," the girl says. "Pop back if ever you want to talk. Bye Imogen. Thanks for coming."

As Imo climbs the staircase towards her flat, she mulls over the rep's words. Could she be right? Maybe she does need to focus on herself. Are her memories of the tragedy at home clouding her judgement? She can't let Sophia go, but that's no reason to cling onto Amber.

Chapter 22

Tuesday 4 October

Imogen

The glass vibrates against her forehead as Imo leans on the train window. Being in the countryside is a reminder that there's a world outside Abbeythorpe. It's as if the train has pierced a bubble. Jagged hedges flash past. Dips and hollows, mounds of verdant earth, escarpments. Tips of trees are speckled yellow and copper although most leaves are still green, clinging to twigs, to branches, to solid trunks. But soon they will shrivel and fall.

Sheep dot across a field, eating grass. Above the horizon, skies are pale blue and vast. Imo is a speck on the earth. Like the sheep.

Her phone vibrates and makes her shiver guiltily. Is it Mum? Does she sense Imo's on a train despite her promise never to travel on one alone? A blur slams against the window and she jumps. It's a train going the other way. How would it be to fall in front of it? Life extinct in a nano-second. No more uncertainty, no more waiting.

That was what Inspector Hare thought at first and he coordinated searches along the Nottingham line. He advised Imo's family to stay away, but they watched it live on Sky News. Lines of anoraked civilians in a synchronized sweep of the embankment. Eyes down, brogging the undergrowth with sticks. Looking for a corpse.

Imo opens her purse for the tenth time to check for her railcard and the bangle, wishing she had a box or an envelope. It's going to look weird plonking it in Mrs Murphy's hand. But as the woman must already have doubts about Imo, Amber's weird flatmate, it probably won't matter.

She had a dream again in the night. Amber appeared on one side of a badminton net with the welfare rep on the other. They batted *Get me, won't you* and *Forget about it* between them with Imo scouring the spectators for Sophia. By the time it was light, Imo, drenched in sweat, knew she had to speak to Amber's mother. The bangle occurred to her halfway through the phone call. So she told Mrs Murphy she wanted to return it without the risk of it getting lost in the post. The woman reluctantly agreed, but explained Tuesday was her only day off this week from her garden centre job. Imo offered to go immediately and mentally composed a grovelling speech to Dr Wyatt to explain her absence.

The train slows and trundles past a farmhouse. Rusting equipment languishes in the yard. It would have been pristine once. A wall of hay bales wrapped in black plastic sheeting divides a field. One side is meadow. The other has been cleared to flat, bare earth. The train enters a tunnel, bright with graffiti. Big, sharp-edged words that say nothing.

Finally a platform appears alongside and people at Chadcombe station wait to board. After a screech of brakes and a lurch, the train halts. Imo gets out. It's chilly after the train but not as cold as Abbeythorpe. It's like everyone says: the climate is better down here.

There's a rank of taxis outside the station. She gives the address to the first driver in the line and gets in the back. The journey passes in silence. He pulls up outside a solid semi-detached. Privet hedge, neat lawn, fuchsia bushes in the flowerbed. The house must be worth a lot this far south despite the flaking paintwork. Imo worries no one's home as there's no car in the drive, but a dark-haired woman in her early twenties answers the door. She wears black trousers and a purple shirt with *Pizza Pedro* embroidered on the breast pocket. Imo gives her name.

"Come in," the woman says stiffly. "Mum's expecting you."

Imo follows her through a narrow hallway and into the cosy lounge. Quality three-piece suite, worn on the arms. Velvet curtains, open fireplace.

Mrs Murphy stands up and points to an armchair. "We've just made a pot of tea. Would you like a cup?"

Imo accepts and sits down, feeling nervous and wondering whether she has made the right choice in coming. Amber's mum retakes her place on the sofa, looking tired.

"Thanks, Jade," she says when the young woman brings in the tray.

Jade serves the tea and sits on the other armchair. Both women look at Imo. She balances her cup on her lap and retrieves the bangle from her purse. Takes a deep breath.

"This is Amber's. At least I think it is. We found it on the ground at uni."

Mrs Murphy puts it on the arm of the sofa. "That's kind. I'll make sure she gets it when she comes home." She swallows, her eyes pensive.

The reaction doesn't surprise Imo. Even if the woman's not worried about Amber going travelling, she must want to know when she'll be back. It's her other daughter's reaction that strikes Imo as odd. Jade glares at the carpet and shakes her head.

Imo notices three photos on the mantelpiece. One shows Jade smiling into the lens, with a figure on either side raising champagne glasses towards her. Mrs Murphy on her left. A Goth girl with jet-black plaits and thick eyeliner to her right.

"That was taken two years ago," Mrs Murphy says, following Imo's gaze, "when Jade got made branch manager."

"So that's …" Imo looks at the Goth.

"Amber in her gloom phase. It's funny how your children change." Mrs Murphy's eyes fall on one of the other photographs. A dark-haired girl of about thirteen has her arm round a younger, auburn-haired child. They look to be at a theme park. "They both had curly hair in those days. All that straightening can't be good for it."

Imo points at the third picture – a bride and groom. "Is that you and Amber's dad?"

"I still miss him, so do the girls. He'd turn in his grave if he knew how things had panned out."

Imo's confused. Amber told them her father was an accountant in London. She remembers how Amber went on about "in Town". "When did your husband pass away?"

"Jade was eighteen and Amber thirteen. Heart attack on the tube on his way to work. Our world turned upside down. Jade was due to start university the following week. She'd done most of her packing, but that got put on hold." She looks at her daughter. "But you'll get there one day, love. And you're doing all right, managing a top family restaurant."

Jades gives her mother a weak smile and her eyes come to rest on Imo.

"It must have been hard for you both," Imo says, feeling lame. She turns to the mother. "Hard for Amber too."

Mother and daughter exchange a glance and Imo feels the room chill. Mrs Murphy slouches in her seat, looking even more exhausted. Jade brushes lint off her trousers.

Eventually Mrs Murphy says, "Amber seemed to take it worst. She was thick as thieves with her dad. After his death she retreated into her own world and came out now and again as different people. That's how she came to dress like that." She glances at the Goth girl in the photograph. "She got in with a bad crowd for a while."

Jade's head shoots up and she stares at her mother.

"But it was a stage of the grieving. We have to understand that." Mrs Murphy looks at Imo as she speaks, but Imo's sure she's addressing Jade. "Her wildest time was around fourteen, fifteen. By sixth form she'd calmed down and managed to take her A levels." She takes a breath. "Perhaps she'll go back to studying when she's ready." She glances at Jade. "You both will."

There's silence and Imo sips her tea. What more is there to say? Amber didn't settle at university because she's still finding a way to mourn her father. Five years is a lot of grieving, but Imo can understand it. The light went out of Imo in February. Until then, she thought families like hers only existed on TV news and true crime documentaries.

She gets up and thanks them for the tea. This family has its own tragedy. They don't need Imo poking her nose into it. She has to let Amber go.

Mrs Murphy shows her to the door and promises to give Amber the bangle. When she sees her. The sentence is punctuated in half by a deep sigh.

There's ages until Imo's train so she decides to walk to the station. Jade catches up in the street and walks beside her. "Just so you know. Amber's not the sad girl lost that my mother paints."

"That's okay," Imo says, walking on. "You don't have to explain." The welfare rep was right; she needs to concentrate on her own uni experience. It was Amber's choice to leave; her text home proved that. Time for Imo to get back to Abbeythorpe.

But Jade has more to say. "Amber must have put on one hell of a performance for you to come all this way. But then Amber's good at acting: grief-stricken daughter, Goth, junkie. She even acted pretend-pregnant for months. Broke Mum's heart with that one."

Imo walks faster, regretting her visit even more, but Jade keeps up, filling the air with bile.

"Then she went one worse, told us she was psychic and trying to contact Dad. I'd have chucked her out but Mum forgave her every time." She touches Imo's arm and stops walking. Imo has to stop too. "It's a mile and a half to my restaurant but we don't have a car any more. Mum sold it to pay Amber's uni accommodation fees. And now the ungrateful madam vanishes and leaves us to pay a term's rent for no reason."

"I'm sorry," Imo gasps, the word *vanishes* having sent her heart rate into freefall. "I guess I didn't know Amber at all."

Chapter 23

Amber

New pains – ankle and knee. Payback for all the times in the last few days when she's faked them. Amber's head clangs with Tegan's imagined laughter: *Serves you right*. The spite is sharp, then muffled, then sharp again. A din to be endured.

She opens her eyes, but it stays dark. Her brain is mushed like in the old days, back under the bridge with her true friends. Everything bathed in a chemical shadow.

For the first time in years, her head feels the same whoosh and buzz. And the smells: pee on concrete, unwashed flesh, stale food. Only the sweet, fusty scent of weed smoke is missing. Maybe if she inhales deeply enough, it will be here too. A rush of warmth; she's home. It's nice to be back at the bridge.

Then she remembers Danno. She can't stay. Broke him once, mustn't again. The thought triggers an older memory: through the unfamiliar cottage window in Derbyshire, a serene world of white outside. Doubled over, hand pressed against the glass, wanting the pain to be over. Wanting her mum.

She must leave before Danno gets here. But when she tries to stand up, her leg doesn't move. Her head hurts too much to work it out. She curls up and sleeps.

Chapter 24

Tegan

When she hears Imo's door being unlocked, Tegan resists sticking her head out into the hallway. None of her business where the girl's been all day. But when footsteps go from Imo's room to the kitchen, she picks up her coffee mug and joins her.

"Thought you'd done an Amber."

Tegan's tone is jokey but Imo doesn't smile. It looks as if she's been crying. Tegan's school friends were the same, always blubbing. Maybe she's the odd one, hard-hearted. She clenches her hands around her empty cup, forces a smile. "Lectures, was it?"

Imo shakes her head and flops onto a seat. "Why am I such a bad judge?"

"Too trusting." The words are out before Tegan realizes it's a rhetorical question. She sits beside her. "Has something happened?"

"I went to see Amber's mother."

"At home? In … where is it she lives?" Tegan asks, wondering how she's ended up with these flatmates: a disappearing fantasist and now an obsessive.

"Chadcombe. I skipped a lecture."

There's a question in her voice. What does she want – a bollocking or reassurance? Tegan doesn't give a toss if Imo misses lectures. Tegan plans on missing most Accountancy classes unless the lecturer Hennessey bucks up his ideas.

"I feel stupid," Imo continues. "Her mum was nice and everything, but it was obvious from what she told me that she wasn't surprised Amber's gone travelling. Then Amber's sister filled me in on some of the stunts Amber's pulled over the years. This disappearing act is mild in comparison to other things she's done."

"I always thought she was a liar." Tegan winces after she's said the word. Storyteller would have been kinder, but now that Imo's seen the light, the truth will do.

"I should have listened to you and Phoenix. Remember when she told us her dad was an accountant in London? It turns out he died five years ago."

Tegan stiffens and feels a moment of empathy with Amber. Maybe the girl had good reason to pretend her father was still alive. Tegan has made up a fair share of tales about hers.

Imo stands up. "Amber lasted two days. That was her choice. Why should I care?"

"Some people don't want to be helped," Tegan says.

Her phone buzzes. It's bloody Ivor in Flat 7. He's been a limpet since the pre-s party. She reads his text: Papa sends his love. Ivor's attached a photograph of a postcard, the words *Montreux Chillon* in yellow print over a photo of a waterfront castle on Lake Geneva.

Papa? He can't mean …? Tegan feels a flurry of interest. Has her dad actually sent her a postcard, put pen to paper? He hasn't done that since she was twelve. These days he manipulates his ex-wife, her mother, into speaking for him. Is this a sign he's changed? But the silly idiot must have got her flat number wrong: 7 instead of 17.

"I've got to pop downstairs," she tells Imo. She'll get the card from Ivor straightaway. But before she's out of the kitchen, Ivor sends another photo: the back of the postcard.

"Darling Tegan. Switzerland is fine place. Sorry you not here. Back Thursday. Give Dad a call? Love Dad, Kanya and Dylan."

Of course, her dad hasn't written to her. It's his Thai bride's handwriting. *Give Dad a call* not even *your dad*. Just *Dad*, like she thinks they're part of one happy family. And why mention the kid? It's not like Tegan's ever going to play big sister to their brat.

"Changed my mind. I'll make some drinks," she says, coming back to the kettle.

Chapter 25

Imogen

Imo's limbs still echo with the motion of the train journey. Her eyes stay closed despite the distracting moonlight through the curtain gap, but her mind won't switch Amber off.

Vanishes – Jade's word to describe her sister's actions.

Something was troubling Amber. Imo remembers the night she was drunk and puking into a plastic bowl. Amber rambling about her father. When Imo thinks of it now, it's obvious the girl was mourning. But she mentioned something else too, someone. Was that another of her tales, or the only time she spoke the truth?

Amber. Sophia. Imo's head is loud with both. She forces the student rep's words into their place and relives her patronizing tone. *Are you getting enough sleep?*

Her thoughts eventually settle on allowable worries. How is she going to explain to Dr Wyatt why she missed the lecture? When she fails the exams at the end of the year – and she's bound to fail – she'll be dumped off the course. No concessions for skivers. She tots up her missed sessions in her head. And it's only Tuesday of the second week. She checks the time on her phone: 2 a.m. It's Wednesday. Another bout of coughing forces her onto her other side. The new position relaxes her and she drifts into sleep.

Dreaming again, Sophia's face flickers into focus. She's looking down on her.

"It's dark in here. I can't hold out much longer," Sophia whispers.

Imo wakes in a sweat. For a moment she doesn't know where she is. All she knows is that the nightmare has found her again.

***

The familiar weight presses on her chest when she wakes in the morning. After the nightmare she must have slept soundly but the memory of it has brought her grief to the fore. It's a monumental effort to get out of bed and shower. After she's dressed, she's exhausted. The only eighteen-year-old running on empty. Phoenix will have jogged off with her Mech Eng crew and Tegan, immaculately coiffured, will have zoomed out in her convertible. And Amber … What if Amber's changed her mind and come back? Imo rushes through the hallway.

But Amber's door stays closed no matter how loudly she knocks. When Riku comes through the front door with a parcel, she points theatrically at Amber's door. "Have you seen her?"

Riku shrugs and disappears into his room.

To her surprise, the door opens when she tries the handle. Amber's belongings sit in half a dozen cardboard boxes. Scissors and brown tape rest on top of one. Imo sighs sadly. Soon Amber will be packed away and gone forever. She closes the door behind her.

Back in her own room, she checks her laptop. Still no Facebook posts from Amber, but Dr Wyatt has emailed a two-thousand-word essay and a reading list. Imo throws on clothes and trudges to the library. The campus is busier this week because the second years have arrived. Lots of them are hanging out on the central concourse, oozing confidence and recounting their glorious summers.

Inside the library, she feels like a girl overboard, not knowing in which direction to swim. No staff in sight, how's she supposed to find the German section? Lauren is at a desk with a stack of books. She beckons Imo over.

"The German books are down there on the right. They've got multiple copies of everything on Dr Wyatt's booklist."

"Thanks," Imo says and glances at Lauren's pile. There's a *Mother and Baby* magazine beside the German textbooks. "Frankly, I'd rather read that."

Lauren reddens and pushes it to the next desk. "It was here when I sat down. It's not mine."

In case the magazine owner intends coming back and taking the seat, Imo says goodbye and goes to find a free table. She stupidly picks one that looks out onto the smokers' courtyard. They huddle in packs, stay ten minutes, then leave. The camaraderie is obvious. Imo wonders if she should take up smoking.

She finds the German section where Lauren said it would be. After flicking through a few titles, she picks three that look the most relevant to the essay question.

Hours and chapters pass and she needs the loo.

The toilets are in the foyer next to the coffee machine. When she comes out of the ladies, she sees a man sitting over a Styrofoam cup. There's something familiar about his hunched shoulders.

When he sees her, he tries to smile but looks like he's given up. "I left my class. Just walked out. They told me my teaching was pointless. We all make mistakes. I live with mine."

It's Imo's Accountancy lecturer, Sean Hennessy. He must recognize her from the last lesson, because she had been the only one paying attention.

"I told them I felt like Reggie Perrin, so now they're all googling Reggie Perrin because they haven't got a clue who he is." His head sinks towards his drink.

Imo smiles politely and, when she gets back to her desk, she looks up Reggie Perrin. It's a TV comedy from the 1970s. She keeps on breathing but feels a hole grow in her chest as she reads. The main character thinks his life is pointless, fakes suicide and disappears.

Chapter 26

Imogen

It's seven o'clock when her rumbling stomach finally makes her call it a day at the library. Tegan and Phoenix will have gone to the canteen without her, but she can eat a tin of beans in the flat.

Back in her room she finds herself thinking about Amber again. Five years isn't really that long to grieve for a father. To mourn any loved one.

She has an overwhelming urge to talk about Sophia. But who to call? Dad's the practical one, organizing posters, visiting Sophia's favourite places, leafleting her university. Mum retreats to Sophia's room and sits in silence for hours. Freddie acts like it hasn't happened, but through his closed bedroom door Imo's heard him sobbing. Grandma's the one who wails in public and lets Imo wail with her.

If Imo's parents have gone away to search for Sophia, Grandma Jean will be at their house. She used to go there to babysit her three grandchildren, now it's the house she sits with. Someone must be there when Sophia comes back.

But it's not Grandma Jean's turn today and she answers

her home phone. Air catches in Imo's throat as she pictures her alone in her high-backed chair waiting for the phone to ring.

Her grandmother's voice is bright. "Hello, Imogen, sweetie. You've just caught me. I'm meeting Freddie for a drink."

"My brother?" She's astonished.

"We're making it a fixed thing, every Wednesday at the wine bar, now he's working locally."

A pellet of envy forms in Imo's chest even though she knows he took the low-paid job to be close to home. The unsaid *one out one in* rule applies more than ever. Imo occupied her parents' offspring-shaped hole when Freddie managed to return to his graduate placement in Birmingham. Now it's his turn to plug the gap while Imo's away. But they both know it's a chasm they'll never completely fill. Only the third sibling can do that.

"What about you, sweetie?" her grandmother asks. "I expect you're finding it hard to settle."

"What?" Imo snaps, hating the way she's been found out. Then she moderates her voice. "Of course, what else?"

"You mustn't worry about everyone."

Imo stands up and paces her bedroom. "I'm not, I don't." The floor space is tiny so she gives up and sits on her bed again. Why deny it?

"It doesn't have to be like …" Grandma swallows. "It breaks me to know what you've all gone through."

"I know." Imo lies back on her pillow, hacking. She shouldn't have phoned.

"That's a nasty cough. Been kissing too many boys?"

Imo has to sit up again to clear her throat. She's relieved by the subject change despite knowing what will come next. *A pretty girl like you.*

"A good-looking lass like you must be fighting them off."

And next: *Never mind about your skin.*

"How's your acne? Did you get the brownies? I baked gluten-free. I read somewhere that wheat is bad for the complexion."

Damn, the parcel she never collected from the post room. "Delicious. Thank you." Keeping the lie out of her voice, and the guilt. "How are you?"

Her grandma's voice drops. "Getting there. I tell myself Sophia wouldn't want us to mope. We're a strong family and I've got good friends."

Imo can't speak. She thinks of the *good* friends, the ones who clutch her arm and, in hushed tones, ask, "Have you heard anything?" Don't they know it would be on every bloody news? Or are the "good friends" Grandma's other buddies who change the subject whenever she mentions Sophia? *Move on; she's gone.*

Grandma Jean breaks the silence to talk about *Strictly*, their go-to subject when Sophia gets too much.

Imo barely listens. How strong are they as a family? Not as robust as they were at first. In numbing shock, they shuffled into a formation. Dad knocked on doors. Freddie designed the poster – the only one who knew how. He and Imo left the smiling Sophia in mortar board and gown on lampposts, in shops, on fences around the railway station. Mum waited at home.

They went on outings: Slimbridge, Alton Towers, Weston-super-Mare – favourite places from Sophia's childhood in case she'd gone there. But the excursions have dwindled. Too much disappointment is corrosive.

Their lives, their days, turn on a sixpence. A trip to Tesco, Mum's hospital shift, Dad's quiz night, all disrupted by another suspected sighting. The anticipatory rush to Inspector Hare, barely breathing for the happy end, only to have hopes dashed. Not their girl. Often not a girl at all.

Is Sophia even missing? Isn't that a label they've given her? She could be alive and well and living the life she's chosen. Sometimes Imo hates her for getting them into this. Normal families don't have this. A sob swells inside her as Jean continues to speak.

"… so I think Anton will go next week, don't you?"

"Sorry, Grandma, someone's at the door. I'll ring you back."

Imo ends the call and lies on her side, coughing and crying for several minutes. Why is she the only one who can't move on? Her throat closes. She knows why.

Chapter 27

Imogen

A day in June. Four months after Sophia vanished. Another wave of grief-laden inertia has hit Imo's mother. Signed off work for a week, she spends her lethargic hours between Sophia's room and the patio where Sophia sunbathed as a teenager.

Then that Wednesday morning, Mum gets up and throws clothes into a suitcase. "Falmouth," she says.

"You want to go there, today?" Dad asks warily, not quite believing.

"The cottage we stayed in during the London Olympics."

"Well, great." Dad, sounding excited, casts a hopeful glance at Freddie and Imo. "Do you mind?"

"They have to stay here. In case." Mum's tone is firm. They all know what she means.

As they back out of the drive an hour later, Mum winds down her window. "We'll bring her home, I promise."

Through the windscreen Imo sees her father's face plummet. Seventeen-year-old Sophia went with them on the holiday to Cornwall. Mum has decided the missing twenty-two-year-old is there again.

"Could be worse," Freddie says, waving them off. "At least he's got her away for a few days."

It does get worse. That afternoon Inspector Hare visits the house. His expression is grave when they tell him Mum and Dad are on their way to Falmouth.

"We're going to have to ask your parents to return."

"But they can't," Freddie protests. "Dad's finally got her out of the house. Tell us what you want to tell them. I'm Sophia's twin brother. No closer kin."

Inspector Hare thinks for a moment, then looks at Imo. "You're eighteen, aren't you?"

Imo nods, bracing herself. Time for Sophia's little sister to grow up.

Inspector Hare takes a breath. "We've found a body."

A boulder falls on Imo's chest. She wants to cry but knows she can't; Inspector Hare would think she's a kid and stop talking.

"A young woman, we believe to be Sophia, was found at the bottom of a terminal building at Bristol airport. It seems she fell off the roof."

"Fell?" Freddie asks.

Inspector Hare looks at them with his world-weary eyes. "We have to wait for the coroner's report, but it looks like suicide."

Imo does cry then. All these weeks Sophia has been nearby. The airport is less than five miles away. Why didn't she get in touch? Why didn't she say goodbye?

Through her tears, she hears Freddie. "I'll do it. I'll make the identification. We only need to tell my parents if it's confirmed. It can't be her."

"That's very good of you, son. And you're quite right: it might not be Sophia, but ..."

"Of course it won't be her," Imo snaps. They've been here before, many times. "Even the girl at Nottingham station wasn't her."

"And I can't tell you how much we regret that," Hare acknowledges. "There's no need for either of you to view the body. We can match the DNA from the samples you both gave. But I have to tell you she was carrying Sophia's purse. She had her bank card and university library pass."

"I want to see her," Freddie steps forward suddenly. "It's the only way my family will believe this."

"I want to see her, too." The words escape before Imo thinks of the consequences.

***

Inspector Hare drives them to the hospital mortuary. Beside Imo, Freddie's face is grim, his shoulders stiff. Is he hoping it's mistaken identity or does closure matter more than seeing his sister's fractured body on a mortuary slab? Imo can't blame him; each media appeal is the trigger for every saddo and sadist to crawl out of their sewer and spatter the family and the police in the shit of fake sightings and psycho theories. Social media is rife with threads that hashtag Freddie as rapist and killer. Yet Freddie insists they do the appeals anyway. To give up on Twitter and TV campaigns would be to give up on Sophia.

Are they about to end Freddie's nightmare and start a new one? A chill pinches Imo's arms and she wishes she'd brought a cardigan. Hare has the car's air-conditioning on. Outside, midsummer rages and she has to twist away from the brilliant sunlight in her eyes. Even though she's sitting, she feels unbalanced. A thought crosses her mind. Is that what happened to Sophia? Not suicide. On the airport roof, looking at planes. A glint of sun in her eyes, a slip of her footing?

Shame shoots through her, bringing prickles of sweat to her back and scalp. Her sister is dead and she's trying to make a better, softer version of it. Now Imo pictures it in its full horror. Ribs splintered. Legs and arms shattered. Mouth filled with broken teeth and blood. Suicide or accident, what does it matter, Sophia has suffered a terrible death.

There are designated police parking spaces at the hospital that Imo has never noticed before and Hare leads them through an entrance straight into the mortuary foyer. It's as brightly lit and stuffy as every other hospital department. Staff in white tunics cross the corridor, carrying clipboards and pushing equipment trolleys. Hare takes them into a small waiting room. Squeaky vinyl-covered chairs and OK! magazines on the coffee table. A kettle for waiting families to make their own drinks.

"Can I get you anything?" he asks.

"We'd just like to see her," Freddie replies.

Hare nods. "I'll take you. The body suffered considerable trauma and you will see some discolouration to the skin. You may not recognize her immediately."

Imo follows Freddie and they speed along another corridor to match Hare's long strides. Adrenaline races until she feels herself free-falling, every bit of her loosened.

When they reach the door of the viewing room, she squeezes her eyes tight shut. "Please God, please God," she prays. Heart racing, breath shallow, body trembling, she steps in after Hare and Freddie. And opens her eyes.

Chapter 28

Imogen

A knock at the door disturbs her thoughts. Imo wipes the tears from her face and struggles into a sitting position. *That* memory again. No matter how hard she tries, she never goes more than a couple of weeks without reliving it. And now it's followed her to Abbeythorpe. Pain jabs in her ribs as she moves and, when she gets up, her head screams almost as much as when she viewed the body.

"I know you're in there." Phoenix knocks again. "Tell me to beggar off if you're entertaining your Tinder likes." But she stops joking when Imo opens the door. "What's happened? Have you had an accident?"

"It's nothing."

"I've seen more colour in a corpse." Imo looks away and Phoenix smiles sympathetically. "You look a bit under the weather, that's all. Would a glass of wine perk you up? Tegan and I are sharing a bottle."

With every bone and every muscle aching, Imo follows her. As she walks down the hallway, the memory lessens. The body wasn't Sophia. But seeing the lifeless girl, dead after falling – and imagining what happened when she hit the floor – had made Imo afraid of heights ever since. How could Hare have ever thought the badly cut hair and snap-thin face could be her beautiful sister? Police identified the girl later as a local glue-sniffer, known for pick-pocketing airport travellers. Far from closing enquiries, the body posed more questions. Had Sophia been at Bristol airport when her purse was stolen? Where was she going? And where is she now?

"Sit down before you fall down," Tegan says when they join her in the kitchen. "I'll get you a glass."

As soon as the first mouthful hits her tongue, Imo knows Tegan didn't buy it in the all-night garage. She glugs more greedily, as happy little fireworks go off in her head. Alcohol always helps for a while.

"There weren't any handouts; you didn't miss much," Tegan says. "It was that weirdo we had for Accountancy. He stropped out before the end."

Imo's halfway through her second glass before she registers what Tegan has said. She's missed a Business lecture. She puts down her glass, remembering that their lecturer, Hennessey, spotted her skiving in the library.

Phoenix gives her a concerned look. "Have you had dinner? Shall I make you some toast? I'll make coffee too." But when she presses down the toaster, there's a flash and it goes dead.

"That's bound to be my fault. Things always break around me," Imo says. Her voice buckles.

Phoenix and Tegan exchange a glance. They must see another flaky flatmate, more unstable than Amber. Imo buries her misery in a big gulp of wine. It's then that she notices what the others are wearing. Tegan's in a lacy red dress, Phoenix in a pale blue jumpsuit. They must be going out. She's keeping them waiting.

"I'll get changed." She folds a slice of bread and shoves it in her mouth.

Not until she's in her room does it occur to her that she

doesn't have to go out with them – might not be invited – but she's no strength of will to resist. A night out might separate her from her memories. For a few hours.

They're on a second bottle when she returns. They applaud as she sits down.

"I said leopard print leggings and a pink crop top," Tegan explains, her voice sounding uneven. "Phoenix reckoned suede mini-skirt, but you got us both. I love your jacket."

Imo pours herself another glass. Mum bought her the jacket when she was in Year Ten, real biker chic, but then ruined it by stitching her name inside the collar. Her mother drains the fun out of everything, more so since February.

"I don't want sand in my car, though," Tegan says, apparently picking up a conversation she and Phoenix were having while Imo got changed.

Phoenix explains that they're planning a trip to the coast before winter sets in. "I should be able to borrow my parents' van."

"You can drive something that big?" Imo asks.

"I grew up on private land and drove HGVs as soon as I could reach the pedals. We all did." Her eyes struggle to focus. Imo reckons she's had more of the second bottle than Tegan. But the alcohol hasn't made her boastful. She speaks modestly, matter-of-fact. It makes Imo feel even more inadequate.

"My theory test expires in April, but I won't be ready for the practical," Imo says. "Not then, not ever. I've been … distracted." She hasn't driven since her birthday. If she passed, her parents would have to decide whether to give her Sophia's car. After the police had searched it and found no evidence for where she'd gone, Dad fetched it back from Nottingham. When he got home, they all climbed in and sat in silence for several minutes, as if some familial telepathy would locate their missing relative. Dad got rid of his racing bikes to make space in the garage. No one's been in it since.

"Not everyone learns to drive," Phoenix says. "Friends of my mum's in Canterbury never bothered."

"Well, they wouldn't need to in Canterbury," Imo says. "They can ride round on camels."

Tegan and Phoenix stare.

"It's in Australia, isn't it?" Imo adds.

Phoenix refills her glass. "Don't ever change." She pats Imo's arm.

Tegan chokes on her drink and covers her face with her hand.

But Imo's mood stays cloudy. She remembers Tegan and Phoenix laughing about Amber and realizes she's taken her place as the Flat 17 joke.

"I know I'm stupid," she says. "I know nothing about geography, can't drive, can't even sleep. No coordination except in dance and that's not a life skill and I'm not even good at that apparently. And on top of that it turns out I'm a bad judge of character. My grandma reckons I care too much, but I bombed out with Amber, didn't I?"

She stares at the table, waiting for the others to laugh at her, but Phoenix's expression is serious.

Phoenix clears her throat. "For what it's worth, I don't think Amber had any intention of binning university. Trust your gut, Imogen. I don't know what we can do about it, but I don't think you're wrong."

Tegan shares the last of the wine between the three glasses. "I think you're a good judge. You're friends with me, for a start." She drinks up.

They decide to abandon their plans to go clubbing and stay in the kitchen eating custard creams and drinking coffee. The refreshments aren't enough to blot up the alcohol and Imo's head stays spinning. But it's a happy spin that manages to fling ominous thoughts of Sophia and Amber to the edge of her mind.

Chapter 29

Thursday 6 October

Phoenix

Another Riku special, Phoenix assumes, when she answers the door to a dark-haired woman, holding a parcel. She offers to take it.

The woman explains she found it on the doorstep and asks whether she can come in and wait. "I'm meeting someone from university maintenance at ten to help clear my sister's room. I'm Jade Murphy."

Phoenix shakes her hand, appraising her. Early twenties, defined cheekbones where Amber's were plumper, but the same blue eyes and freckles. "We can probably get straight into the room. Imo said it was unlocked yesterday."

"That must be the Imogen who came to see us. Is she here? I'd like to apologize. I think I sounded ungrateful."

Bitter was how Imo had described Jade Murphy, fed up to the back teeth with her younger sister. But as she sits down on Amber's bare mattress she just looks disappointed.

"At least I haven't got to pack it," she says, reaching forward to one of the cardboard boxes on the floor. "My mum must have done all that." She checks her phone. "I should be all right for time. My friend doesn't need her car back until five."

"Have you driven up from Chadcombe this morning? You must be gasping for a drink. I'll put the kettle on while you wait for the maintenance people. Imo might be back by then too."

But as soon as Jade accepts the offer, Phoenix regrets suggesting it. What are they going to talk about while they sip their tea? Amber is their only common ground but, after what Imo said, Amber might be an off-limits topic for Jade.

Without knocking, she leaves the parcel outside Riku's door. To her relief, Tegan's in the kitchen, making herself a drink. Phoenix shoves teabags in two more cups, pours on boiling water and persuades Tegan to sit in Amber's room with them while she drinks hers.

Jade has spread the contents of one of the boxes onto the bed. A rainbow of clothes: purple jumpsuit, tartan dressing gown, floral knickers, vest tops in pink, green and orange, silver sandals, three pairs of neon trainers, black lace-up boots. When Phoenix sees the trousers that Amber claimed belonged to her gypsy grandmother, she can't resist checking the label. Primark. Of course.

"They seem to be full of clothes and shoes." Jade knocks another box with her foot. "I wonder what she packed to go travelling. Every jumble sale outfit I can ever remember her wearing is here."

Tegan looks up from her drink. "Is there a red wig and a turquoise kimono in one of them?"

Jade shrugs. "Not that I can see."

"Do you mind if we check?" Tegan asks, but she's already upended one of the boxes onto the floor.

Phoenix twigs why Tegan's checking and rummages through another box. Jade spreads the clothes from another one on the bed. Between them, they check all six boxes, but the outfit Amber

127

wore at the Freshers' Fair isn't there. Tegan glances at Phoenix. The nagging doubt that Phoenix has felt since they went back to the Freshers' Fair resurfaces. She's sure she witnessed something, some kind of deception. But by whom? One of the stallholders – the woman on the parents' stand, the chess boy, the LGBTQ girl? Phoenix's skin heats: no, not Keren, not *her*. Riku, then? Why was he there, staring at everyone?

"Did your mum take some clothes home last week?" she asks.

"Mum lugged a suitcase back on the train. Amber's bedsheets and duvet, and a few posters. Nothing else."

Phoenix feels her belly squeeze. Tegan, wide eyes still looking at her, seems to be experiencing a similar thing. On the edge of something.

"What's going on?" Jade looks from Phoenix to Tegan. "Did Amber go off with your clothes, is that it? I'm pretty sure they were hers. I remember the kimono. She looked a right idiot."

The indignation of being accused of having a wardrobe like Amber's flashes across Tegan's face. She swirls her tea dregs as she struggles to suppress it. "So as far as you can see, all she took was her passport, phone and purse?"

Jade seals a box with brown tape and bends down to snip off the end. "Yes, that's right … No, wait, her passport must be at home. Mum keeps all ours in a fireproof box. Unless Amber brought it here. Doubt it, though; she's not that organized."

Phoenix chews her lip. Whatever Amber's text to her mother said, she hasn't gone abroad. So where is she?

But Jade beats them to it. She sits down on the bed and folds her arms. "Of course, she hasn't gone travelling. Why would she start telling us the truth after five years of bullshit?" Her eyes are pinpricks and her jaw is hard. This must be the bitter Jade that Imo experienced.

"Where do you think she's gone? Without her passport and possibly wearing a kimono." Tegan sits beside her and softens her voice. "That's what she was wearing the last time we saw her."

Jade lets out an ugly laugh. "She'll have beggared off to a squat with her druggy mates. And I wouldn't worry about what she's wearing. That girl walked around with a cushion shoved up her belly for four months." She glances at Phoenix. "Didn't Imo tell you? My darling little sister went off the rails when Dad died. Decided an appropriate way to grieve was to get pissed, smoke dope and hang out at the Chadcombe Bridge with a bunch of junkies. Mum put it down to a phase. I'd lost my dad too and my place at uni, but you didn't see me carrying on like that." Her voice goes up in a question. Phoenix nods reassuringly.

"After a year, she stopped going out, and seemed to pack in the drink and drugs too. Alleluia, normal service resumed. But no, she announces she's *pregnant*. Even Mum couldn't forgive that one, couldn't bear to look at her. But luckily the woman next door took Amber under her wing. They went to antenatal classes together. The neighbour was due about a month or so before Amber and glad of the company because, well, there was no boyfriend on the scene."

"Amber never told us she had a baby." Tegan talks into her teacup as if trying to process the shock by saying it aloud to herself.

Jade turns to her. "That's the point: she didn't. She was never pregnant. How could she lie like that to our mother?"

The doorbell rings. Phoenix sighs and so does Tegan; neither wants to answer it.

Keys turn in the front door to the flat and a man calls out, "Hello. Maintenance here." He knocks on a door in their hallway. "Another one for you, sonny." He must have picked up Riku's parcel from where Jade and Phoenix left it outside his door.

"So what happened?" Tegan asks, on the edge of the bed, facing Jade and ignoring the activity they can hear in the corridor.

"Cheryl, the neighbour, twigged in the end and caught her out."

"Hello, ladies, are you decent?" The maintenance man taps his keys on the door.

Tegan rolls her eyes at the interruption but gets up to open the door.

"Just these lot, is it?" He piles two of the packing boxes on top of each other. "Can you go ahead and open the doors, duck?" He nods at Tegan. She hesitates, clearly annoyed at being likened to pond life, then steps out ahead of him.

Jade picks up another box.

"Why would Amber make up something like that?" Phoenix asks when the man has gone.

"God knows. She's an attention seeker. Her stunt ruined our friendship with Cheryl. She stopped speaking to us and left a few months later. No idea where she went. We've got new neighbours now, a snooty pair." She heads out with the box.

Phoenix takes another and follows her. It must be full of shoes because it's heavy. She's used to load-lifting at home and keeps up with Jade on the stairs. "That's a shame," she says, not having a clue what snooty neighbours mean. Hers are like family.

"I'm glad Cheryl left, though. It was humiliating for Mum having her next door. Amber had used Cheryl as a grieving post to mourn our dad and didn't care how cruel she'd been."

Tegan and the maintenance man wait by the only car in the loading bay. Jade puts down her box and unlocks the boot. The man goes back inside for another.

Jade says, "So now you know my sister. We thought her big tricks were behind her, but it looks like this vanishing act is her starting up again. I'm sorry she dragged you two into it. And Imogen."

After they've waved her off, Phoenix gets out her phone to send a text. The tension she's had on and off since the second visit to the Freshers' Fair tightens across her shoulders. "Something doesn't feel right."

"You sound like Imo. Please don't," Tegan says. "One fruit cake's enough in this flat."

"Amber's neighbour vanished and now Amber."

"Hardly. I don't blame the neighbour for not leaving a forwarding address with Amber's lot. Why would you want to stay friends with someone who made a mug of you for months?" She eyes Phoenix's phone and smirks. "Who are you texting – MI5?"

"I'm asking Imo for Amber and Jade's address. If I can get onto an old electoral register, I might be able to find the neighbour's full name and then work out where she's moved to."

Tegan gives a big sigh and holds up her hands. "Great, Imo's paranoid enough without you winding her up."

Phoenix takes a breath, knowing that what she's about to say will promote her to number one fruit cake in Tegan's eyes. "What if something's happened to them both?"

Chapter 30

Tegan

The disabled spaces are taken even though none of the vehicles display blue badges. Tegan parks crossways, blocking two in. Lights are on in several rooms of the geography tower. Amber would go mental at the energy waste, but Tegan's grateful as they indicate which windows she doesn't need to scan. He'll be lurking in a darkened room, like a woodlouse.

After ten minutes she's fed up of craning her neck. Where the hell is he? She's sure he's chosen the geography tower as his regular vantage point. The highest building on campus with 360-degree view of paths, roads and other buildings. The best place to keep a lookout, even though she'd rather he beggared off and left her alone.

She gets out and sits on the bonnet, playing with her phone while she waits. Still nothing, so she leans back on one arm and lifts her feet off the ground. To add to the effect she plumps her hair with the other hand. A siren luring sailors onto the rocks. There's movement at a third-floor window. Result. But when she looks up, two figures shoot out of sight and she realizes they were students. As she's outside the geography department she assumes they are ogling the car, not her.

When she honks the horn, the sound reverberates off the building and brings people to several windows. She rests against the car for a minute, brazening it out, but climbs in when the last few watchers linger.

Bloody typical; now that she actually *wants* to speak to him, he's nowhere. She asked him once why he kept on after she told him to get lost. *Just following orders*, he said. Wasn't that the excuse the Nazis used at their war trials? She'll have to ask Imo, the German student.

Remembering what else he said – *I'm here to make you safe* – she gets out and, with a germ of an idea, opens the bonnet. Hand clutching her forehead, she steps back theatrically. Needing more props, she gets the car manual out of the glove compartment and hauls a never-opened tool box from the boot.

No sooner has she begun flicking through the manual than she hears the hum of an engine approaching. Bingo. The Mercedes pulls up in front of her open bonnet, boxing in two more cars in the disabled spaces.

"Trouble, ma'am?"

Tegan manages not to laugh. *Ma'am*? That's a new one, and she thought she was the one acting. Or maybe he's taking the piss. God knows what goes on inside that hoodie; he never takes it off.

"Good to see you." She shouldn't have said that; even a numpty like him knows she's never pleased. Giving herself thinking time, she returns the tools to the boot.

Marlon stands with his feet apart, hands clasped across his crotch. Dark hair in a topknot, two-day shadow, black trousers. The only flash of colour is a bling-watch on his wrist. Reward for faithful service? Her stomach hardens.

She forces a smile behind her eyes. "I need your help."

He hesitates for a moment, no doubt considering the likely possibility that she's on a wind-up – it wouldn't be the first time. He nods, steps towards the open bonnet and rolls up a sleeve.

"The engine's fine; I've fixed it," she says quickly, aware that people are at the geography windows watching. It's not beyond possibility someone will call security. Even from that distance, he might not pass for a student. She'll have to hurry up.

As he rolls his sleeve back over his thick, tattooed forearm, she gets her bag and fetches out the piece of paper that Phoenix gave her. The girl had pored over digital electoral registers like a geek from a *CSI* episode until she found the full name of Amber's old neighbour. But that wasn't enough to put her sleuthing escapade to rest. Then she declared she needed 'specialist' help.

"Cheryl Judith Burdett." Tegan offers him the note. "I need a DVLA search to find her current address."

Not taking it, he looks at the paper as if he might need to detonate it. "Who is she?"

"Nobody, probably."

"Why are you asking then?"

"My clever friend found out her full name at her old address but we don't know where she's moved to. I thought you could ask one of your … associates."

His body stance softens. "Sure, I know people. I'll run it past the boss."

"Don't bother my father with this." Her anger slips out, before she can stop it. "He's not back from holiday until tonight," she adds in a calmer tone. "We need the information today. Can you help us?" Her voice slips into a simper.

But he's still suspicious. "Why don't you get your clever friend to do it?"

She smiles while her thoughts race to find a plausible answer. Phoenix knew how to gain access to the electoral register legally but wasn't about to hack into vehicle licensing databases. Tegan pops the scrap of paper into his hoodie pocket and pats it. "We need a more specialist service, and fast. But if you're not the man for the job, I'm sure my father could suggest someone else."

He straightens. "Leave it with me, ma'am." He climbs back into the Mercedes, places the note on the dashboard and is on the phone by the time he gets the car in reverse.

Ma'am. Again. It's a wonder he didn't salute.

Chapter 31

Tegan

When Imo joins them on the kitchen chairs in her usual hood-up, head-down state, Tegan asks how her German conversation class went and makes a supreme effort to seem interested in the answer. Imo sighs out a tale of how fluent everyone else is and tells her that the PhD student taking the class hates her. When she stops speaking, she squints from Tegan to Phoenix. For a girl who's slow on the uptake she's hot on detecting atmosphere.

"What's going on?" she asks. "Were you bitching about me?" The sulky, martyred look stays on her face until they tell her about Jade Murphy's visit to collect Amber's things.

Imo brightens. "So that's why you texted me for Amber's address. Where do we start looking? Chadcombe's down south, isn't it? Maybe she's gone the other way, far north. Does Amber know anyone in Wales?"

Tegan shakes her head, not bothering to challenge Imo's quaint knowledge of geography. "Amber caused a rift with her neighbour when she pretended to be pregnant."

"Jade told me about Amber's lies, but it was years ago," Imo says. "What makes you think she's gone off because of that?"

"We don't," Tegan says, "not necessarily, but something from her past could have made her scarper."

"And we're starting with her old neighbour, Cheryl," Phoenix adds.

Imo frowns. "If her next-door neighbour knows something, don't you think her mother would have asked?"

Tegan shrugs at Phoenix. *Your call.* They'd agreed not to tell Imo that neighbour Cheryl had done the same into-thin-air trick as Amber, but Imo proves brighter than they gave her credit for.

"What's happened to her?" Imo asks.

"She left." Phoenix clears her throat. "Without a forwarding address."

"Disappeared?" Imo stands up, her voice coming out in a gasp.

"Give it a rest, Imogen." Tegan rubs her throbbing temples. "Get this into perspective. Very few people vanish."

Imo's eyes flare. "Over three hundred thousand a year. One percent are still not found after a year. That's three thousand daughters, sons, mothers ... sisters ... never heard from again. It happens." She leans closer to Tegan. "One minute you're an ordinary family, the next your ... father goes missing and you spend the rest of your life in hell."

In stunned silence, Tegan and Phoenix exchange a glance. What's Imo's story? Tegan realizes how little she knows about her.

Sitting back in her chair, smaller now as if her fire's gone out, Imo continues in a calmer voice. "Let's find both these women, Amber and ...?"

"Cheryl," Phoenix supplies.

"And Cheryl. Stop them becoming another statistic. Agreed?" Imo peers at Tegan.

"Agreed." It sticks in Tegan's throat – no way has Amber's neighbour gone missing – but what else can she say?

Imo bounces in her seat, on a roll now. "I'll take the train to

Chadcombe again and seek out some of Amber's old friends. See what they know."

"Not yet."

"No."

Phoenix and Tegan speak at the same time. If Jade is to be believed, Amber's mates are drug-addled gang members who live under a bridge. And Imo is no Ross Kemp. They can't let her go there.

Imo deflates.

"You can come with us to visit the neighbour if we ever find her," Phoenix says.

Imo slips her hood back and flicks her hair, apparently happy with this concession. "How will you get her new address?" she asks.

"You'll be the first to know." Tegan stands up. An evening in the car outside the geography tower awaits her because she stupidly didn't agree a time with Marlon. She could be stuck there all bloody night.

"Can we come with you?" Imo asks. She's done it again. Tegan didn't say where she's going but Imo seems to have guessed it's to do with Amber.

Tegan's phone rings before she can think of an excuse. It's a number she doesn't recognize.

The voice is dark and shockingly familiar. "It's me."

"How the actual hell?" Tegan's whole body trembles and she drops the phone. They were supposed to meet by the car, but Marlon's got so far into her life that he's inside her mobile.

Phoenix hands it back. There's silence on the line. Tegan wonders if he's peeved about her tone, but figures it's because they both know the answer to her unfinished question. Her father, that's how he got her number.

Eventually he speaks again: "There's no record of Cheryl Burdett having a car after she left the address you gave me, so there's no new address at DVLA."

"That's bullshit."

Phoenix and Imo look at her quizzically. She needs to calm it down, to keep him on the line. Her voice softens. "That can't be right, can it?"

"Eddie ran the search and he's one of the best."

Tegan doesn't know an Eddie but concedes that only the best stay on the payroll. Mess up and you're dropped.

She kills the call.

Despondency grows on Imo's face as Tegan explains that Cheryl's Chadcombe address is a dead end.

Phoenix frowns. "Who was that on the phone?"

"The vehicle licensing people."

"The DVLA? Phoned you?" Phoenix tilts her head, her eyes narrowing on Tegan. "At this time of night?"

"Does it really matter?" Tegan snaps. "All you need to know is there is no record of a car, no record of Cheryl. That's as far as we can go."

"Does that mean Cheryl sold it when she left Chadcombe?" Imo rests her chin on her hands. "Has she gone abroad, like Amber?"

Tegan's eyes meet Phoenix's. Imo catches their exchange and looks suspicious. Any minute now she'll twig what they're thinking: Amber's passport is unlikely to have left Chadcombe. Amber isn't abroad; Cheryl probably isn't either. The last thing they need is for Imo to freak.

Phoenix bails them out. "All we know is Cheryl hasn't registered a car at a new address. Perhaps we can find another way of tracing her." She paces the kitchen. "Where else are people registered?" She counts on her fingers. "Job agencies, optician, dentist, doctor." She claps her hands. "That's it. Cheryl's a parent so she's bound to have made use of hospitals and doctors. Her details would have been updated when she moved." Her expression changes. "But we can't access NHS data. That would be illegal." She sits beside Imo and they look down, dejectedly. "This is getting us nowhere."

Tegan takes a breath. She's known these girls less than two weeks and university's not a team sport. Flat sharing is making her soft. She'll rent a room in the town centre next year. So why has she already pressed redial on the last number received?

"I might know a way," she says.

Both girls grin and raise their hands to high-five her, but she moves away, walks out of the room with the phone to her ear.

Chapter 32

Tegan

After half an hour of waiting for Marlon to call back, their enthusiasm wanes. Riku comes in twice, pours boiling water on two Pot Noodles and leaves without saying a word, despite both Imo and Phoenix trying to engage him in conversation. A nod and a grunt is as far as he goes, which is more than Tegan offers him. And he makes the kitchen stink of synthetic chicken.

Tegan opts for the fragrant sanctuary of her bedroom, assuring Imo she'll text her if she gets Cheryl's address. By 9 p.m. she is halfway through a marketing summary when there's a knock at the door. "Come in, Imogen," she calls, mildly irritated.

Her door opens, but Marlon stays outside, shifting his weight as he looks about the hallway.

She balls her fists. Of course he can get into her flat. Close surveillance is what he's paid for. That and something she'd rather not think about.

"The boss says you have to do it yourself." He fishes two folded sheets of printer paper out of his pocket. "Eddie emailed these instructions."

Riku's door opens and he stands, arms folded, glaring at

Marlon. The other man's shoulders tense and his fingers flex. His eyes rest on Riku's open-toed sandals and Star Wars socks, but Riku's gaze is steady, dead ahead. Tegan feels a moment of admiration that, even dressed in half-mast tracky bottoms, he has the guts to face-off a thug. But she wishes he would do one, so she can make the thug give her the information she needs.

At that moment Phoenix comes out of her room and gasps. The hallway grows too crowded for Marlon. He thrusts the printed pages at Tegan and ambles off without another word. Riku watches him until he's out of the flat, then goes back into his room.

"Great. Now what do I do with these?" Tegan brandishes the pages in Phoenix's face.

"That was *him*, the stalker," she exclaims and follows Tegan into her room.

"Don't be stupid." Tegan smooths the instruction sheets out on her desk, her hands shaking with rage. How dare Marlon come here? How dare …?

As Phoenix leans over her desk and reads the paperwork, a flush of colour grows from her throat to her ears. "A friend of yours?" she asks suspiciously. "Where did he get this?"

"He's a part-time postgrad I got talking to in the Abbi bar." The lie brings bile to Tegan's throat. She flicks her hair, thinking fast. "I told him about Amber and persuaded him to help. He works in the NHS. Physiotherapy. He took some convincing but he has a daughter himself. Ginny." She stops before she develops the lie into a three-bed semi, his mother-in-law's gout and Ginny's first ballet exam.

There's a scrunched expression on Phoenix's face. "That guy's a physiotherapist?"

"Yeah, you'd never think it, would you?"

"I thought he was the low-life I've seen skulking around campus. Riku must have thought it too. He seemed to be playing bodyguard."

Riku a bodyguard. As if. She points at the instructions. "Will you help me?"

"It's illegal."

"Not really, only a bit." Tegan shrugs, trying to act casual.

"Isn't that like being a bit pregnant?"

Amber managed it. Tegan nearly says it aloud but thinks better of it. "If we can locate this Cheryl woman, we can park these conspiracy theories and get on with our lives."

Phoenix goes to the window and peers out. Her expression is reflected against the darkness. Pained conflict above the cheekbones. Tegan gives her a minute to come round to her way of thinking. But Phoenix stays pondering for so long that Tegan gets up and snaps shut the blind.

"Do you want me to beg?"

Phoenix sighs. "I'll do it. But only because we're worried about Amber." She sits down at Tegan's laptop and takes up the first page of the instructions.

Tegan puts her hand over the keyboard. "Not here; it can be traced back to me. We'll have to hope one of the open access terminals in the library is free."

"What about Imo? Should she come with us?"

Tegan shakes her head. "Send her a text, if you must. But let's keep this vaguely sensible, shall we?"

Chapter 33

Tegan

The lift in the library is out of order and they have to trudge up four flights of stairs to get to the computers. Luckily the study room is deserted, the new academic year not having kicked in completely. Phoenix tells Tegan to open up the screen while she makes sure they're alone. Tegan is glad of this division of labour; she needs a breather after the stairs.

When Phoenix comes back, Tegan moves aside to let her sit at the keyboard. Her nimble fingers follow the printed instructions. It takes a while but eventually she's onto the second sheet.

The door from the stairwell opens and a man with an ID card round his neck approaches. It's the librarian who told Tegan she was in the wrong place for the library induction talk. He still hasn't ironed his shirt. Phoenix closes window after window, as he walks closer and closer. Her typing gets more and more frantic, but they're still hacked into the National Health Service when he stops next to them.

"Working late, girls?" he says, wheezing after the stair climb.

Tegan stands between him and Phoenix, trying to block his view of the screen. "Open twenty-four hours, isn't it?"

"Yes, yes. No problem." He doesn't move. "Tricky essay, is it?"

It takes a moment for Tegan to realize what he means. "Something like that, but we're managing."

Behind her, Tegan hears Phoenix desperately clicking the mouse. What now? Make conversation and risk him hanging about?

All three of them look up when the door opens again. Imo, in a skin-tight zebra print dress. "There you are," she breathes. "I've been looking everywhere for you." But when she moves in close to the librarian, it's clear she's talking to him, despite squinting straight at Tegan. "I'd like to know where the German section is." She puts her hands on her hips.

The man tries so hard not to look at her boobs that his neck bulges. "Ground floor. You can't miss it."

"Will you show me? Please?"

Imo's breathless voice is clearly nothing to do with the stairs. Either she's drunk or she's pouring all her acting skills into getting the man away from them.

When the librarian follows her swaying backside to the stairwell, Phoenix has to retrace her steps through the instructions. The librarian's interruption has cost them several minutes.

It's an age before the NHS logo appears on the screen. After more minutes and more clicks, there's a box for the patient's name, and another for the town of residence.

"We've only got her old address," Phoenix murmurs. "Let's hope the name is unusual enough for a match."

As Phoenix types, the door opens again. The librarian. Fair play to Imo; she kept him away for quite a while, but probably scared him off in the end. Tegan doubts he's been that close to a woman in a dress before, except other librarians in tweed. Maybe if she ignores him he'll go away. She keeps her eyes on the computer screen, her heart rate racing. There's one Cheryl Judith Burdett on the system.

But the man steps closer. "Do you know how to use the library search engine? All the search results have been peer-assessed."

Tegan stands up to head him off. "We're good thanks."

Phoenix takes a sharp breath and Tegan sees why. *New Name: Jane Brown*.

"Has the firewall blocked you?" The man looks at Phoenix and rubs his neck. "I can show you what to do."

He's still walking towards them. Tegan's about to say again that they don't need his help when a better idea comes to her. She smiles.

"Actually, can you take me to where you left our friend? She's a whizz at computer stuff. We need her here."

"Anything I can help you with?"

She bites her lip then grins, feeling rather like the snake in *The Jungle Book*. "How kind. We're researching gynaecology and need anatomical images."

He rubs his neck. "I'll show you where your friend is."

As Tegan leads him away, she sees Phoenix frown at the screen.

Chapter 34

Tegan

By the time they get downstairs, Imo has gone so Tegan dreams up a Business Studies query to keep the librarian downstairs. When she sees Phoenix walk out of the exit, she invents an urgent phone call and leaves him to re-shelve a pile of books.

Back at the flat, Phoenix is at the kitchen table, leaning over a coffee.

"Did you get the address?" Tegan asks.

"Are you sure we should be doing this?" Phoenix looks pale.

Tegan sighs. She hates it when people get all moral after the fact. If Phoenix didn't want to hack into the NHS, the time to get a conscience was before.

"No regrets. That's the best policy, I always find," she says briskly.

"You don't know what we could be getting into," Phoenix murmurs.

Tegan's senses sharpen and she recalls Phoenix's intense expression as she left her in the library reading the screen. Phoenix was the one who reckoned Cheryl had vanished without a trace, but now they know she's alive and living under another name. So why isn't Phoenix relieved?

"What else did you find out?"

Phoenix opens her mouth to say something, then shakes her head. "Just the name change and new address."

Tegan's spent a lifetime with liars. Phoenix's deception is obvious, but she decides not to challenge it. There'll be time later to find out what she isn't telling her. "That's great then."

Phoenix takes a sip of her drink. "I've been thinking. Maybe we should tell Imo I couldn't find Cheryl and not mention the name change."

A sense of disappointment comes over Tegan that she can't understand. The others dragged her into this business and now Phoenix is offering her an out. Why isn't she grabbing it?

Phoenix looks up. "And maybe we ought to accept that Amber doesn't want to be found."

Before Tegan can think, Imo bursts into the kitchen. "I heard that. I thought you wanted to find her as much as I do." She trips in her high heels and grabs at the wall to right herself. "When I got your text, I went to the top floor of the library to help you. Do you know how hard heights ...?" Her skin darkens. "You said I should trust my gut, but you're just humouring me, aren't you? Then laughing behind my back."

"No one's laughing," Phoenix says gently. "I'm having doubts for myself, not for you." She fishes a piece of paper out of her pocket and slaps it on the table. "Here's Cheryl's new name and address. You can follow it up if you want to."

When Daisy Was Two Years Old

Daisy sits at her play desk, drawing unicorns. Mummy is in the kitchen, cooking tuna pasta bake. Occasional wafts of melting cheese make Daisy's tummy rumble. But her thoughts stay on the chocolate mousses she saw get unpacked with the shopping and she hopes they're for pudding.

Her baby unicorn has a curly horn. Daisy's tongue rests between her gappy teeth as she concentrates on keeping inside the lines with her pink felt-tip.

When the doorbell rings, she ignores the noise and opts for blue for the mane and tail. But it rings again. She clutches her ears, trying to block the sound.

"Shall we see who that is?" Mummy heads for the door, wiping her hands on her apron.

But after she's looked through the spy thingy, she ducks away, her finger on her lips. She runs over to Daisy, keeping low. "Let's have a little sleep," she whispers and Daisy finds herself plucked away from her drawing. The doorbell rings as they head for the bedroom quietly and Mummy tells her to shhhhh.

They snuggle in Mummy's bed, but Daisy wants her tea. Mummy doesn't realize, but her hand has slipped over Daisy's mouth and she doesn't like not being able to speak.

The bell rings again.

"Let's do your counting," Mummy whispers. "In our heads to ten."

One, two, three. Daisy's heart beats faster. Five, three, four. It doesn't help that she can feel Mummy's heartbeat too. And with the covers over their heads, Mummy's breath smells sour.

Long after the bell has stopped ringing, Mummy lifts her out of bed. "Right, sweetie, you can finish your picture while Mummy serves up supper."

She kisses the top of Daisy's head. "I'll just give your face a little wash. You've got pen on your cheek."

Daisy barely notices that the blue felt-tip is still in her hand.

Chapter 35

Tegan

Off the M4, up the North Circular, left onto the A40 at Hangar Lane tube station.

In a rare moment of kindness, Tegan told Imo that if finding Amber's neighbour meant that much, she'd drive her to the address herself. Now she wishes she'd checked the piece of paper before opening her mouth. The address is bloody Ealing and her car guzzles petrol.

Imo's been fiddling with Facebook for the whole journey. Tegan reckons she could have driven her to Edinburgh and she wouldn't have noticed.

"We'll be there soon."

Imo puts her phone on her lap. "It was worth a try. I might have got lucky with the first few."

"How many have you checked?"

"Ignoring the ones that show a maiden name and the ones who say they're retired, I've looked on a lot of profiles." She rubs her forehead. "Maybe forty or fifty."

Tegan whistles out a breath as she overtakes a bus. There must be hundreds of Jane Browns on social media and they don't even know what she looks like. A needle in a rats' nest.

Imo's eyes move out to a squint as she stares through the windscreen. "The more I think about it, the more I know there's something off about Cheryl changing her name."

Tegan shrugs. People must change their names for lots of reasons. She toyed with it herself when she filled in her university application. The idea of arriving as a totally new person tempted her.

Traffic is chocka, the worst Tegan's ever driven in. Cardiff seems like a sleepy village in comparison. And why all the bloody hooting? No one's getting there quicker.

"Is that it?" Imo points to an apartment block in a service road on the left.

The sat nav is flashing *Destination Reached* but the automated voice has packed up. Tegan has to take a sharp left or risk shooting on to the next junction. Adopting the local lingo, she flicks a V to the irate driver behind and doubles back into the service road.

They park in a designated visitor space and sit in the car for a moment, looking up at the building. One, two … five floors, with a roof terrace. Better than the shoeboxes Tegan imagined London housing to be. Each apartment must be worth half a million, more? Her mind ticks through a projected profit and loss sheet. Maybe in a couple of years she could consider an investment here, if the prices haven't skyrocketed in the meantime.

A tower in the same red brick has been appended to the front and interrupts the sleek art-deco features of the rest of the building. Health and safety regulations must have required a wider entrance and fire escape even though the original building survived the Blitz.

A dog bolts round the building and heads straight for the car.

A snarling, barking mound of fang, tongue and claw rears at the windscreen. Imo squeals and cowers in her seat.

"Now what do we do?" she gasps, head buried in her arms. "We're trapped. We'll have to wait until the owner calls it off."

Sod that, Tegan's paintwork won't last long. She flings open her door, steps out and shouts, "Woof!"

The dog shrinks away, head down like Imo on one of her off days. After a half-hearted final yap it stalks around the back of the building.

"Are you coming or what?" she says to Imo.

"How did you do that?"

Tegan shrugs. "All dogs need a master." Her jaw tightens as she remembers her dad saying it to someone down the phone once. She was too little to know what he meant. She knows now. She moves towards the building in angry steps.

"Don't walk so fast, Tegan. Wait for me. What if the dog comes back?"

She halts until Imo catches up. "It won't."

As she guessed, the tower extension is now the main entrance to the building. Imo locates the bell for Flat 413 but Tegan grabs her hand before she can press it. "Don't warn her we're coming; she might not let us in."

"But … she wouldn't do that, would she?"

"Come on, Imogen, we've knocked on your door countless times and you haven't answered, even though we've known you're in there. Hiding."

Imo's face clouds and Tegan regrets adding her final one-word sentence. If Imo wants to hide, let her. It's better than spilling her mood over the rest of them.

Looking over Tegan's shoulder, Imo breaks into an unexpected smile. "Let me get that for you." She holds the front door with her bum and helps a Nigerian lady lift a pushchair up the steps.

Tegan takes hold of the internal door after the woman has swiped it with her keycard. "Do you need a hand?"

"The elevator should be working, thank you," she replies. Her little boy says bye-bye when the lift shaft opens. Imo waves him off.

When the lift returns, they step inside and study the buttons. "Fourth floor," Tegan says.

"Fourth?" Imo's voice wavers.

The lift door closes and Tegan presses number four before Imo can back out. When they reach the floor, Imo steps out like she's expecting quicksand. Tegan strides past and taps on the door they believe to be Jane Brown's.

"Hi, Jane, it's me," she calls confidently, hoping Jane's curiosity will get the door open.

But there's no reply and none of the neighbours answer either when she knocks on their doors. She sits on the floor with her back against Jane's door, cursing the time and money spent getting here. All for nothing.

"She must be at work." Imo still sounds nervous, keeping her back to the wall. "We might as well go downstairs and wait in the car. We'll see when anyone comes to the main entrance."

Tegan's not waiting anywhere. They've found out the address exists, so the Cheryl–Jane woman must be fine. Tegan made the gesture to drive Imo here but now she wants to return to real life. There's a Business Studies meeting first thing and she wants to be there to ensure they go with her idea for their project. If they leave Ealing now, she can have the whole evening in Abbeythorpe to prepare.

"That dog might come back. Let's call it a day while the coast's clear," she says, feeling shitty for playing on Imo's fears.

But Imo's not moved. "You can bark at it again."

A door across the hall opens. An old man, thin hair, even thinner arms, stares at them from its frame.

Imo's charm kicks in. "Good morning. I wonder if you can help us. We've come to see one of your neighbours, Jane Brown. Is she around?"

He glides his liver-spotted hand up his grey braces. When he cracks into a shaky smile, Tegan thinks they're in business but he disappoints.

"Don't know, dear," he says.

Undeterred, Imo ploughs on. "Have you seen her today?"

"Don't know, dear."

"Well, do you know where she works?"

"Don't know, dear."

Tegan stands up, muttering: "Thanks anyway" and pulls Imo towards the lift.

"Did you shoo that dog?" The man peers at Tegan. "It's the only peace from its bloody barking I've had all week. I can even hear the damn thing when I'm on the roof garden. It plays havoc with the roses."

Tegan spots her opening. "Does the dog disturb Jane too?"

"The lass in that flat, you mean?" He nods towards number 413. "She's not here much. At college, probably."

"What college does she go to? What's she studying?" Imo asks and turns to Tegan. "We could go there now."

"Colleges are all the same to me. I'm afraid I don't know, dear." The old man shakes his head and retreats behind his door.

Imo steps forward with her hand out ready to knock and ask him more.

Tegan tugs her away. "Leave him be. He said he doesn't know where she is." And she doesn't want to waste time driving across London to the designated college. It's time they called it a day.

"Now what do we do?"

"We go home, Imogen. He's confirmed he knows her." Tegan calls the lift. "She lives here; she's not lost."

Imo's eyes flash and Tegan braces herself for another barrage of crime statistics. But Imo says quietly, "It could be weeks since a definite sighting. Trails go cold."

In the close proximity of the lift, Imo's dejection makes Tegan pause. "I get that you're passionate about this, and maybe something's happened to make you ..." She clams up, not going there. "But realistically, Imo, this woman isn't missing."

Imo gives a reluctant nod and studies her trainers as they descend.

"I think you're right," she says, getting her second wind as they reach the car. "She's not missing, but she might know where Amber is."

"Come on, Imogen. That's a stretch."

"Does your sat nav say how far it is to Chadcombe? You know that stuff Jade Murphy told you about Amber getting into drugs, what if the neighbour was the supplier? It would explain the name change if she's a criminal. Maybe Amber's fallen back into her old ways. We could go to that bridge Jade talked about, see if Amber's addict friends are there. They could be part of the jigsaw. We might as well now we're down here."

"Enough now," Tegan snaps. "We're not Scott and Bailey. We've done our best to find Cheryl but that's the end of it."

Tegan starts the engine and senses Imo staring at her as she backs out. She's given up a day and a tank of petrol to indulge Imo's detective fantasy. Imo can gawp at her all the way back to Abbeythorpe if she wants, because that's where Tegan's heading, and no detours.

Chapter 36

Tegan

It takes over an hour to drive from Ealing to Chadcombe. Tegan knows she's been played but, when Imo announced she'd get the train there tomorrow, Tegan had no choice. Letting Imo wander into a drugs lair on her own would be like dumping Snow White in an apple orchard. The detour became a necessity.

The Chadcombe Bridge is easy to find as the dual carriageway into the town goes over it. The River Thames below is a picture of designer yachts and riverside bars. The local council must have done a clean-up operation since Amber used to loiter here. It's hardly the den of iniquity that Amber's sister Jade painted.

Once over the bridge, Tegan takes the first exit and parks in a metered space by the river, but doesn't bother paying; they won't be here long. As they walk along the promenade they see a figure on a bench, a sleeping bag rolled up beside him.

Before Tegan can stop her, Imo goes to him, waving her mobile. Tegan sighs and appraises the tramp. Thinning ragged hair, mottled skin. Fortyish? If he legs it with the phone, they might be able to catch him.

"Have you seen this girl?" Imo asks, putting the phone into harm's way.

The man looks at the screen, without taking it. "I seem to have lost my spectacles." His voice is surprisingly cultured. "Blind as a bat really."

And smelly as a badger. Tegan shifts downwind. "She's about five six, meat on her bones, short bleached hair."

"How old?" He casts his gummy eyes towards her and then turns back to Imo for the answer.

"Eighteen, but she used to hang around Chadcombe a few years ago."

"The youngsters congregate under there." He points a chapped hand towards the bridge. "Be careful, though, some of them are, well, not themselves. Drugs, of course."

"Thanks." Imo presses something into his hand. "Can you get a coffee round here?"

He pockets the money. "I'll take a cup of tea at the kiosk in the marina." He twists a business card in his hands. Imo must have given him it with the coins. "Can't read it but I can guess what this is. Alas too late for me. But I appreciate the gesture." He hands it back to her.

"Take care," Imo says and walks on.

They see the bridge's underbelly of concrete-coated joists. Half a dozen figures huddle round a fire even though the early afternoon is warm. What's the life expectancy of a junkie? If Amber hung around with a crowd when she was fourteen, they're likely in prison or dead by now. This lot will be the next no-hope generation, unlikely to be as rational as the tramp.

She touches Imo's arm. "Let me do the talking this time."

"I'm not scared, if that's what you think."

"Suit yourself." Tegan shrugs.

The bridge casts a dark shadow. Tegan shivers and Imo folds her arms. The fire is in a metal brazier the junkies must have nicked from somewhere. The light from the flames flickers across their putty-white faces, but they don't look up when Tegan and Imo approach. Two boys in tracky bottoms and dirty parkas share a fat, stubby smoke.

Tegan and Imo halt four feet from the fire. By some unspoken agreement, they've decided this is the group's threshold; any closer and they'd be marching into their private space.

A girl lifts her gaze from the fire and looks in their direction, but her eyes are bleary and unfocused.

"Our friend used to come here," Imo says simply. Tegan notes that she doesn't show her phone this time.

The girl coughs. Tegan can't tell whether she's trying to answer, or if it's the effects of the smoke. As if exercising some muscle memory from a past life, the girl covers her mouth politely. Her grime-coloured fingernails are bitten down. The sleeve of her loose, grey jumper slips to reveal a slit-slat stave of scars inside her wrist. Tegan wants to cough too, or puke; behind the smoky air is the distinctive smell of urine.

Their presence finally registers with the others and six pairs of glittering eyes look at them. But nothing else in their faces, or their bodies, reacts.

A lorry judders across the bridge. A chip wrapper presses against a graffitied bridge joist in the wind. But there are no sleeping bags or cardboard boxes. Where do these people go at night – back to middle-class mummy and daddy? Is that what it was like for Amber's mother – the constant dread of what state her daughter would roll home in?

"Our friend is Amber Murphy," Imo says. "Did you know her?"

The girl who coughed stands up and lolls closer to them. Her face crumples. Imo and Tegan step back. "Amber … hurt too much," the girl says. Then her mood changes and she turns to walk away.

Tegan takes out a five-pound note. "Was Amber a friend of

yours?" She holds the money out to the girl. "Are you still in touch?" She winces; schoolgirl error. She's given away her cash on a stupid question.

The girl snatches the money and blinks at Tegan, rocking from foot to foot. The air is thick with the dank, decaying smell of her. "Never the same after Leo."

"What you saying, Vee?" a voice calls out. A tall figure walks towards them from the other end of the tunnel. His boots ring out as he approaches, his phlegmy cough echoing in the silence. Tegan tenses and wonders whether they have just made a big mistake. But as he gets closer, Tegan relaxes slightly. He's just a boy. His washed-out blond hair matches his skin. There are scabs around his mouth, a black bruise on his cheek.

The girl looks away. "Doesn't matter, Danno." She rejoins the group at the fire.

The two boys with the spliff stare morosely into the flames. The tall boy's eyes flit between Tegan and Vee.

"Did you know Amber?" Tegan asks, but fears it's another stupid question. He'll say yes if he's seen the fiver that went Vee's way.

His eyes widen and he takes a step closer, causing Tegan's heartbeat to rise. She grips her car key, ready to jab, but his shoulders buckle before he can take another step. "They wouldn't give him a funeral, told her he was born dead." He gets down on his haunches, gazes into the fire.

Imo keys something into her phone. Vee hugs her skinny arms around herself and rocks back and forth, continuing to stare at the fire. A pleasure cruiser coasts by on the river, with a brunette in sunglasses on deck. She doesn't look their way, her landscape unspoilt.

Tegan's phone buzzes. She reads the screen. It's from Imo: Fake father? Imo stares at her expectantly. At once, Tegan sees what she means and swallows a gulp of smoky air. It hadn't occurred to her that Amber's pregnancy charade might not have

160

hurt just her family and her neighbour, that there could have been a duped boyfriend too. This poor sod is grieving for a kid that never existed. When Amber got bored of the joke, she must have told him his son was stillborn. Is that why he's under this stinking bridge? Grief harder to shake off than the drugs?

"We're sorry for your loss." Imo steps forward to put her hand on the boy's filthy jacket.

But Vee knocks Imo's arm away. "Leave him. He doesn't need you stirring that up."

"Don't worry, we're going." There's an edge to Imo's voice. "Come on, Tegan." They start to stride away, but after a few metres, Imo stops. She pauses and turns. Goes back a final time, her tone softer again. "Do you stay here all night?"

"We've got places," Danno says.

"None of your business." Vee takes his elbow to pull him away.

Imo gets out a card and holds it out to them. "One text, that's all, nothing more."

When they don't take the card, she lays it on the ground. "Families worry. Believe me."

***

The brooding silence in the car gets to Tegan and she finds herself driving carefully, concentrating hard on mirror, signal, manoeuvre every time she overtakes an Eddie Stobart. She wants to know what Imo's thinking, but the girl sits ramrod straight, eyes dead ahead.

They're level with Oxford when Phoenix calls Imo's mobile. "Just checking you're surviving Tegan's driving."

"Watch it, you're on speaker." Tegan laughs, relieved at having someone to talk to. "We'd have been back hours ago but for a pointless detour to crackhead-land."

"Not completely pointless," Imo snaps. "We now know Amber's not worth finding." She explains to Phoenix about the father of Amber's fake baby. "You should have seen him. He looks like the walking dead. Amber did that to him. I thought she was a victim – missing – but those people we saw today, they're the vulnerable ones."

Good, thinks Tegan, *she'll drop it now.* She imagines Phoenix thinking the same thing.

"Did you go to Ealing?" Phoenix asks.

"Nothing doing. We found Cheryl–Jane's flat but a neighbour told us she was out at college."

"Good, good." Phoenix sounds relieved. Hardly surprising as she was the one who wanted to duck out of the whole Cheryl business after she'd done the NHS search. She never did tell Tegan what she found. And Tegan's not about to ask, not now that even Imo has lost interest.

But then Phoenix says, "Maybe the reason for Amber's departure lies at the Abbey."

"Unlikely," Imo says. She looks out of the window, as if detaching herself from the phone conversation. Tegan wishes Phoenix could see Imo's disinterest and end the call.

Instead Phoenix says, "Amber went weird on us at the Freshers' Fair. What if it's got something to do with that?"

"What, like: she was terrified the chess nerd would ask her out?" Tegan calls as she pulls past a lorry.

Her sarcasm fails to reach Phoenix, who carries on. "Not him. Something came over her when we were near the Deaf Students' information stand and the Parents' Group. Do you remember?"

"Not really." Tegan sighs. "I think I'd moved on." *Like I wish you would now.*

"And the LGBTQ girl was there," Imo says. "She was nice, wasn't she?"

There's a pause on the line.

"Phoenix, are you still there?"

Phoenix speaks again. "I've been mulling it over for a few days. It might be something, might be nothing, but did you

162

notice the woman on the Parents' stall when we went back to ask about Amber?"

"What about her?" Imo says. Still looking out of the window.

"Her body language. She was holding back. I might be wrong, that's why I haven't said anything. But I know a couple who do a mind-reading act. They taught me a bit about understanding people. It's all about the tells."

There's a pause. Tegan toys with lobbing Imo's phone out of the car. Is Phoenix trying to wind Imo up again? *Mind-reading* act? Where does she find such weird friends?

"Spit it out, Phoenix." She taps the steering wheel, annoyed at her own curiosity.

"When Imo asked her if she'd seen Amber, the woman moved her leaflets across the table as if creating a barrier between her and Imo. She started on about mature students and a family barbecue, but barely looked at Amber's photo."

Tegan knows a con when she sees one – she can read the signs too – but she doesn't buy Phoenix's interpretation. "You're reading too much into it. Why would some random woman know anything about Amber quitting uni?"

Imo bounces in her seat. Oh crap, she's hooked again. "I noticed that thing she did with the leaflets."

"Exactly," Phoenix replies. "You didn't get close to her, Tegan, but her eye movements said she wasn't telling the truth when she claimed she'd clocked off early on Tuesday. And we *know* she was still there; we saw her. She was still there when Amber flounced off. I reckon she saw something and for some reason she wouldn't tell us. The problem is; I don't know how to find her. The Freshers' Fair's finished and I tried accessing the Abbey Parents' Group on Facebook, but it's invitation only, so I can't see members' profiles."

Imo turns to Tegan. "Can you hack in?"

Tegan's grip on the steering wheel tightens. "I thought you said Amber wasn't worth bothering with. Why do you care?"

"I don't ... I can't explain ... If this woman saw what happened, she might know where Amber went. I need to find her and get her to say what she saw. Then I can forget about Amber. We all can. So will you hack into Facebook?"

Tegan narrows her eyes. Is that what they think of her: a computer hacker, a criminal, her father's daughter? She can't hack into anything – even if she wants to – not without help. Her foot slips on the accelerator as another thought parachutes into her head. No way – she couldn't, could she? The car behind flashes its lights and she speeds up. *No way.*

But she hears herself ask, "When's the family barbecue the woman told you about?"

"Tomorrow lunchtime. Why?"

"If you're both so desperate to find that woman, you should go. She's bound to be there."

"It's for parents only, like the Facebook group," Phoenix says.

Tegan hesitates, doubting her idea. Why should she help? It's not her problem. Phoenix seems as hooked as Imo – she can leave them both to it and get on with her life.

But Imo is still looking at her with expectant, puppy-dog eyes. "So how can we get into the Parents' Group?"

Tegan takes a deep breath. "Time my son and I joined."

"Tegan!" Imo gasps. "You've got a baby?"

There's silence on the phone and Tegan imagines Phoenix with the same open-mouthed expression as Imo. She smiles to herself as she keeps them hanging.

"I'm not that stupid," she says eventually. "But I know where I can borrow one." She pulls off at Cherwell Valley services and resets the sat nav.

Chapter 37

Amber

Her fingers trace the rut in her scalp. Not so soft today. A scab has started to grow. Rough and brittle. Itchy. She examines her fingernails in the gloom. The bloodstains aren't just from where she's bitten them to the quick; her head bled again yesterday when she stupidly scratched it through her greasy hair.

Was it yesterday? Hours and minutes merge because of her blackouts. A weak light ebbs and flows in the corner of the wall, but she's not sure it signifies night and day. What can a patch of flaking plaster blistered with cotton-wool mould tell her? All she knows is the damp, pervasive smell of spores and a thousand imaginary beetles that feed on the pus around her tied ankle.

At first she thought it would be easy to slip the knot, but the ring of twine tightened into her bone with every futile effort she made. She'd tried biting the slack between her foot and where the cord was fixed to the bedframe, but couldn't bend that far however hard she stretched. And with her belly in a permanent growl, she'd run out of energy to persist. She devoured the sour apple and soft crisps ages ago. There's been no food since then.

Her body trembles. Sweat prickles out of every pore. Someone will find her, won't they, even though she knows now this isn't the bridge? Who did she tell? She tries to remember, shuts her eyes tight. If only her head would clear. Her memory goes over the same ground, retracing her steps, and her thoughts return once again to the Freshers' Fair.

***

On shaking legs, she makes it out of the Great Hall and stands on the steps outside. Students stream past, chatting happily. She paces around the building to the back and into the shade. Cars jockey for space in the small car park. She walks on, past a service entrance and a bin store. And eventually returns to the afternoon sunshine.

Her steps have reached a rhythm and she follows the same route again. Three times around the building. Five. Rubbing her bracelets up and down her forearms as she struggles for what to say and how to say it. Composing, editing, rehearsing. At the back of her mind lurks the self-doubt and humiliation that made things collapse as they did.

At the front of the Great Hall again, she decides it's time to act, confront her past. Her heart races as she approaches the steps. A bangle slips off her wrist and she stoops to follow it. The silver bracelet spins away. Bounces down the steps, glinting in the sunlight. The Great Hall doors open again. She gasps as two figures cast a fresh shadow over the steps. Her blood stills, freezes in her veins. Time stops.

***

There's no memory of what happened next, but she knows in her aching, hungry gut that she told no one. She holds a half-drunk bottle to her lips, but she's shaking so much that water dribbles down her chin and wets the front of her kimono, already stink-damp with sweat and blood.

Chapter 38

Imogen

The nearer they get to Cardiff, the more Tegan's body seems to tighten over the steering wheel. It makes Imo nervous and she keeps needing the loo. But asking Tegan to stop at every other service station doesn't help the mood. Imo feels like she's done something wrong, even though the decision to drive this way was entirely Tegan's.

Is she still angry that Imo dragged her to Chadcombe Bridge, a world she usually tiptoes past? Imo was the same until Sophia.

Her dad went to London on his own the first time. He planned to stay a week but lasted two days. He looked sheepish when he got home. "Sorry, love, I couldn't … so many homeless, just kids. I'll go back, I promise." He cried. Mum hugged him. Her turn to be strong.

He did go back and Imo and Freddie went with him. Put up posters at Paddington, Euston, King's Cross and Waterloo, and wandered through the royal parks. Imo saw a world that hadn't been there on previous visits to the capital. The world of sleeping-bag mounds, parkas tied with string, quiet dogs and vacant eyes. Imo soon realized it had been there all along, just not visible to her. They took helpline cards with them, sensing deep down they wouldn't find Sophia but, if just one homeless kid took their card and phoned, their trip wouldn't be pointless. Imo still carries the cards in case she sees a duvet in a shop doorway. The gaunt face is never Sophia's, but she moves on a card lighter.

After the Severn Bridge and several motorway junctions round Newport, the sat nav delivers them onto a B road. Tegan ignores the signs for a bird sanctuary and the Severn Estuary, turns left and stops in front of a tall, wrought iron gate with a lodge cottage beside it.

An elderly woman comes out and greets Tegan over her garden wall. Imo doesn't understand a word but the tone sounds friendly on both sides. Tegan reads her phone screen and taps a code into a panel on the gatepost. The gates swing open, she waves to the woman and gets back in the car. The gravel crunches under the wheels as they sweep up a long drive.

"I didn't know you spoke Welsh," Imo says.

"You're not the only linguist." Tegan grins. "I was brought up with Welsh and English."

The house at the end of the drive comes into view. Imo's mum and dad would love it. It's a gorgeous sandstone colour like Cotswold cottages, although there's nothing cottage-sized about this place. The drive splits into a crescent around a lawn that's in better shape than Imo's lounge carpet. The house must be one of those listed manor houses that have been converted to posh flats. Each leaseholder pays a packet for the upkeep of the grounds.

The gravelled area extends on the far left into the distance to a huge block-shaped building. Through the glass-folding doors, Imo can see a fleet of gleaming motors.

Tegan points at them as they crawl up the drive. "Ancient woodland and a wildflower meadow got bulldozed for that … that dick palace," she splutters and glares at the building. "Wish

I'd joined Conservation Volunteers sooner. We could have challenged it. He shouldn't have it all his own way." She parks in the crescent and gets out. "Come on."

Imo picks her way over the gravel. A flowerbed runs the width of the house. Miniature roses – gold-coloured blooms – not a weed in sight.

The large oak door at the centre of the building opens and a man in a bottle-green suit and matching tie steps forward. "Miss Parry," he says, "welcome back."

"Mr Rogers." Tegan goes inside without looking at him.

Imo smiles and follows Tegan into a ... what the hell is it? Stone pillars in the middle of the floor, wood-panelled walls, a roaring fire in a large, ornate fireplace that's already making her sweat. A modern art print on one wall, the copy of an old master on another, a parquet floor.

"I'll tell Mrs Parry you're here and make some tea." Mr Rogers goes through a door on the right, presumably to his apartment – even though, to Imo, he's acting more like a housekeeper than a resident.

"Tacky, isn't it?" Tegan says when she catches her looking at a mock medieval tapestry beside a leopard skin on the back wall.

"Well ..." Imo hesitates, picking her words. Tegan's family must occupy some part of the building. "Communal areas have to cater for so many tastes."

"Three people live in this house. One is a former maid from Thailand, another is two years old."

"Whose house?"

"My father's." Tegan's voice is glacial.

Chapter 39

Imogen

"Welcome, welcome, so kind of you." A tiny woman with a sing-song voice comes into the hall through the door Rogers used. Her dark hair's scooped into a ponytail and she's not wearing make-up. Although her face is line-free, there are dark shadows under her eyes.

The woman flings her arms around Tegan, who visibly stiffens.

"Hello, Kanya," she says tightly.

The woman releases her and turns to Imo. "You Tegan friend?"

Before Imo can answer, the woman's arms are around her. She smells of summer flowers. Tegan seems to have gone mute so Imo introduces herself.

"Imogen." Kanya repeats the name, pronouncing the last syllable as "gin". It makes Imo smile even though Tegan rolls her eyes.

Rogers comes back with a tea tray and they follow him into the lounge. Cherubs on the ceiling, crystal light pendants, another tapestry, more old masters. Rogers leaves the tray on a coffee table in front of a two-seater sofa covered by a patchwork throw.

A little, dark-haired boy sits on a rug with a Mega Blok tower, his eyes on a plasma screen TV. *Fireman Sam* in Welsh.

Kanya invites them to sit on the sofa and pours the tea. After she's handed out the cups, she sits beside her son on the carpet and turns the TV down to a murmur. The child frowns but Kanya gets his attention on the building blocks.

"Welcome, welcome," she says again. "You're always welcome here."

Imo looks at Tegan, willing her to say something nice.

Tegan takes the hint. "How is he?"

Kanya glances up. A cloud falls over her smile. "In London until tomorrow. I can text him. Maybe he come back early."

"I meant him." Tegan points at the boy. "Dylan." Her brother's name sounds uncomfortable in her mouth, as if she's never said it before. "I wasn't asking about my father."

The bitter tone seems lost on Kanya and she moves the coffee table to the side. "See for yourself. Play with him."

When Tegan doesn't move, Imo puts down her cup and slides onto the floor beside the boy. Reluctantly Tegan kneels next to her, but Dylan buries his face in his mother's shoulder.

"He's not usually shy." Kanya's eyes are anxious, apologetic.

Imo looks at Tegan again: *Say something else nice.*

"Shall we build a house?" Tegan, using the tone she reserves for pitching her jackets, forms a square with some spare plastic bricks.

Dylan peers out from Kanya's chest and puts a brick on top of one of Tegan's.

"You have to put it like this." Tegan moves his brick so it straddles two of hers. "Your house will fall down otherwise." She passes him another brick. "You try."

He puts the new brick next to his first one.

"I suppose Dylan must speak Thai as well as Welsh and English," Imo says. "How clever."

Kanya places the child on her lap and kisses his head. Her

eyes look heavy. "No Thai. My husband say, 'Don't confuse him.'"

Dylan wriggles off her knee to put another block on Tegan's house. While they build, Imo tells Kanya about university. She seems genuinely interested in Imo's course.

"What you like for dinner?" she asks eventually. "You can stay the night." Her voice goes up an octave to the excited tone she greeted them with when they first arrived. Imo thinks it must be lonely with only the efficient Rogers for adult company.

Tegan stands up. "We've got to get back. I've got a course meeting in the morning."

"Sad that Dylan cannot play with his sister for longer." Kanya looks forlorn as she stands up too.

"Actually," Tegan says, rubbing her chin. "I've just had an idea. How about you and Dylan come back with us?" She touches her chin again. To Imo, she's a lousy actress, but manipulative. Kanya has no way of knowing they came here with the sole intention of borrowing the boy.

"There's a family barbecue on campus tomorrow. I'd love to show off the little man." Tegan sounds like a children's TV presenter, but even less sincere.

"What about your father?" Kanya bites her lip.

The fake jollity drops from Tegan's face. "I thought you said he was in London. He won't want to visit me."

"He come back tomorrow. I should be here."

Recovering, Tegan tips her head to the side. "Oh, that's a shame. I've already bought your tickets for the barbecue."

Imo stares at her. Bought tickets? When she's just claimed the invitation to Abbeythorpe was a spontaneous idea.

But Kanya doesn't seem to notice the lie. "So sorry," she says in a small voice.

"I'm sorry too." Tegan's voice is loud in contrast. "Dad will be disappointed that I can't spend time with Dylan. He's always asking me to show an interest."

The two women are small, about the same height, and yet Kanya seems to shrink as she faces Tegan.

"Never mind," Imo says, trying to smooth the situation. "I'm sure there'll be other times."

"You could always let me look after Dylan for the weekend." Tegan's voice still dominates the room. "That way you can be here when Dad comes back. The two of you can spend some quality time together."

Kanya wraps her arms around her body and rocks. "But ..."

Tegan squats down beside Dylan and pats his head. "I don't know why I didn't think of it to start with. Dad will be pleased I'm looking after my little brother."

Dylan ducks away and clasps his mother's legs.

"I don't know," she says, picking him up.

"If you get a bag of Dylan's things, we can get off before the tea-time traffic." Tegan doesn't look at Kanya as she speaks. It's the same haughty way she addressed Rogers. Imo feels a moment of guilt. It's her interest in the woman at the Parents' Group at uni that's making them take Dylan away from his lovely, lonely mother.

"I take it you have a travel cot we can borrow," Tegan says.

"Yes but he's in a bed now he's two and half." Kanya looks close to tears.

"Just for the weekend."

"He's never been away from me." Kanya hugs the boy to her face.

"So the first time should be with his sister. Dad will be thrilled. It's great when Dad's happy, isn't it?"

Kanya hesitates. Lost in a thought. Finally she gives a sigh. "If your father want it. You ring me when you arrive?"

"Of course," Imo says, putting her arms around Kanya. She wishes they could take her too, away from this draughty mausoleum, and, she suspects, an even colder marriage.

By the time they've fitted the car seat that Kanya's given them into the back of the Mini and loaded the boot with other child paraphernalia, Dylan's nodded off in Kanya's arms. She tries to wake him to say goodbye. His eyes open and close again, deep in slumber. She kisses his cheek and fastens him in the car.

Imo touches her arm. "We'll take good care of him. I promise."

He sleeps the entire journey to Abbeythorpe, even when they stop at services and take turns to grab a coffee and use the loo.

"It's hardly rocket salad, this parenthood lark," Tegan says as she looks in her rear-view mirror at her sleeping brother. "A doddle."

Chapter 40

Phoenix

Her flatmates get back from Ealing at about 8 p.m. just as Phoenix is washing up at the kitchen sink. She hears the screams on the stairwell before they reach the flat and goes into the corridor to see what's happened. They come in, Tegan grappling suitcase and travel cot, Imo holding shrieking child at arm's length.

"He's pissed himself," is Tegan's greeting. She dumps the luggage, goes past Phoenix into the kitchen and rushes out with the bowl of washing-up water.

"I don't think the wee leaked through to the upholstery," Imo calls after her. Phoenix follows her into the kitchen.

Still holding the screaming boy, Imo fetches milk out of the fridge. Fighting the boy's wails with her version of "Rockabye Baby", she pours out a full mug. Before Phoenix can stop her, she presses the drink into his tiny fist. He lets go before he's even taken hold, still screeching. Milk splashes onto his already wet trousers. The mug lands on its side and sprays milk in a wide arc across the lino. For a moment it looks as if Imo might start bawling too.

Phoenix takes the child and places him on an easy chair. She finds pyjamas in the suitcase and instructs Imo to mop up the milk while she washes his sore, red legs. But even wiped clean of wee and milk, he still cries. Who can blame him? According to Imo, Tegan has hardly seen him since he was born. As far as he's concerned, he's woken up in the company of complete strangers.

Imo goes back to the fridge and this time retrieves a loaf of bread. "I'll make him some toast."

"I'll do it," Phoenix snaps. There isn't time to wait for Imo to faff with the oven. She was bad enough when the toaster worked.

Imo leaves the bread on the kitchen counter and stalks off to her room with her hood up. Phoenix grills the bread, vowing to apologize to Imo when the current child crisis has passed.

But even with Phoenix's expertly buttered toast in front of him, it turns out that Dylan can eat and scream at the same time. The wailing brings Riku into the kitchen, but he does a one-eighty when he sees the baby. Crumbs slither down the boy's chin in a cascade of tears and saliva, but at least Riku's brief appearance gives Phoenix an idea. She thinks of what she saw hanging on his wall and remembers what she brought to uni. When the child has mutilated as much toast as he wants, she takes him to her room.

Her juggling balls do the trick. The crying stops suddenly as if she's pulled a plug. He sits on her bed open-mouthed as she throws the three sand-filled balls with two hands, one, two, high, then low.

Tegan comes in. Has she waited until the noise stopped? She goes past the child and inspects Phoenix's wall of posters. "This one's sexy," she says, not worrying about her choice of adjective in front of a two-year-old.

Sonny, bare-chested, rolling fire across his forearm. Cloud in front of him, bent backwards almost into crab in her shimmering midnight-blue leotard, a flame swirling from her scarlet mouth.

Phoenix shrugs. Her parents, but she says nothing.

When the child's eyelids begin to droop, she switches to the calmer game of Three Cup Shuffle. She puts her trick beakers on the bed beside him. Head nodding with fatigue, he keeps his eyes on the moving cups but never spots where she's hidden the two-pound coin. Sleep gets the better of him and he curls up. They don't dare lift him into the travel cot, but manage to get him under her duvet without waking him. Phoenix volunteers to stay with him. Tegan brings her a sleeping bag she got from the Conservation Volunteers, before retreating to the child-free refuge of her own room.

Chapter 41

Saturday 8 October

Phoenix

The crying starts, and Phoenix wills her senses to hold onto sleep. But she's awake and the child in her bed is howling.

"Ma … ma." He's still lying down, but putting all his energy into his lungs.

Her joints creak and lock as she gets up from the sleeping bag on the floor. She starts in a soothing voice. "You're all right, Dylan. You'll see Mama tomorrow. One more sleep." But, remembering his arrival last night, she senses urgency. "Let's get you to the toilet."

Propped in front of the toilet bowl he wees, on and on, bladder the size of an air balloon. She wants the loo herself but the boy keeps on going. When he's finished, she washes their hands and takes him to the kitchen. Pacifies him with a drink of milk. Thank God his mother packed his special leak-proof beaker.

She puts bread under the grill and boils the kettle, shaking her head. She pads her hand over the child's car seat which Tegan rinsed and left propped on the kitchen top. Still damp.

Dylan has finished his milk and his chunters grow louder, threatening to reach their previous pitch. Working quickly, Phoenix pours boiling water into a pan and adds an egg. At the back of a cupboard, she finds a wooden egg cup, gives it a wash because there's no telling how long it's been there, and, after three minutes, pops in the egg. The child stops crying and watches her.

Tegan steps into the kitchen in designer jeans and a purple check shirt. Phoenix aches in her onesie after her cat nap on a cold floor. To her annoyance, Dylan smiles and holds out his arms to Tegan for a cuddle. Tegan doesn't reciprocate but at least she cuts the toast into soldiers to dip in his egg.

"Sleep well?" Phoenix asks sarcastically.

Tegan pats her shoulder. "Thanks for everything. I couldn't have managed him without you."

Charmer, Phoenix thinks, but she smiles.

"Can you get him dressed?" Tegan asks, hoisting the child onto her hip. "I've got a Business Studies meeting."

Phoenix sighs. Of course, first charm, then ask for the favour. "I'll show you what to do, but *you* can dress him; he's your brother. Where's his stuff?"

Sulkily, Tegan takes Dylan to her room. Phoenix follows and, to her surprise, Tegan manages to get Dylan washed and dressed mostly by herself, only needing help with getting the toothbrush out of his mouth and untwisting the bib of his dungarees.

Phoenix rewards Dylan's cooperation with more juggling.

"How come you're so good with kids?" Tegan asks. "I suppose you're one of many."

Phoenix dumps the balls in Tegan's lap. "It's time I got dressed."

Shower water bounces off her angry body and she slaps shampoo into her hair. Why do people assume that? People from her community are as mixed as everyone else. Big families, small, one parent, two, some with hands-on grandparents, some without. Then she remembers Tegan doesn't know her background; the question was genuine. She throws on jeans and a sweatshirt, and goes back to Tegan, feeling calmer.

Tegan smiles at her. "I've cancelled my meeting. I think the others were still in bed anyway." Her tone is conciliatory. Maybe she realizes she offended Phoenix, although it's more likely that she's gearing up to ask another favour. She and Dylan are on their knees, rolling the juggling balls back and forth to each other. "Can you give Imo a knock? It'll take her ages to surface and we don't want to get to the barbecue late."

"We? Imo and I can't go. The woman from the Parents' stall will remember that we cross-examined her. If she knows something about Amber, she won't tell us. You'll have to go by yourself."

She throws up a ball and catches it on the bridge of her nose, imagining the panic coursing through Tegan. She's going to have to look after Dylan on her own. The ice queen will never show her fear, but it's enough for Phoenix to know it's there.

Chapter 42

Tegan

"Don't pull my hair. You're not a baby." Tegan releases the buckle on Dylan's car seat and lifts him off the towel she's used as precautionary padding. He's got the same fuck-you look in his eyes as their father. Does she have it too? Probably.

The main car park on the central concourse is full so Tegan parks in her usual disabled spot by the geography tower. They set off walking to the student union but Dylan dawdles like a drunk so she scoops him onto her hip and ups her speed.

They join a pioneer wagon train of parents when they approach the union building. Prams, pushchairs, long-handled trikes. Young parents weighed down with baby carriers, nappy bags, highchairs. A handwritten sign for the barbecue sends them through a side gate into the smokers' garden behind the Abbi bar.

A heavily pregnant woman waves at Tegan. "There's a space here." She's at a wooden picnic bench with two girls about Dylan's age. Tegan doesn't want to get wedged in one place – a quick mingle, find the woman from the Freshers' Fair and leave is what she has in mind – but the girls have Mega Bloks and might be playmates for Dylan. The kid's not so bad; he deserves to get something out of the party.

"Lovely, thanks," she calls out, then whispers to Dylan, "Remember what I said." She puts her finger to her lips. "Double chocolate."

He copies the gesture and balls his fist. Tegan gently knocks her fist against his.

The woman, Sian from Chepstow – learnt Welsh in school but prefers English –introduces her girls, Lowri and Lili. Closer up, Tegan can see one is eighteen months or so older than the other. They have the same flat noses and chubby cheeks as their mother.

Sian's a talker, specialist subject: her children. Tegan hears all the details of two home births and current antenatal arrangements for the twins she's expecting. Tegan's mind drifts. Is this how Kanya fills her days? The thought of Kanya's isolation grates in her head. But it's not her problem. She tunes back to Sian.

Her girls jabber too while Dylan plays it strong and silent.

"Doesn't talk much, does he?" Sian says, between ultrasound stories.

Tegan stiffens. He's only quiet because there's an ice-cream on offer if he keeps his trap shut and doesn't blow her cover.

"He's fine." She sounds defensive and remembers how Kanya apologized for him being shy. Did Tegan intimidate her? She's surprised to find that the thought doesn't make her feel good.

"Do you know everyone?" she asks before Sian can start up again. It's time she got on with why she's here.

"No one," Sian replies. "I picked up a flier for the barbecue at the crèche." She points to a door across the yard. "The crèche is in there. Perfect for Lili when Lowri's at school. I get a few hours' study done. Some of us have started meeting here for coffee at picking-up time. I'm a newbie. Mature student, obviously. Midwifery."

Tegan's eyes glance over her expansive belly. Of course, what else would she be studying? "Nice talking to you." But pointless. She suggests a go on the bouncy castle to Dylan and leaves Sian with an insincere see-you-later.

As he bounces himself stupid, she scans the garden. Plenty of dark-haired women in their thirties but none she recognizes as the woman from the Parents' Group stall. She squats on the rubber mat by a dad who's unfastening his son's shoes and describes the woman to him.

"Do you mean the woman in charge?"

Tegan hesitates. "She might be in charge. I don't know. She has a daughter. Mop of ginger hair. The child, not the mother."

The man laughs. "Yeah, sounds like her. A postgrad. Teacher training, I think. Haven't seen them today but there's a bug going round. It's not just the teenagers who get Freshers' Flu."

Dylan collides with another boy and they both start bawling. Tegan pulls him off the bouncy castle and lets him nestle on her lap until he's calmed down. She finds the sensation of his sweaty little body next to hers strangely comforting. But when she puts his shoes back on, he throws himself on the mat, refusing to move. She manhandles him into her arms but loses her balance when she stands up and knocks into a man carrying two pints of beer. Most of the beer seeps into the grass. She looks up at him.

Six feet tall, black and beau-ti-ful.

"I'm so sorry ..." Her apology comes out like something Kanya would say. Or Imo. She pulls herself together. "Let me replace those drinks."

"No need." Voice deep. Yorkshire accent? "I'll go back to the bar. Hello, little fella." He lightens his tone to address Dylan.

Dylan stops pulling against Tegan and stares. He's as mesmerized as she is.

"Handsome dude," the man says and gives Dylan a thumbs-up. "Gets it from his mama."

He's gone inside before Tegan twigs it's a compliment. He

meant her. She plumps her hair, feeling electric. She likes a man who speaks his mind. But her mood nose-dives when she remembers this is a family barbecue and she's just been chatted up by someone's dad who thinks she's someone's mum. Sleaze.

Sian brings her girls to the bouncy castle. "One of the organizers has told me how to get into the Parents' Facebook Group. If we send a friend request, their convenor will accept."

Tegan gets out her phone, sensing that this is the information she needs. If she gets into the Facebook Group, she'll get a list of the other members. She can pass it to Imo – and to Phoenix – and leave them to track down their Freshers' Fair woman. As per Sian's instructions, she gets up the link but, just in time, stops herself making contact.

"Great. I've done that," she lies. "Best be off now. Dylan needs his nap." She leads him out of the gate, and pretends not to notice how he's twisting towards the bouncy castle.

Chapter 43

Amber

Amber groans and rolls over. It's still dark. Gingerly she touches the throbbing sore in her hair, then feels the cut around her tied leg. Both wounds are caked in dried blood and ooze. The food bowl on the floor is empty again and her stomach cramps with hunger.

Her head spins and she grips the bed, a rush of colour explodes before her eyes. She fights against the familiar cloudy feeling, tries to focus before she blacks out again. Tries to hold onto fragments of memory before they crumble to nothing. The last thing she can picture, before it all goes blank, is a taxi. A white car sitting by the side of the road, engine running. In a panic, she dashes towards it. And suddenly she's on the back seat, gesturing to the car in front. Telling the driver to follow.

***

The driver cocks his head. "Fancy dress, is it?"

Amber has forgotten about her wig and kimono. "Not any more," *she says grimly. "Can we go?"*

He puts the car into gear. "Which car, love?"

Amber glances through the windscreen. To her horror she sees she has two choices.

"That one." A split-second decision. She stabs the seatbelt into its socket as the taxi takes off.

"Friend of yours, is it?" the driver says, giving her a lopsided grin. Amber's skin tingles when she remembers where she's seen him before.

"Not exactly," she says.

"I get it," he drawls. "A boyfriend."

Oh, for something so normal. She clenches her fists as he wastes precious seconds stopping at a zebra crossing to let more students pass. Then she relaxes as he accelerates and catches up with the car.

"Or the ex, is it?" He glances at her, appraising her outfit again. "You're not a stalker, are you?"

Her eyes prick with tears.

"Don't worry, love," he says. "None of my business. You got money, have you?"

Amber pats her hip – a twenty in her kimono pocket – and hopes it will be enough. She doesn't know where this journey will end.

***

Now she knows. Here. Lying on a bed in her own filth. Waiting for no one.

Chapter 44

Imogen

Why can't it rain more? Imo doesn't mind walking so much when she can hide under her hood. But this afternoon is sunny and she might have to talk to people if they see her. She's okay at saying, "Hi," but if they say "How are you?" it's too much. Seven months of lying that she's "fine". It would be ideal if she could stay in her room until the sky clouds over again, but the essay won't write itself. She sets off and wishes the library could be nearer to halls.

And yet it's also a good thing it's not raining as the family barbecue would get cancelled. It's their only link to the woman at the Freshers' Fair. Imo can't explain even to herself why she wants every lead to Amber followed up. Tegan has Amber down as a fantasist and a liar. And she's right, isn't she? Imo should be glad Amber's gone. And yet she can't shake off the stirring doubt. It's nothing like the pinching, cramping fear she has for Sophia, but the nagging is there. Where is she?

There's someone by the geography tower. Imo speeds up, preparing to offer a quick hello and speed past. But it's Tegan, standing by her car. Dylan's finishing an ice-cream.

"Have you got any wet wipes?" Tegan says by way of greeting. "Or a handkerchief." She yawns. "I'm knackered. Is this normal at two o'clock?"

Imo doesn't reply. She's been yawning at two o'clock for months. Nights of what-if thoughts and dark cellar nightmares don't make for restful sleep.

She only has old tissues in her bag, nothing that can be used on Dylan. "Has the barbecue finished already?" she asks. "I thought it would go on all afternoon."

Tegan scrapes a layer of brown off the boy's chin with her little finger and wipes it on a page of her order book from her handbag. "The woman wasn't there, but I got the Facebook group details."

"And?" Imo catches a curl of cream before it falls off the cone.

"I can't join, can I? If I get to see their profiles, they can see mine. Do you think my Facebook profile in any way resembles a mother's?"

Imo thinks of her old profile in the time *before*: pouting poses, WKDs, leopard print leggings. "I take your point."

"Do me a favour and walk him back to the flat while I drive the car. I'll never get his paw prints off the seats if I take him."

Tegan presses the boy's sticky hand into Imo's. The library trip is cancelled before Imo even has time to mention it. Tegan gets in her car and drives away.

"Why did she get you an ice-cream, if she was worried about the mess?" She asks the question to herself but Dylan taps his lips and says, "Doub choc late." Imo has the sneaky feeling she's caught the tail end of a bribe by the Tegan School of Childcare.

They walk back, swinging their arms. She teaches him Little Mix songs and her steps are light. They encounter several students whose expressions melt into smiles when they see Dylan. They ignore Imo and she feels blissful. Can she take him on all her walks across campus?

Dylan clambers up the stairs and goes straight to the door of their flat. How quickly children adapt to change. Imo wishes she could be more like a two-year-old. They find Tegan already in her room with Phoenix, looking at a new Facebook page that Phoenix is creating for her.

"I'll get him washed and changed," Tegan says. She leads Dylan by the wrist, avoiding his sticky hand, to her sink. "Then we can take his photo for the page."

Imo doesn't know what surprises her more: the swift and thorough job Tegan does of washing his face and hands or Dylan's lack of protest. Imo moves off the bed so Tegan can spread out Dylan's suitcase and find clean clothes.

Tegan sits Dylan on the floor in her tasteful room with some of the toys Kanya packed for him and takes several photos on her mobile. When Phoenix fetches her juggling balls, they get a couple of the shots they need.

Phoenix loads them into Tegan's new parent-friendly Facebook page. "You know what would make this better? If there was at least one photo with a dad in it. I know Amber would go ape if she heard me mention that heinous twentieth-century stereotype, but this looks too thin. No grandparents, uncles and no daddy. Even single parents have other people on their profile."

"We can be his aunties." Imo thinks she's come up with a good idea until they remind her they don't want the woman they questioned at the Freshers' Fair to connect them to Tegan. She sits down and pulls up her hood.

"A dad would be the best," Phoenix says, resizing the last shot of Dylan. "What about Ivor in Flat 7? I'm sure if you asked him nicely, he wouldn't mind fathering your child."

"F—" Tegan suppresses the curse when she remembers Dylan's in the room "… off. Besides, Dylan is half Thai. No bloke round here is going to pass a likeness test."

"One bloke round here will." It's out of Imo's mouth before she even realizes. "Riku lives on the other side of that corridor."

Phoenix pushes back Imo's hood and kisses her forehead. "Brilliant idea."

Tegan is less ecstatic. "No way. I'm not asking *him*. And, besides, he'd never agree. You know he's a miserable git."

"I have the perfect excuse." Phoenix grins. "We can say Dylan wants to see his unicycle. I saw one hanging on his wall."

Tegan puts her hands on her hips. "Whether that's a euphemism or not, I'm not letting him slam the door in my face."

Phoenix mirrors Tegan, sticks out her elbows. "Tegan Parry, the businesswoman who never takes no for an answer, defeated by a boy. Well I never."

Tegan hesitates for a moment, glancing from one flatmate to the other, then her face assumes a determined look. She takes the child's hand. "Dylan, there's someone we'd like you to meet."

Chapter 45

Imogen

Imo hears movement inside, slow movement; it's an age until Riku answers the door. Suddenly he's there, filling the doorframe. They've prepared their lines but Tegan and Phoenix become a tableau: Girls Frozen on Threshold. Imo knows it's down to her. She takes a breath. And … Action.

"Hi Riku, Dylan would like to see your unicycle." She takes the boy out of Tegan's arms and sets him on the floor. "In you go."

As Dylan squeezes past, Riku jumps away as if the child is carrying an electric charge. Imo sees the gap in the doorway and goes for it. Tegan and Phoenix are right behind.

Imo's pumping adrenaline, heart pounding at her audacity, expecting to stumble on some sort of bombsite. But the atmosphere inside unexpectedly makes her relax. There's soft, oriental music coming from a speaker and sweet-scented tea lights on the window sill. A poster of cloud-covered mountains with Chinese or Japanese symbols on the side fills the wall above the bed. A white silk dressing gown lies on a lilac bedspread.

"You have a beautiful room," she says, waving her arms to

convey her meaning. But Riku just nods; it's doubtful he understands.

With five people in it, the single study bedroom is claustrophobic. The silence is deafening.

"There." Dylan points to where the unicycle is clipped to the shelf above Riku's desk, reminding the girls why they've barged in.

"Please can we …?" Expansive gestures from Phoenix.

Riku stares at her.

A roll of address labels on the desk catches Imo's eye. One's been filled out to an address in Seoul. That's Japan, right? She'll ask Phoenix later. Another chance to show her ignorance of geography – even though she knows every stop on the railway line between Nottingham and Temple Meads and visits each of them in her dreams, searching for her sister.

Riku must have seen her looking. He puts the roll in the desk drawer and picks up two pads of paper from the desk. One – a block of official-looking forms – follows the address labels into the drawer, but the other – a sketchpad, maybe – he puts on the high shelf, before unclipping the unicycle.

"How kind." Tegan steps forward. "Dylan would like a ride. Can you get it steady?" She speaks at normal speed, no concession to Riku's lack of English.

Somehow he gets the message, squats down and holds the frame with both hands. As Tegan lifts Dylan onto the saddle, Phoenix squeezes between the cycle and the window to take pictures on her phone. Imo steps out of camera shot and notices the pile of parcels under the desk. What does he do with them all?

When Phoenix has enough shots, she puts her phone in her pocket and helps to hold the unicycle. Imo can tell Dylan's in safe hands and finds herself with the random thought that it's not the first time Phoenix has taught a child to ride.

Dylan screws up his face when Tegan says it's time to go, but he has an unexpected ally. Riku opens another drawer and gets out three beanbags and starts to juggle. Less accomplished than Phoenix, it takes him a couple of goes to get into a rhythm but then he's up and running. Imo takes a photograph on her phone. A shot of Daddy on his own might enhance Tegan's fake profile.

When Riku sits down beside Dylan and offers him a beanbag, she suggests a group photo. "Tegan get by Dylan, Phoenix next to Riku."

Both girls cotton on. Tegan shuffles Dylan in closer to Riku and leans in herself. Phoenix sits down but makes sure there's a gap on her side so they can crop her out.

When they've got what they came for, Tegan goes into bad actress mode: "What do you say to the nice man?" But at least Dylan's thank you and goodbye wave seem genuine.

They hurry back across the hallway and burst into silent laughter in Tegan's room. Imo's belly hurts with the effort of not making a noise, Tegan rolls on her bed with a hand over her mouth, and even Dylan smiles before he gets engrossed in the bag of toys his mother packed.

"I thought he'd twig when Phoenix kept diving out of camera shot," Imo giggles.

"I didn't dive." Phoenix tries to land, arms first, on Tegan's bed but slips onto the floor, laughing hysterically.

"How did you know how to handle the unicycle?" Imo asks. "And who taught you to juggle?"

Phoenix stands up. "Let me show you something." She rests her forearms on the floor and pushes her legs into the air. The trousers of her dungarees slip to reveal athletic calves. She drops her legs out to the splits, wobbles and, red-faced, falls on her bum. "I'm out of practice." She sits up and swallows. "I didn't want to tell anyone." She takes a deep breath and looks at them all in turn. "My parents are in the circus. I am too, except in term time."

Imo claps. "I knew it. What's your act?"

194

Phoenix shakes her head. "I chose to go to grammar school. My parents kept touring and I stayed with an ex-circus family near school."

"That sounds like my boarding school but in reverse." Tegan bursts out laughing again. "Do you miss it?"

Phoenix's face grows serious. "Not the danger, I don't miss that." She stops as a memory clouds her face, then looks up. "Keep it to yourselves. I don't usually tell people because of the stupid questions. My parents are fire-breathers and I get sick of people asking me what the secret is. It's annoying."

There's silence but Imo knows she'll explode if she doesn't ask. "So what is the secret of fire-breathing?"

Phoenix sits on her haunches and grins. "Don't inhale."

The three girls laugh until their bellies ache.

Phoenix recovers first and sets about loading the photos from her phone onto Tegan's laptop. The images make them laugh harder. The group shot that Imo took is better. Riku looks bemused rather than terrified, and Tegan's smile is less despotic.

Phoenix resizes the image, cutting herself out of it and loads it, plus the best ones of the unicycle bunch. Satisfied with her new fake self, Tegan sends a request to the convenor of the Parents' Facebook Group. Imo and Phoenix scroll through Tegan's profile and high-five at their accomplishment. When Dylan tries to join in, they notice he still has one of Riku's beanbags in his hand.

Phoenix offers to take Dylan to return it. After they've gone, Tegan's laptop pings.

"They've replied already. I thought they'd still be at the barbecue." She clicks a link. As she reads the screen, her eyes widen and the colour drains from her face. She snaps the laptop shut.

195

Chapter 46

Imogen

"Come on, Tegan. What does it say?"

Imo feels anger rising, like when Inspector Hare says they've investigated a sighting and ruled it out. He never explains why. How can he be so sure that they haven't given up too soon?

"You've gone to the trouble of getting Dylan here, you can't bail now. Tell me what the message says."

"This is bullshit." Tegan opens the screen and reads. "'Welcome. Your request to join the Abbey Parents' Group is accepted. You can access our page from the link in your inbox. If you see this message in time, why not go along with your son to our family barbecue this afternoon. Sadly I'm not there as my little girl has a nasty cold. That's parenting for you! Feel free to contact me or any of our members. We're a friendly bunch. Jane.'" She points to the thumbnail-sized image of a dark-haired woman. "Reckon that's the woman at the Freshers' Fair? The name must be a coincidence."

Jane Brown.

Imo's pulse quickens. "It couldn't be, could it? The name

Amber's neighbour, Cheryl, now uses. What if her college isn't in Ealing like the old boy thought? It's here. It's the Abbey."

But Tegan puts on her dismissive voice. "Hold on. Don't get carried away. It doesn't make her Amber's neighbour. That happened years ago and two hundred miles from here. There must be thousands of Jane Browns, probably half a dozen in Abbeythorpe alone."

Imo, deflated, nudges Dylan's wind-up tractor with her toe. Something made Amber freeze that Tuesday afternoon. Coming face to face with a woman she lied to years before could be what made her bolt.

Tegan closes her laptop. "I'll contact the group in a few days to see if this Jane person's kid is better. We can decide then how to play it. This woman might know something about Amber, or she might not. Dylan hasn't had any lunch apart from ice-cream so why don't I take us out for a pizza. There's bound to be a place that does colouring sheets and plastic toys while kids wait for their food. Afterwards we can take him on the swings in the town park."

Imo thinks of Amber's sister Jade managing her pizzeria. Would she make them welcome if they lived nearer? She might recognize the tiny image of Jane Brown as her ex-neighbour. Imo's about to suggest another trip to Surrey but decides not to risk upsetting Tegan's mood. It's great to see her taking an interest in her brother.

"And I was thinking," Tegan continues, "when we drive him home tomorrow, we could stop at Waterworld. Make a day of it. I can buy him swimming trunks and arm floats when we get there. I bet he'd love it." There's a knock at the door and she gets up to answer it.

"What the hell do you want?" Tegan's light tone vanishes.

Imo gets off the bed, expecting Ivor or even Riku to be the cause of her sounding angry. But her breath catches in her throat. It's the stalker from the nightclub, from the audition. Black hoodie, topknot, sunglasses. Tegan was wrong about him being harmless. He must have taken Amber and now he's come for them. Her hand creeps towards her pocket but her phone's still on the desk from uploading the pictures. They're cornered. Dead.

"The boss wants the kid." His voice is hard, uncompromising. Imo's insides are leaden.

"I've got Dylan until tomorrow." Tegan's tone is haughty. "I arranged it with his mother."

Imo covers her mouth. What? You don't mess with people like this. She needs to plead; this weirdo wants to snatch Dylan.

"Mrs Parry made a … mistake," he says.

This man knows Tegan's stepmother? The way his mouth twists on "mistake" makes Imo shiver.

"What's he done to her?" There's a tremor in Tegan's voice.

"Mrs Parry is fine, ma'am. The boss says the kid comes back tonight."

"Why would my father entrust you with picking up his son?"

Imo gasps. This psycho, who's stalked them across the campus since they arrived, must work for Tegan's dad. Another piece of ballast snaps its rope. Is nothing in Imo's life anchored? Tegan, her supposed friend, a girl she lives with, denied knowing this thug when she raised her fears.

"The nanny's in the car," he says.

"Dylan doesn't have a nanny; Kanya looks after him herself," Tegan replies.

"New arrangements."

A lump forms in Imo's throat; poor Kanya. It's doubtful she had any say in the change of plan.

"I'm supposed to hand over my brother to a woman he's never met? Well, he's not here." Tegan waves her arms. "So you can't take him."

Imo gives a grim smile. Tegan's tone is tigress. Was it only yesterday that she baulked at calling him her brother?

Through the open door, they hear Phoenix come out of her

room with the child. She calls out: "Riku's not answering but we went to find my beanbag set. Dylan wants to show you his trick." Her voice trails off when she reaches them.

"Tegan's postgrad friend?" she says, looking at the man and holding Dylan close.

"Did *she* tell you that?" Imo moves towards the doorway. A lie. This man is no one's friend.

"I'll bring him to the car," Tegan croaks, as if holding back tears. She scoops Dylan up and kisses his hair.

Phoenix offers to help carry his belongings.

"Marlon will do it," Tegan says, her face hardening. "He's a loyal donkey."

The man's face remains impassive behind his shades.

Chapter 47

Sunday 9 October

Imogen

The muzziness isn't only in her head; it's seeped through every vein and bone. Fifteen hours in bed, and crying for Sophia for most of them, she's ravaged, like an addict on a come-down.

Already afternoon? A flurry of lightness in the molten lead of her mood. But her phone taunts her that it's not twelve yet. So much of the day to kill. Which day? Monday again, more lectures missed? But her memory lands on Sunday.

She feels pinched and pummelled all over. It's how her body was after Sophia had been missing a week and her composure finally snapped. The pain of every organ twisted. The realization that the toxic uncertainty could last forever. It's a memory that refuses to dim. She has a hazy sense of her dad lifting her onto the sofa. Someone – Freddie – putting a cushion under her head. Her body in shiver-spasm, only days later able to process what went on as she lay there. The raised voice of Grandma Jean seeing off more door-step journalists; Dad's repeated phone calls to Sophia's friends; another sombre-faced policeman, filling the lounge with unexpected aftershave. And then the recollection of animalistic shrieks, not recognizable as her own even though they must have been. Worst of all, Mum's silent tears, turned away from her.

Somehow her mind still holds room for pictures of her life before: with Sophia, screaming in delighted terror on Colossus at Thorpe Park; at the village hall with her final bow as Violet Beauregarde, Grandma and Freddie on their feet applauding; *Hurry-up-and take-the-photo-Dad* through gritted teeth as she poses in her Year Eleven prom dress. She mourns the loss of normal Imogen almost as much as she grieves for Sophia.

Her mind stretches from her family photos to Tegan's fake Facebook profile. How deceptive images can be. The woman – Jane Brown – what does her profile say about her? Something stirs in the fog. She only caught a glimpse of the screen before Tegan shut it down, but Jane Brown's profile starts nagging. It niggles her out of bed, into her dressing gown and to Tegan's door, even though she's probably out with the Conservation crowd and Imo's done being friends with her anyway; she doesn't need a friend whose father hires henchmen and lies about it. Tegan's omission is a doubt too far.

When Tegan opens the door, Imo decides to get to the point. "I'd like to browse the Parents' Facebook account. See what it says about Jane Brown."

"Good for you." Tegan starts to close the door.

"So can I have your password?"

Tegan opens the door again. "Is that it? That's all you've got to say to me after last night?"

Imo blinks. What does she mean? It takes her a moment.

She blushes with shame. "I'm sorry about Dylan. How are you feeling?" How could she have got so wrapped up in Tegan's deceit that she forgot Dylan?

"How do you think?"

Imo's never seen her looking less than immaculate before, but her hair is uncombed and her face bare. The way she fronted up to that Marlon man must have been an act. Inside she was probably as scared as Imo.

"Do you think he'll take care of Dylan?"

"My father?" Tegan's voice croaks and breaks into a cough.

Imo thinks of the birdlike, friendly, lonely Kanya. What has their jaunt with Dylan cost her?

"You mustn't blame yourself," she tells Tegan. "We went along with it."

Tegan looks at the floor and shakes her head. It's the first time Imo can remember Tegan breaking eye contact with anyone.

"I'll come back later. Perhaps we can go for a walk." Imo cringes. People keep telling her to go for a walk and now she's suggested it. What the girl will really want is to be left in peace. "If I could just get that password off you."

Tegan steps into Imo's space, craning her neck. "Is that all you can think about? You can't make normal decisions like have a shower or care about your real friends, but you fixate on a girl you knew for two days." She points at her, her eyes wide with anger. "You let me bring my family into this, my baby brother, and you still can't leave it alone. You want to drag some poor woman from the Parents' Group into it too. If she is Amber's neighbour – and that's doubtful – don't you think that girl's brought her enough trouble?"

Imo backs away.

Tegan calls after her: "Let's face it, Amber legged it because she's ashamed. She led her family, her boyfriend, her neighbour on a merry dance and you want her to lead us on another one. Grow up, Imogen."

When Daisy Is Three

"I don't want to get out," Daisy wails as Mummy drags the arm floats down her arms. Mummy is being too rough. She usually gets them off in the showers but they haven't shampooed today and Daisy still has the stinky swimming pool smell on her.

The changing room is empty so Mummy spreads their things along the bench. They've never had this much space before. Daisy cries harder because the others are still swimming.

"Hush, sweetie. It's time to go." Mummy peels her out of the wet costume and sits her, naked, on the bench.

"It's not, Mummy. The swim lady hasn't done the Goodbye Song."

"Quick, quick," Mummy says, holding out Daisy's fluffy snow-flake towel with the hood.

Daisy leans back and feels immediately cosy.

"How's that?" Mummy says, dabbing Daisy's nose with a corner of the towel. "Are you warm now?"

Daisy tries to wriggle free in a noisy, sobbing sulk.

"You'll be cold," Mummy says sharply. "Up to you."

Daisy stops wriggling and studies Mummy, trying to gauge how cross she is. She seems to be in a hurry. Her shoulders are still speckled with water droplets but she's putting on her clothes. Keeps glancing towards the door. Eventually she smiles. "Would you like a breadstick? Or strawberries?"

"I want crisps," Daisy says petulantly.

Mummy rummages in the rucksack. "We don't have crisps. Nasty, salty things."

"The other mummies have them."

That funny smile crosses Mummy's mouth. The one she keeps for people she doesn't like. She opens a plastic tub and places it on the bench beside Daisy. The strawberries glisten and their sweet tang makes Daisy's mouth water. But she turns away, folding her arms.

"Why can't I swim?"

"You know why, Daisy." The towel on Mummy's head has pulled her forehead, lifting her eyebrows. "Mummy said you mustn't speak to anyone. We only came because you promised."

Daisy bursts into fresh tears. "We always talk to the swim lady."

"Not today."

Silent tears roll down Daisy's cheeks as Mummy tugs her into pants, vest and tights.

"Are we going to the café?" They usually have beans on brown toast with the other mummies and children. Daisy's not sure what will happen as the others are still swimming.

Mummy zips up Daisy's boots. "We're going straight home."

Her skin grows stone cold and she shivers. "I don't want to."

Mummy looks up. "Eat your strawberries."

"Home is scary, Mummy. Funny noises." And a big bang woke Daisy in the night.

Hurriedly, Mummy packs everything into the rucksack, including the strawberries. Her face glows a fierce pink. With Daisy on her hip, she gathers the bag and coats and heads for the door. Daisy's bathing suit is still on the bench.

"You've left my costume, Mummy." She stretches her arms and legs towards the bench but her waist is clamped to Mummy and they keep moving away.

"It's the unicorn one," she says urgently. "With the pink bows, Mummy."

But the door closes behind them and they speed past the pay place to the car park.

"The pink bows," Daisy sobs.

Chapter 48

Monday 10 October

Phoenix

An admin office has been transformed into an *X Factor* audition queue. A zig-zag cordon of red rope conducts the long line of students to desks where secretaries receive their assignments and take their signatures.

They've come together in Tegan's car because they were both running behind the 9 a.m. deadline. No reply from Imo; Phoenix assumes she's already set off. Tegan is in charge of signing in her group's Business Studies project proposal. Phoenix has written an essay. Blood, sweat and apostrophes – it's years since she's written anything of length, having ducked out with A levels in Maths, Physics and Design Technology.

"I'll know to get here at ten next time," Tegan says, sighing at the wait ahead of them.

Having Dylan taken away hit her hard. Phoenix can tell she's still not herself, otherwise she'd be working these queues with her sales pitch, shifting jackets.

"Did he get back all right?" Phoenix asks.

Tegan folds her arms and shrugs. "Suppose so."

Phoenix raises her eyebrows. Surely Tegan phoned to make sure the stalker returned her baby brother? Phoenix has no siblings, but she likes to know where the younger kids are when they're touring. Families look out for each other.

"I'm steering clear," Tegan says. She must see the surprise on Phoenix's face and adds: "It's best for Kanya. Dad will play happy families for a few weeks then beggar off to London. I'll get in touch then."

Phoenix nods and it dawns on her that, despite Tegan's bad mood, something's shifted. She refers to her stepmother as Kanya now. But Phoenix is still uneasy. How can Tegan be sure the hired thug returned Dylan safely?

"How long has Marlon worked for your father?" she asks.

"He took Dylan home if that's what's bugging you. He's back here now. Look." She pulls Phoenix by her shoulders through a gap in the queue. "Can you see out there? Keep looking."

Phoenix watches the busy foyer, for a moment stepping out of the queue as it shuffles up. Then she spots him. Man in black, hood up, take-away coffee, mobile to his ear. She gives Tegan a sympathetic sigh. What words of comfort do you give a girl whose father has sent a minder to watch her every move? *It's only because he cares?* Bollocks, she can't say that. Phoenix's parents care but they let her go her way, always have. Real love, even after Cloud's accident.

Glancing into the foyer again, Phoenix senses someone looking her way. Expecting Marlon and pretending she's not intimidated, she makes eye contact. But it's not with Marlon – no sign of him now. The person watching is petite with dark hair in a ponytail. The Parents' Group woman from the Freshers' Fair. Phoenix thinks of smiling but the eye lock has gone on too long. She presses her palms under her armpits and feels the dampness on her fingers.

Eventually the woman slips her gaze. Phoenix is relieved until she realizes she's shifted it onto Tegan, frowning as if she's working something out. What if she recognizes Tegan from the fake Facebook profile? Though it hardly matters. Tegan and Dylan won't be attending the Parents' Group any time soon. She wants to nudge Tegan but figures the woman is off limits as much as Imo. Both led to her gaining Dylan and losing him again.

Suddenly the woman's puzzled expression changes and she hurries away, leaving Phoenix to make sense of the flash of anger she saw in her face.

Eventually, Phoenix and Tegan move forward in the queue, near enough to the reception desks to hear what's said.

"Have you got your Accountancy assignment too?" one of the secretaries asks.

"I haven't got one, have I?" Grey uni hoodie, crumpled jeans, wavering voice. Imo is at the front.

"It says here, you're due to hand in German for Dr Wyatt and Accounting for Mr Hennessy."

Phoenix expects Tegan to make a sarcastic comment about Imo's incompetence, but she pushes her way to the woman's desk, frowning. "We weren't set an Accountancy paper." She turns towards the crowd. "Do any of you do Business Studies?"

A few nods, a wave, a couple of "Yeah"s.

"Did Hennessy set us an Accountancy assignment?"

Vigorous headshakes. A chorus of "Nope"s.

"Looks like the Business Studies department made a cock-up," Tegan tells the secretary.

"Thanks," Imo says, but Tegan looks away.

The secretary smiles apologetically. "They're academics; they're not expected to get things quite right."

Phoenix catches Imo's arm as she leaves. "Time for a coffee?"

Imo lifts her bloodshot eyes and manages a smile. "Okay, but I have a lecture at eleven."

"Tegan, will you join us?" Phoenix calls.

Tegan gives a firm head shake, causing her thick locks to bounce on her shoulders, and reaches the reception desk. She doesn't look round.

Chapter 49

Phoenix

Phoenix wishes there was time to go back to the flat for a drink instead of coming to a campus coffee shop. Imo's appearance might put other customers off their latte. The lank strands of hair that poke out of her sweatshirt hood could fry chips, and the corners of her eyes are crusty.

Phoenix pulls out a clean tissue. "Do you mind if I just …"

Imo closes her eyes while Phoenix dabs the worst of the crud off them.

"You remind me of my mother," she speaks awkwardly as Phoenix grips her chin. "When I want to go out, it's like getting through airport security. Worse since … Doesn't matter. Do you know what it's like to sleep badly?"

"Not every night," Phoenix answers. Some winters in the caravan it's hard to sleep even with the heater on. "Have you phoned your mum lately?" That's what Imo needs, a heart-to-heart with family. Phoenix phones Cloud most days and they text all the time.

"What would I say?" Imo rubs her eye.

They stare into the drinks. Phoenix suspects Imo's mood is

down to her argument with Tegan. The flat's walls are thin and she heard what Tegan said yesterday. No point in broaching the subject; even if she could talk Imo round, Tegan is still fuming.

Imo rests her head in her hands. "Everything's pointless; we all die anyway."

Phoenix's heart rate increases and she looks around her. Animated students sit at other tables, chatting, texting, eating. No one's watching but she sees Imo through others' eyes. The girl is struggling, needs help. Phoenix feels out of her depth.

"Have you ever talked to … someone about how you feel?"

"The welfare reps say, 'Tell me your problems, I'm here to help,' but they don't listen. I wanted to talk about Amber but the woman started asking about *me*."

"It might help though." Phoenix peers over her cup. "To talk with a … professional."

Tears trickle over Imo's uneven, red skin. "How can they work me out when I've never worked myself out? Have you noticed when you see a big Celebrations tin on a coffee table, it never contains chocolates? It's stuffed with scissors or elastic bands. That's what it's like inside my life."

"What about your mother then?" Phoenix brings the conversation back to where she started, clutching at straws. "Maybe you're right about counsellors but your mum knows you."

Imo rubs her eyes and peers through her fingers. "My mother has three children, but is consumed by one of them, and it isn't me."

Phoenix sighs. Sibling rivalry. She wasn't expecting this.

"Not like that. I'm not jealous." Imo forces out a laugh. "We're all consumed by Sophia. Always will be, I suppose, until we know." She swallows. "That's why I worry about Amber."

Here we go. Phoenix rubs her mouth, contemplating what to say. Decides it best to let her talk. Get Amber out of her system.

"If she turned up right as rain, I'd have more questions than she could ever answer. I've had night after night to wonder, to make up my own what-ifs. Could I cope with the betrayal? I want her to be fine, I love her, but might end up hating her if it turned out she left of her own accord." She looks up, her eyes hungry for reassurance. "I'm not mad, am I?"

Phoenix takes a breath as she sees what's been in plain sight ever since she met Imo. This isn't about Amber, not really. "Who do you mean?"

Imo blinks out tears. "Sophia, my big sister." She struggles to control her voice. "We reported her missing on my eighteenth birthday. Strictly speaking, the next day because it was long after midnight when Dad made the call. She was supposed to come back from university to take me and my friends out clubbing. Mum was furious when she didn't turn up. Didn't think we'd be safe on our own. We waited until ten and finally persuaded Mum to let us go without her." She looks directly at Phoenix. "Did you see the appeals? BBC, ITN and the others."

"I don't think so …" Between circus performances and faulty electricity generators, she doesn't see much TV in the caravan. Even term time at Carla and Antonio's she was head down with revision. Her skin heats with shame; her own family secret pales next to Imo's.

"And you've heard nothing since?" she asks gently.

"There were several sightings at Nottingham railway station on my birthday so it looked like she intended to catch a train to my party. Police thought it was down to three possibilities: something happened at the station; on the train; or when she arrived at our end. But they never found anyone who saw her on a train. They wasted ten days until a young woman came forward who matched the CCTV images they thought were Sophia at Nottingham. The sightings had all been mistaken identity. The police interviewed Sophia's flatmates again in her hall of residence and it emerged that no one had actually seen her for at least three days before Dad reported her missing." She wipes her eyes. "Police say the first twenty-four hours after the last sighting are the Golden Time. We discovered our gold was base metal. Police know less now than when they started."

Suddenly she's on her feet and pacing, oblivious to curious looks from two girls at the next table. "I can't find Sophia, but Amber's trail is fresher. What if she's in danger? Will I let her down too?"

Without thinking, Phoenix stands up and takes her hands. "Listen to me. You're exhausted. Go back to the flat after your lecture and get some sleep. I'll help you with this, I promise. We'll find Amber together."

Phoenix watches her trail out for her lecture. With any luck, afterwards, she'll sleep through until the morning and Phoenix will have had time to think of how the hell she can keep her promise.

Chapter 50

Imogen

The seat nearest the door of the Accounting lecture room is empty. Imo puts her stuff on the desk but has to stand up to let the class nerd through. He knocks her mobile with his rucksack as he brushes past. Imo catches it before it spins onto the floor, doesn't expect an apology and doesn't get one.

When Tegan appears, she stands up again to let her sit in the row, but Tegan walks to the back of the lecture theatre without acknowledging her.

Hennessey arrives ten minutes late, manages a "Hi, guys" into his briefcase. He can't find what he wants and pulls the contents onto the empty desk beside Imo's. A dab of bloodied tissue sticks on his jawline and his pale blue collar is speckled with red. Among the printed sheets and what looks like students' Accounts homework, Imo spots a handwritten page. She studies the title out of her eye corner. *Death of a Dying Rose*. A poem? He shoves everything back into the briefcase apart from another handwritten sheet – too scrappy for Imo to read – which he takes to the whiteboard and copies from it in red marker pen.

"Profit and loss accounts ..." He addresses his crib sheet rather than the students.

As hard as she tries, Imo realizes she's only deciphering every fifth phrase. Elbows on the desk, she pushes her fingers under her hood. They slide easily through her greasy hair. Has it only been three days since the trip with Tegan to Wales? She screwed up. So absorbed in her pursuit of Amber, she lost sight of how much Tegan was hurting. She knew from the first day of term Tegan wouldn't want to be her friend, but it's worse than she predicted. Tegan isn't just ignoring her; she hates her.

"The balance sheet is a snapshot of ..." Hennessey points at the board.

Imo rests her hands in the front pocket of her sweatshirt. Two weeks in and Tegan's found her out. *Grow up, Imogen.* And what Phoenix said this morning about promising to help. Something to humour her, along with *Go to bed after your lecture.* Phoenix is friends with Tegan, not her. She blinks hard; she's on her own.

***

It's the after-school, tea-time rush and the restaurant is packed when Imo gets to Chadcombe. But she can't leave it any later if she wants to catch the last train back. She aims to return to Abbeythorpe by midnight. Little chance of seeing Phoenix for the talk she promised. Good; she prefers Tegan's open scorn to Phoenix's condescension, only saying she'll help find Amber to pacify her.

Harassed-looking staff speed across the dining floor. Should she take a window seat in the take-away area? As she resigns herself to a long wait, a waitress appears. She's dressed in a uniform like the one Imo saw Jade Murphy wearing the previous week, except the waitress's shirt is red and hangs off her skinny shoulders. Jade's was purple and showed off her figure.

"How many of you?" The waitress takes a menu out of the

stand. "Just the one? If you'd like to follow me." She takes her across the busy restaurant to a table for two next to the toilets. Wedged behind a larger table where two mums are feeding bolognaise and pizza slices into assorted children.

"Welcome to Pizza Pedro. I'm Tasey and I'll be looking after you." The waitress has also squeezed through the gap and launches into her spiel. Imo's seat and the toilet door match Tasey's shirt. "We have a buffet and a specials board." She waves her arms like an air stewardess identifying safety exits. "Your choices include: Pasta Paradiso, Simply Spaghetti and Pedro's Perfecto. There's also—"

"I'll have a margarita," Imo says. "And a Coke. Is Jade here this afternoon, the manager?"

"In the kitchen; we've had a late delivery. I'll see if she can serve you." Tasey scurries away before it dawns on Imo she must think she's requested to see the manager to complain about something. Poor kid. Imo senses a kindred spirit.

A few minutes later Jade approaches with her pizza and steps aside to let the mums vacate their table and retrieve a pushchair. "Thanks for coming. Have a lovely evening." Her smile fades when she sees that her new customer is Imo. "What are you doing here? Did you request to see me?"

Imo apologizes for disturbing her at work. "I want to ask you about your neighbour. You mentioned her to my friends when you collected Amber's things."

Jade puts down the pizza. "Then you've come a long way for nothing. Thanks to my so-called sister ..." She remembers where she is and whispers, "I haven't seen Cheryl for years."

Imo pulls out the other chair. "Two minutes, please."

"That's all I can spare." She sits down. There's a definite kink in the hair she's scooped into a ponytail. No time for the straighteners that Mrs Murphy disapproves of.

"How well did you know your neighbour?"

"She was my friend more than Amber's. We were closer in

age although she was a good bit older than me. Amber had been kicking off for months, ever since Dad died. I used to confide in Cheryl. A bitch fest really, but I could hardly mouth off to my mum, could I? Then Amber spoils everything. Cheryl was thrilled to announce her pregnancy but then the kid next door gets knocked up too, stealing her thunder. To her credit, she took Amber under her wing when Mum couldn't cope. But there was no time to hang out with me. Amber's needs got in the way of mine as usual."

Tasey comes to the table, apologizes for the interruption and says Jade's required on the phone. Imo moves her face into a friendly smile, not wanting to upset the waitress again even though she's ticked off at her timing.

Her pizza's already been cut into sectors and Imo eats a slice with her fingers. She's hungry, realizing this is the first thing she's eaten all day. It's a long way to come for food, but it looks like food is all she'll get. Jade's at the bar, cradling the phone to her ear while interrogating a computer screen.

To her surprise, Jade returns after a few minutes and sits down. "Not only was my sister drunk, stoned and running wild every night, she ruined my friendship with Cheryl. Mum had to go on sleeping pills. She hadn't needed those when Dad first died, but Amber's antics made her a nervous wreck. The only good thing about her fake pregnancy stunt was she stayed away from Verity and her bridge crowd cronies."

Verity? Known as Vee? The girl Imo met at Chadcombe Bridge with Tegan? Staggering, incoherent, arms etched with five-bar gates. Said she knew Amber, but would have known Taylor Swift if Tegan paid her enough. Imo remembers something she said.

"Who's Leo?"

Jade stares at her for a moment and lets out a big sigh. "Amber kept that going, did she? She went back to her pisshead phase after she'd destroyed us with the fake baby scam. Mum thought she was settling down, but I wasn't surprised when she started up again. She'd forgotten what being normal was by then." Jade pauses, as if losing her thread.

"Leo?" Imo prompts.

Jade shrugs. "A name Amber rambled in her drunken stupors. No doubt another 'friend' from the bridge." Jade snaps her hands in the air in angry inverted commas.

There's a crash and the sound of shattering glass. The restaurant noise lulls and two boys applaud until their mother shushes them and conversations continue. Red-faced, Tasey squats on the floor, picking shards out of a brown puddle.

Jade jumps up. "Let me do that. You get the mop, love." Her tone is kind. Kinder than when she talks about Amber.

"One last question," Imo says, thinking how much easier it would be if Tegan let her access the Facebook profile. "What did your neighbour look like?"

"Cheryl? Dark hair, slim, fairly small. Why?" But she doesn't wait for an answer and goes to help Tasey.

Chapter 51

Phoenix

Hoping that Imo's finally asleep, Phoenix doesn't call on her when she gets back from her lecture. Would helping her give false hope? About her sister as well as Amber? Unable to face her, she goes straight to her room and googles Sophia Smith.

Oh God. Hundreds of hits. And images. A pale-skinned graduate with Imo's blue eyes. And a couple in their forties huddled outside a railway station. The same couple flanked by police officers at a press conference. And several out-of-focus shots of a girl and boy, always hidden in hooded coats or sweatshirts. More than likely Imo and her brother. No wonder the poor kid is obsessed with Amber. Can't contemplate another loss. Phoenix closes down the search, unable to bear the knowledge of Imo's pain.

She starts the maths exercise the tutor wants ready for the next seminar. An hour in, she reaches for a textbook from her shelf and sees Riku's beanbag. May as well see if he is in now.

His door is ajar but not properly closed. She knocks and calls hello. He must have popped out to make a drink; she heard noises in the kitchen as she went past. When she nudges the

218

door, it opens halfway so she tosses the beanbag onto the floor and turns away. But before she's reached her room, she feels unkind for not returning it more graciously. She goes back, intending to leave it on his desk with a note. He must have some Post-its, but the only things on the desk are a roll of address labels and a sketchpad. He might not like it if she messes up a label, but surely he can spare a page out of the pad.

She picks it up and opens it. Reels away as if her fingers are on fire. There's a head-and-shoulders sketch. The detail and accuracy are breath-taking. Sweetheart mouth; large, dewy eyes; short, soft hair framing the wholesome face. It would be beautiful if it wasn't so sick.

Amber.

Chapter 52

Tuesday 11 October

Tegan

Despite having no lectures, Tegan's up early and parked in the High Street. A cash and carry behind the Co-op has signed an order for her jackets and she's composing an email to her supplier on her laptop. If this keeps up, she'll have to find a bigger factory. Shame really because her current supplier took on her product when no one else would and it's going to mean dumping them just when their belief is paying off.

Never visit a cash and carry before 8.30 a.m. – she's learnt that this morning. It was like Sainsbury's on Christmas Eve, except with flatbed loaders instead of shopping trolleys. Every convenience store owner within a ten-mile radius was stocking up. She had to stay in her car until the rush died down. She's returned to it now, pushing her luck on a double yellow line.

At least her other reason for an early start has worked out. No sign of a black Mercedes. But is that what it's going to take: sneaking out under cover of darkness to stand any chance of not being followed? She presses her eyes closed and grips the steering wheel. Is this her life? Forever? Her father's heavy following not only her but her friends too? What happens when she meets someone – a boyfriend? Will Marlon stalk him? Or, if her father decrees it, worse? She shudders and folds her arms.

Her phone rings and she jumps in her seat. Is it him? But when she checks the screen, the caller is Phoenix. Not again. Tegan kills it, not ready to hear a plea for a truce with Imo. Phoenix follows up with a text: Phone me urgent. A bombardment of texts from Phoenix, all like this one, started last night. Why does she care all of a sudden?

A red-faced woman jog-walks up the road, heaving a boy of about six after her. Late for school.

A different man used to follow them when Tegan's mother took her to primary school. Did he have to run to keep up with them sometimes? A skinny guy with a craggy, pitted face. Tegan was never scared; she thought every family had a man looking out for them, especially families where the father worked overseas. It was one of the first things she asked her new friends when she started at boarding school. "Has your guy come with you?" No one got what she meant and pretty soon the idea of a man following her faded out of her mind, replaced by hockey club and fencing lessons.

The craggy man came back when she went home during the holidays and that's just the way it was. How old was she when it dawned that they weren't like other families? Around twelve, she thinks, when Mum stopped the charade of Dad working overseas. Tegan was a daddy's girl in those days, checking the dormitory pigeon holes three times a day for a postcard or a letter. There was only ever one mail a week from him but it didn't stop her checking. In hindsight she's not even sure they were from him; the postmark didn't add up with what she later found out.

The craggy man – she never did know his name – collected

her one half term and drove her home. When she got there, she saw that her mother had been crying again. She told Tegan that her father was leaving them. Had asked for a divorce. Tegan rounded on her, adding mental blows to the physical ones that marked her mother's throat, and yelled that it was the lousy wife he was leaving, not his daughter. But for once her mother fought back and spat out the truth about his extended "overseas" work: three years in Swansea Prison. And now he was free and tucked up in his tacky country manor with a woman he'd met on the internet.

Two blokes in a grubby white van crawl past, appraising the convertible. When the passenger notices Tegan, he winds down his window and licks his lips. She wields a V-sign and screams a "Fuck off" with more venom than the guy deserves.

When her mother first told her, she still loved her daddy, hating the justice system nearly as much as she loathed his Thai bride. The charge against him, whatever it was, must have been jumped up. And her dad confirmed it when he came back into her life after he left her mother. The craggy man started driving Dad to her school on weekend visits. They picked up where they'd left off before he went to prison. She was thrilled to see him and he brought her little gifts: jackets, shoes, jewellery.

It was during an ICT lesson that everyone got the idea to do internet searches of their parents. It was a wealthy school populated by families of overachievers: a novelist, an opera singer, actor, TV scriptwriter, rugby coach. As the actor's daughter squealed delightedly about his ten thousand search hits, Tegan typed in her father's name and felt sick to her stomach. Hand trembling, she closed the page. How could she not have known?

She didn't have a smartphone in those days and had to wait until the holidays to search the internet alone. Sneaking a chance to use her mother's computer, she opened a nauseating Pandora's Box. Every search hit referred to her father's drugs network across South Wales, hinting that clever lawyers, bought with his dirty money, had got him a reduced charge. Tegan's whole world shifted out of kilter.

In her rear-view mirror, a traffic warden in a grey uniform walks towards her, about six cars behind. His progress is slow as he photographs each vehicle and types into his tablet. Tegan knows she'll have to drive off before the man reaches her.

Her dad still makes gestures. Nothing for months, then the car, an iPhone. She thinks of the postcard Kanya sent from Montreux. He reeled her in like he did Tegan's mother. The charm, the gifts, the soul-bearing seduction. Tegan once asked her mother if he still had her followed. She shook her head. "I'm off the payroll, thanks to wife number two." How much longer will her father bother to have Tegan tailed now that he has Dylan? Heir to the empire. Her poor, perfect, little brother.

She puts her forehead on the steering wheel, her shoulders shaking with sobs. A text comes through and she reads it, glad of something else to think about. Phoenix again: Need to speak to you both urgently. Meet at flat after my lecture?

You both means she's texted Imo too. Tegan's tears dry. The pair of them can shove it. She's not making up with Imo any time soon and if Phoenix was a true friend she'd understand. She reaches for her laptop and opens her fake Facebook profile to delete it and be done with Imo and her Amber hunt.

The cursor hovers over *Delete My Account*, but she sees a photo of Dylan. More tears threaten. A look of wonder on his face as he sits on the unicycle. And he's leaning his weight on her, his stubby hand resting on her forearm. He trusts her, his sister, not to let him fall. In another photo, he's smiling into the camera. The picture was taken on Imo's phone. Imo makes people smile, gets people to do things. Tegan knows she shares the same skill of manipulation, but hers is planned, grafted, whereas Imo doesn't even have to try. People want to please Imo. Her fists clench; that's how she ended up visiting Kanya and taking Dylan, all to placate Imo.

It's also because of her that she has these photographs, these memories. Without Imo, she wouldn't have got to know Dylan. And Kanya. The Thai bride turned out not to be so bad.

Her fingers open and she cancels the deletion request. She clicks on *Change Password*. She won't be friends with Imo but she'll give the girl access to the fake profile so she can stalk the Parents' Group woman to her heart's content. Tegan doesn't have to get involved.

Old password: JonParryBastard666
New password: DylanParryPrince111

***

Twenty minutes wasted, parking at the hall of residence and knocking pointlessly on the girl's door, then another twenty finding somewhere to park and ending up back at the geography tower. She finally locates Imo, worrying over an assignment in the library.

"My lecturer hates me," Imo whispers. "Look how much she's scribbled." She thrusts the page at Tegan.

No awkward silence then. When Tegan searched the library, she half hoped she wouldn't find her. Who would apologize first? Tegan didn't intend it to be her, but it seems that Imo's wrapped herself in another drama and forgotten their argument.

Tegan lifts the feedback sheet to see the grade on top of the paper. "You daft mare, you got seventy-two percent. She's put all these development points because she knows you can take it." She pushes the work back to Imo, remembering how she told the girl to get out of her self-obsessed mope. Is it worth telling her again?

"I'm … sorry about Dylan," Imo says, peering out of her hood. "I shouldn't have cornered you into taking him. And you're right, I need to grow up." She looks at her assignment. "I guess I'm not doing too well so far. Can we be friends?"

Tegan has an urge to hug her and offer her own apology, but remembers that's not the way she rolls. She writes her new Facebook password on Imo's feedback sheet. "Knock yourself out."

Before she can explain, the bearded librarian comes over to tell them to be quiet. "You can chat in the foyer, girls."

As he moves away, Tegan wonders fleetingly if she has another stalker. Whenever she's in the library, he finds an excuse to sidle over. Perv.

"Amber would have something to say about him calling us girls," Imo whispers.

Bloody Amber again. Tegan explains what the password is for, and, with that, she's done. Her involvement with Amber is over. The Parents' Facebook page is open on Imo's screen and should keep her amused for hours so Tegan stays where she is and sets up her laptop to update her order spreadsheets. Her phone vibrates. Another text from Phoenix: Where are you?

Imo also checks a message on her phone and returns to browsing Jane Brown's profile page. After a few minutes she grips Tegan's arm. "I've got a bad feeling about this."

Tegan glances at the images on Jane Brown's profile as Imo clicks through. Several with her little kid: eating spaghetti; standing in front of the Eiffel Tower; on a donkey at a beach.

"How am I going to find her now you're not going back to the Parents' Group?" Imo asks. "We can't get her uni address from this, can we?"

Don't start that, lady. Tegan wants to leave before she gets asked to hack again, but Imo's digging her fingers into her arm.

"Why don't you try the uni crèche?" she says. "A woman at the barbecue told me it's behind the Abbi bar." She silently thanks pregnant Sian. "The mums meet there for coffee." She checks the time on her phone. "Some might be there now."

But Imo grips tighter. "Will you come with me?" She looks straight at her. "I won't ask you for anything else, I promise."

Tegan stares back. Never believe a promise. Life's taught her that – *I'll never hit your mum again no matter how she winds me up* – so why is she hesitating? Damn this girl with her watery eyes that manage to be naïve and persistent at the same time. She'll do this last thing for her and then she's done.

"Let's go."

She presents her middle finger to the librarian's back on the way out.

Chapter 53

Imogen

Not more walking, please. Imo's whole body sighs when they reach Tegan's car and find that a uni maintenance van has boxed it in.

"Bollocks." Tegan kicks one of the van's tyres. "We'll have to walk, but that van better be gone when I get back."

Imo wonders what she'll do if the driver doesn't move. Call her friend Marlon? He must be good at removing unwanted items. Imo feels a chill and stops to fold out the jacket she bought from Tegan. It's the first time she's worn it and it smells like new plastic.

"We could call Student Services," she suggests. "They might be able to contact the driver."

"No chance. I'm in a disabled space and Student Services already put a warning notice on my windscreen last week." She kicks the tyre again.

A piece of paper under Tegan's wiper catches the breeze. "Looks like you've got another. Sorry," Imo says.

Tegan storms to the front and grabs the note, but her attention is on the bonnet. "What the absolute fuck? Some bastard's keyed it."

Below the windscreen, there's a cross about three inches long gouged into the dark blue paintwork. The paper is not a parking ticket. It contains one word: *Don't.*

"Who … who would do this?" Shuddering, Imo takes the note. Handwritten, block capitals neatly spaced. She hands it back and sees Tegan's hands are trembling as much as hers.

"We should call the police," Imo suggests. "They'll arrest Marlon."

Moving her finger across the scratch, Tegan seems to contemplate the idea but then dismisses it. "He wouldn't dare. And it's not his style; he'd go for kneecaps."

Imo winces. What the hell are Tegan's father and his henchman mixed up in? "Who do you think did it then? And why?"

"The why is obvious." Tegan screws up the note and lobs it into the bushes. "Someone wants to scare the shit out of me." She straightens to her full five feet three. "But they'll have to try harder. Come on. We've got yummy mummies to stalk." She sets off, her face grim.

Silent as they walk, although Imo's sure Tegan must hear the fearful rattle in her breathing. A tough bird like Tegan might be able to brush off a threat but Imo can't. If they ignore this, what will happen next? When a few spots of rain dash a darker blue into the shoulders of Tegan's blouse, she opens an umbrella without breaking stride. Is everything water off a duck's back to her?

"Aren't you cold?" Imo asks.

Tegan glances at Imo's jacket. "Not *that* cold."

Forgetting the threat for a moment, Imo feels a fool, duped into buying a raincoat that even the designer won't be seen dead in. Her phone rings. Phoenix again. How many times is that? She kills the call, cringing at the memory of telling her about Sophia. Phoenix follows through with another text. Phone me urgently. Imo puts the phone in her pocket and speeds up as the rain intensifies.

Tegan leads the way into the Abbi bar, a large, open-plan space on the ground floor of the student union building. Surprisingly busy for 11.30 a.m. although, rather than necking pints, most students sit hunched over screens with coffee cups at their sides.

Tegan folds her umbrella and scans the room. "It doesn't look like the mummies are meeting for coffee today. Let me check with the bar."

She finds out that the first crèche session finishes at twelve and the next one starts half an hour later. "According to the bar woman, parents drop their kids off at the back entrance to the crèche on the far side of the garden. If we sit by the window, we'll see your woman arrive."

Imo bristles. Tegan makes it sound like she's obsessed with Jane Brown. Maybe she is. "There aren't any spare seats. Should we come back some other time?"

But Tegan marches up to a boy in an easy chair by a big window that looks out onto the garden. He has his feet on the chair opposite, laptop on his knee and textbooks spread across the seat next to him.

"Are these taken?"

He pulls out his earphones, frowning.

Tegan moves closer. "Actually, we'd prefer to sit on this side."

For a moment he stares at her, but, apparently realizing he's out-glared, moves himself and his textbooks to the opposite pair of seats.

They don't have to wait long before mums and dads gather under an awning in the garden. Most look like typical students, but the empty buggies, pastel-pink lunchboxes and kiddies' raincoats give away their parental status. It's hard to get a clear look at anyone under their anorak hoods and umbrellas, but no one resembling Jane Brown stands out in the crowd. At 11.55 a.m. they go through the crèche entrance and trickle out again five minutes later. Their children are now with them, some in newly supplied raincoats, others in buggies with the rain covers over and eating from their lunchboxes. By ten past, they've all gone, except for one woman holding a baby inside her coat. She moves under the canopy. When she tips back her hood, Imo thinks she's met her before but can't place her.

The woman with the baby paces, speaking into her mobile, unsmiling. She ends the call, stuffs the phone in her pocket and starts out across the pub garden. A man hurries towards her. It's Sean Hennessy – coatless, soaking wet. He throws his arms up towards the woman in what appears to be a gesture of apology, but she barges past him. Instead of exiting the garden by the gate that the other parents used, she carries the baby through the bar.

"Bloody hell," Imo gasps as the woman hurries past their seats. It's Lauren, minus her Gothic eyeliner and crow cape. Face red and tearstained. Imo's world shifts again. How can Lauren be a mother when she seems like a bigger kid than Imo? Someone else play-acting. Does no one tell the truth any more? Did Lauren forget to mention over coffee and cookies she had a child? Maybe she just didn't trust Imo enough. Then Imo remembers how she thought she saw her with Amber at the start of term, but at the audition Lauren denied knowing her. Another lie. What else is Lauren hiding?

Hennessey remains outside in the pouring rain. He moves to a picnic bench under the awning and sits with his head in his hands.

Tegan has also witnessed the scene. "Trouble in paradise. That's what happens when you shag the students." Imo gawps and waits for Tegan to carry on. "Apparently he got it together with a first-year drama student. Nothing serious – not on her part anyway. Next thing you know: bun's in the microwave. She's had to repeat the year."

Imo can't believe it; not Hennessey. With *Lauren*. She actually liked him. Another deceiver. "But isn't that against uni rules?"

Tegan shrugs. "She's over eighteen, not one of his students. Judging by the look of him, he's come off worse."

He's on his phone now, shoulders hunched, obviously freezing. The families for the afternoon crèche session start to gather under the awning and block him from view. Parents cling onto their toddlers who look as if they'd prefer to splash in puddles in the pub garden. At half past, the crèche doors open and they go in. The baton-pass in this direction is swifter and the parents bolt out again in under three minutes. Hennessey has disappeared.

A woman, carrying a child, arrives late and has to dodge the exodus to get into the crèche. Her little girl's auburn curls have corkscrewed in the damp air.

"Was that Jane?" Imo asks.

"Looked like it," Tegan says. "Let's go and wait on the front steps. She'll end up there when she comes out through the gate."

"What will we say?" Imo feels a nervous flutter in her belly. Explaining anything to Jane Brown will surely expose how far-fetched her ideas about Amber have become.

"We don't speak, we follow and find out where she lives. Put your hood up." Tegan fetches one of her jackets out of her handbag. "Needs must," she says, looking at it with obvious distaste.

"I thought you only sold pink," Imo says, recognizing it as a navy-blue version of the one she's wearing.

"Prototype I'm trialling for men." She smiles at the boy on the seat opposite as if about to open a sales pitch, but thinks better of it.

They need their hoods as they shiver in the driving rain on the front steps of the union building. Tegan puts up her umbrella again but stuffs it away when a gust of wind blows it inside out. Jane Brown hurries past them when she comes through the gate. She's turned her collar up against the rain. When she's ten metres in front, Tegan indicates that they should go after her.

"Do a pretend text," Tegan whispers and Imo scrolls her phone, trying to look casual.

231

Jane approaches a line of parked cars and holds out a key fob. The lights of a Ford Ka flicker.

"I thought she didn't have a car," Imo whispers. "We can't follow her now. We should have checked the DVLA under her new name." Despondency descends and she feels the cold even more.

Tegan looks at something over Imo's shoulder and grins. "Don't be defeatist. Come on." She sprints back to the student union, with Imo following.

Chapter 54

Imogen

Riku, in a giant black raincoat, stands on the steps of the student union with a parcel in his arms about to step into a taxi.

"Wait," Tegan shouts. "Let me help." She scoops the parcel out of his hands and leans in to speak to the driver. "Can you follow the little blue Ford that's about to pull out?"

"We're sharing," she adds when the driver looks up at Riku for confirmation.

Riku scowls and for a moment Imo thinks he's going to protest, but he watches his parcel disappear into the front passenger seat with Tegan and climbs in behind her.

After Imo gets in, the driver puts on his windscreen wipers and moves off behind Jane's car. "*Hawaii Five-O* round here, init?" he says. Imo realizes it's Hamid.

"Don't get too close," Tegan orders. "We don't want her to notice us."

"What if she drives onto the motorway? It'll cost you."

"She won't."

Her tone silences him. Imo never thought she'd see Hamid lost for words.

Jane drives through the rain at twenty until she's off the campus, then picks up to thirty, turning right at the traffic lights into the town centre. Imo is aware of Riku beside her – straight back, arms folded, like a sheet of angry metal.

"Been to collect a parcel, have you?" she asks.

His eyes move in her direction but his head stays forward.

"I had to go there the other day. Took me ages to find the post room. It's like Narnia."

His head tilts a fraction.

"You know Narnia? I don't know if it's been translated. Has it?"

Riku doesn't respond.

"He doesn't give you much to work with, does he?" Tegan calls from the front seat.

Riku's expression is unchanged.

"My parcel was from my grandma," Imo says. "A cake – well, brownies. Gluten-free because … it doesn't matter. They were stale by the time I got them."

Riku stares straight ahead.

"Proper conversation-hogger, isn't he?" Tegan says and grips the armrest as Hamid takes a sharp left when Jane turns without indicating.

Imo puts out a steadying hand and catches Riku's thigh. "Sorry." His face remains impassive but she thinks she detects a nod.

They turn right into a road called Victoria Lane. Imo remembers it as one of the places that was mentioned at the accommodation talk at the uni open day.

When Jane pulls into a driveway, Tegan instructs Hamid to go past. The house looks like its photo from the open day display: a sprawling three-storey dwelling, early twentieth century. The kind of place to find solicitors' offices or a dental practice, but it's been turned into student digs. When they've gone another hundred metres up the road, Tegan tells Hamid to stop.

"Right, that'll do for now. We can go home," she declares. "Ask Chatty Man where he wants dropping."

"How do you know she lives there?" Imo asks. "She might be visiting."

"She's carrying Lidl shopping bags. That's her grocery shop going into her own house."

Imo peers out of the misted-up rear window as Hamid executes a three-point turn, and sees Jane push the front door open with her hip and take in two heavy carrier bags.

"Ask him then," Tegan says. "You're the linguist."

"Where do you want to go?" Imo asks Riku, but the side of his face presents an unflinching wall of silence.

Hamid comes to her rescue. "It's the halls on campus. That's where I was booked for."

Imo reaches forward and takes the parcel from Tegan. She points to Riku's name and uni address on the front. "Here?"

He grabs the parcel, cupping his body around it and away from Imo. He stares out of the rain-spattered window for the rest of the journey. When they arrive outside the halls, he gets out, slams the door and disappears through puddles into the building.

"Charmed, I'm sure," Tegan calls after him.

Imo pays Hamid an extortionate twenty pounds.

"Unexpected fare rate, but I've done you a discount," he assures her.

Back in their hall, Phoenix meets them at the top of the stairs. "I've *got* to talk to you. Where have you been? I've been trying to call you."

Imo reddens as she recalls the stuff she told Phoenix. Another heart-to-heart won't help. But the look on Phoenix's face tells Imo that this is about something else. She unlocks her door.

"This can't wait," Phoenix's voice is low and urgent. "It's about Amber."

Imo feels a prickle of concern, but before she can ask Phoenix what she means, Riku comes out of his room with an expression like stone. How he must hate them. She gives him an apologetic smile and turns again to Phoenix. But the girl is already backing away, her skin suddenly as pale as their magnolia walls, her eyes fixed on Riku.

"What did you want to tell me?" Imo asks.

Phoenix shakes her head, enters her room and shuts the door.

Chapter 55

Imogen

Dr Wyatt's morning lecture is a lengthy post mortem on the classic errors people made in their assignments. Imo feels like she's being told off, even though most of the criticisms don't apply to her work. She only half listens, still puzzled by Phoenix's behaviour yesterday. Imo tried knocking on her door a few times, but she didn't let her in.

Lauren, who got sixty-eight percent, makes a point of folding over her feedback sheet and pushing her paper up her desk so the grade is there for anyone who cranes their neck to see. Imo doesn't know anyone else's score but, given the close attention they're paying to the bollocking, there must be plenty of room for improvement. Imo feels a speck of joy at her own seventy-two percent although it's still tinged with umbrage at all the areas for improvement in Wyatt's feedback.

On the way out, Lauren taps her on the shoulder and suggests they get coffee. "I've got twenty minutes."

Before you have to pick up from crèche? Imo doesn't say what she's thinking, but decides to accept, hoping to tackle her about the baby.

"What did you get?" Lauren asks as they queue at the café counter. Her smile slips when Imo tells her. "Ah … well done. What did you get for the translation question?"

"Eight."

"I got nine," she exclaims. "Translations are what'll get us a job when we graduate, don't you think?"

Imo spots the opening she needs. "I suppose as a translator you'll be able to work from home. Handy when you've got kids."

Lauren looks down and chews her cookie. Eventually she chuckles. "I think we're a bit young to worry about that." She takes another bite and concentrates on sweeping crumbs from the table into her hand.

"Didn't I see you outside the uni crèche yesterday?" Imo persists.

Lauren pours the handful of crumbs into her saucer. "Not me. Didn't even know there was a crèche." She brushes her hands together, dismissing the topic as well as the remnants of biscuit.

"There's someone on campus who looks just like you," Imo says. "And remember when I thought I saw you with my friend Amber? That must have been your doppelganger, too."

Lauren shrugs. "Must have been." She locates more crumbs and picks them off the table.

Sickened by the bare-faced fakery, Imo's about to make an excuse to leave, when Tegan appears.

"You don't check your phone, do you? I've been waiting."

Before she can think of an excuse, Tegan has led her out of the queue. Imo gives Lauren an apologetic wave and follows her flatmate to the car, feeling relieved. Anything's better than making conversation with someone whose every utterance seems to be a lie.

"We haven't got long," Tegan says as they drive out of campus.

"Jane Brown will be back from dropping the kid off at the crèche by one." And adds in a low voice, "Then I want to get a quote for the paintwork."

"I see." Imo shivers, recalling the threatening note and damaged car bonnet. "Where are we going?"

"You want to find out about the woman, don't you?"

***

It's bin day in Victoria Lane; black and yellow dustbins occupy the length of the pavement. Imo didn't get much of a view in the rain yesterday but today's sunshine is doing justice to the attractive detached houses and leafy gardens. Jane's place is the biggest, more than three times the size of the others. Dark red brickwork, stone lintels, sash windows. Four dustbins lined up by the front wall. It's a contrast to the state of the rubbish in Imo's halls. She and Phoenix take it in turns to drag their kitchen bin liners to the skips at the back of the building. Most students aren't accurate in their aim and bin bags end up on the ground for the seagulls to peck. And no one takes glass for recycling. Empty spirit bottles adorn every kitchen window like sports trophies.

They park on a side road, beyond Jane's building, and walk back.

"What shall we ask?" Imo says, dodging round a yellow dustbin. "Do you think she could be Cheryl?"

Tegan stops dead, causing Imo to run into her. "I don't much care whether she's Cheryl or Lady Gaga, but if we can establish it once and for all, you can go back to worrying about how to work the toaster and forget about this Amber crap." She walks on.

There's a lump in Imo's throat and she suddenly wants to turn round and run home. Tegan clearly hasn't forgiven her for getting Dylan mixed up in this. But she's right; maybe if they can rule out this woman as Amber's former neighbour, Imo's anxieties might lessen.

"What are we going to do?" she asks.

"You'll see."

There are no names on the doorbell panel, so Tegan presses the first button. After a crackle in the intercom, a girl says hello.

"Morning. I'm Trish from Student Services." Tegan has adopted a convincing local accent. "I'm here because one of your flatmates still hasn't registered her daughter with us."

"Can't be our flat," the voice says. "None of the three of us has kids."

"Are you sure?" Deep in character, she holds out an imaginary clipboard. "It says here Jane Brown, Flat 11."

"This is Flat 1. I don't even think there *is* a number 11, and no one called Jane lives in our flat."

Tegan apologizes for disturbing her and presses the button for Flat 2. When there's no reply, she tries 3 and repeats her spiel. She works her way through the doorbells but, of the eight who answer, only one has any idea about Jane. The bleary-sounding man in Flat 10 recalls seeing a woman with a child go into a flat downstairs. He thinks they live alone but he doesn't know the flat number.

"Jane must live in 2 or 4 then," Tegan says after he's gone. "The ones that didn't answer." She pushes the front door of the building. "We're in luck. The dopey bloke has buzzed us in."

Imo steps back. "We can't break in."

"She'll never know."

"But … why? She's not going to have left her Cheryl Burdett birth certificate lying about."

"Of course not, but I seem to recall one of your wilder theories was that she was a drug dealer, supplying Amber and the bridge crowd. I'll soon know whether she's a criminal."

"How? Syringes and s-stuff?" The thought makes Imo shudder.

"Stashes of cash, expensive jewellery, paintings, ornaments. Unexpected signs of wealth."

"How do you know that?"

Tegan's jaw tightens. "I just know. Are you coming?"

Imo hesitates and checks her phone. It's twenty to one, Jane might be back from the crèche any minute.

"You keep guard then," Tegan snaps.

Before Imo can respond, Tegan shuts the door, leaving her outside. Even if she wants to follow her in, she can't. She goes to sit on the front wall by the bins, not wanting any part of what Tegan's up to. It's a sunny spot on the wall but she can't relax. The street is empty, silent. Respectable. What can some random woman from a Freshers' Fair know about their former flatmate? Imo feels suddenly guilty, not only for being here but for dragging Tegan into it, again. For giving in to her obsession about Amber. About Sophia. She needs to get some sleep, pull herself together. As soon as Tegan comes out, she'll go back to their flat and concentrate on being normal.

She sits for a while, making a point of not thinking so she can blank all what-if thoughts of Sophia. Idly, she lifts the lid on the yellow bin and glimpses empty water bottles and soup cans. Lidl brand. She smiles to herself. They might be grown-ups round here but they still eat like average students.

Her breathing skips every time a car drives past and it goes into overdrive when she hears a child's voice. Jane Brown must be back with her little girl. But a woman on her bicycle comes out of a drive further up and pedals off to the left with a toddler in the bike trailer.

The grinding noise of a bin lorry fills the street. Men step off the back, jog across the road, and gather the bins in bigger groups. Imo stands up when a middle-aged black guy with a cheerful grin gets the bins near her. She smiles, wondering how he copes with the noise and smell every day.

Then it happens. To the right, a hundred metres away, a blue car approaches. Imo can't be sure from that distance that it's Jane's. Just in case, she gets out her mobile to call Tegan, but there's no answer. She hurries to the front door and hammers. Pretty sure that Tegan's broken into one of the flats where they got no reply, she presses the buzzers for numbers 2 and 4. *Come on, Tegan, come on.* But no one answers.

Chapter 56

Imogen

The blue car pulls up at the house and Imo stands frozen on the doorstep, her heart belting. Jane Brown gets out with a grocery bag.

The colour drains from the woman's startled face. Imo braces herself when her expression changes to anger. But the fury vanishes almost as quickly as it arrived.

"Can I help you?" she asks reasonably as she manoeuvres the dustbins to the side of the driveway with her spare hand.

"I'm looking for you, actually," Imo says, trying to summon the brass neck that Tegan wore when she spoke to the other residents through the intercom. "I want some advice." She hopes Parents' Group organizers are like welfare reps, who love it when you ask for their help and they can poke into your business.

But Jane eyes her suspiciously. "How did you find my address?"

"Let me just … I've got to send this." Heart and mind racing, Imo fires a text to Tegan: get out. The thinking time helps. "Sorry about that. I live round the corner and saw you on this doorstep once, so I assumed you lived here."

"I thought freshers are housed on campus."

Oh, God, she's recognized her from the Freshers' Fair. Now what? "I don't actually ... My boyfriend does. He's a postgrad. I spend a lot of time at his place. Halls are juvenile, you know how it is." She tucks her hair behind her ear, hoping it looks like something a grown-up would do.

Jane stares at her and Imo doubts she's ever seen a more immature-looking student, but she presses on with her fabrication. "The problem is my boyfriend's flatmate has a baby. The situation's a nightmare."

Jane's eyes narrow to piercing and Imo braces for a tongue lashing, then the woman smiles and shakes her head. "There's nothing nightmarish about parenting." Her tone is light, indulgent.

Imo feels sweat drip from her hairline. "What I mean is she – my boyfriend's flatmate – hasn't got any help and stays in all the time. Can't face meeting people, doesn't eat properly, can't sleep. The whole thing is too much." She stops herself saying more, afraid of blurring lines between fiction and fact. There's still no reply on her phone. *Get out, Tegan, get the hell out.* "I wondered if you could tell me ... what help's available for young parents."

"If she joins our group, she can access the website." Jane moves past Imo to reach the front door.

"Wait." Imo catches the woman's shoulder and then pulls away, embarrassed. "Sorry. I'll suggest the website, thank you, but it's hard to get her to do anything she's so low. Can you give me any tips? Let me just get my notepad up." She hammers out another text: now!

Jane laughs, nodding at the phone. "No need to take notes. I've got leaflets on dealing with depression and isolation. I can get you one." She gets out her door key.

Imo steps in front of her, blocking her way. "I don't want to put you to any trouble. A couple of thoughts will do."

Jane stares at Imo, frowning. Then she walks back to her car. "I might have a leaflet in here." She climbs in and starts the engine to move the car onto the drive now that the bins are out of the way.

Imo's head whirs. She leans against the building, panting, her neck damp with sweat.

"Can't find it." Jane hurries past her before she can think of another delaying tactic. "Must be in the flat." She unlocks the door and enters.

Imo follows into the foyer, too nauseous to stop her.

"Wait here," Jane says as she opens the door to Flat 2, then closes it behind her.

Imo's ears thud with a noise like the bin lorry. Her concern for Tegan merges with her fears for Sophia, for Amber. But mainly for Sophia. She thinks of the smiling graduation photo that appeared on news channels for a while. Does her sister even still look like that? How much can someone change in seven months? Especially if they're … The foyer spins in black and white.

A million miles away, Jane returns with a leaflet. Her lips move but Imo can't hear her above the thrumming in her head. She nods – she thinks she nods – and takes the leaflet. In a daze, she goes outside and makes it to the front wall. The fresh air calms her breathing and she starts to relax until she realizes Jane's stayed in the flat. Where the hell is Tegan? Hands shaking, she scrolls her phone.

Suddenly Tegan appears on the pavement from the left of the street. Imo rushes forward and flings her arms around her, relieved to smell her expensive perfume again.

"Steady on. I haven't been to war."

Imo lets go, feeling foolish.

"I went into the wrong flat. A man was spark out on the sofa in the lounge so I crept off through the patio at the back. A path leads to the road where we parked. We'll have to come back and try again tomorrow." She checks the time on her phone. "Shame – we're not going to be late to the Business Culture lecture."

Still recovering from her panic attack, Imo shivers and stumbles against the wall.

Tegan studies her. "If you're gonna puke, you're walking back."

Chapter 57

Amber

Her lips crack and hurt with thirst. She stretches her untethered leg towards the water bottles on the concrete. Panting for breath, every movement an enormous, aching struggle. She grips the rusty bedframe and stretches further. Finally, her toes touch plastic. The bottle is full and hard to roll but gradually she moves it nearer.

Fighting dizziness she picks it up and collapses back onto the bed. Manages to lift herself up and greedily tries to open the bottle. But her fingers are numb and stupid, won't turn the lid. She tries again, hands shaking. It won't move. Tears wet her face, mixing with the blood and dirt on her cheeks. A wave of exhaustion takes hold. She stops to catch her breath, rests her throbbing head against the bare mattress. *Sleep now, drink later.* Darkness clouds her vision as consciousness slips away.

The bottle falls from her hand and tumbles through the air. Bouncing across the floor into the others, knocking them out of reach. The noise brings her back and she opens her eyes. She tries to cry out, but her throat is too dry. The room seems to shift under her and she shivers, teeth chattering. Through the gloom she can see the scattered water bottles. Lying like forgotten victims in the cold.

Chapter 58

Thursday 13 October

Imogen

In the morning Imo feels like an invalid. A recollection from yesterday's Business Culture lecture on Groups and Norms flickers into her mind. A prison guard, incarceration. Tendrils of dread grow along her back as she realizes she's taken on fear for two people. Sophia hasn't been found. Is Amber lost forever too? Are both in danger right now as she cold-sweats in her bed?

She lies still until her breathing settles and she checks her phone. Three texts from Phoenix: Let's talk today … I keep knocking. Where are you … Meet in kitchen 11am. The leaflet Jane Brown gave her is on her bedside. *A Ten-Step Guide to Beating the Blues.* She reads no further than Step 1: *Tell a friend how you feel. The blues get bluer if you stay alone.* But her blues are getting blacker. She's got to stop her imagination from doing this.

It's ten past eleven when she joins Phoenix and Tegan in the kitchen.

"We don't mind if you want to have a shower first," Phoenix says gently.

"Clean your teeth while you're at it." Tegan moves back in her chair.

Imo sinks her gaze to the floor, taking in a splodge of mayonnaise, a crushed Pringle and an empty lager can under the coffee table. Is this what they see when they look at her: the dirty, scabby remnants of previous forays into making an effort? God, she hates herself.

Phoenix sits on the coffee table and pats her knee. "You'll feel better if you put on a clean T-shirt. I've got something weird to tell you and you need to be clear-headed."

Like a naughty girl sent upstairs by her mum, Imo goes back to her room, cleans her teeth, pushes a wet flannel round her body, and puts on clean knickers. The sweatshirt and jeans are the ones she wore yesterday.

"Let's talk in my room," Phoenix suggests when she comes back, her voice lowered to a whisper.

"Who are you expecting to eavesdrop?" Tegan asks, as they follow her into the hallway.

Phoenix puts her finger to her lips, shooing the others into her room. "Be quiet; he'll hear you." She makes sure her door is closed.

"What's this about?" Tegan puts her hands on her hips and accidentally knocks an unopened water bottle off Phoenix's bedside locker. It rolls under Imo's legs and she picks it up.

An electric shock shoots through her. A month after Sophia went missing, their mother became convinced she was trapped somewhere without water. She made Imo and Freddie carry water everywhere so they didn't meet the same fate. Mum's anxiety rubbed off on Imo and she often fears Sophia is alone and dying of thirst. She drops the plastic bottle and grits her teeth. She becomes aware of Phoenix holding her shoulders. Gradually she stops shivering, but she's left with a dark sense of misery.

Phoenix and Tegan exchange a glance.

"You reckon I've lost it, don't you?" Imo says. "But I think Amber's in trouble." She looks away. A blurred view of one of Phoenix's circus posters swims in front of her. A muscle-toned duo harnessing the power of fire. How she envies their control. Her gaze stays on the poster. She can't face looking at her flat-mates and seeing their disbelieving faces, or worse their pity. But she daren't close her eyes in case a what-if vision of Sophia, or Amber, is there.

Phoenix clears her throat. "I've been trying for a couple of days to talk to you and wish I'd tried harder. If what you think has any truth in it …" She lets out a deep sigh. "I don't know how the hell to say this."

She walks to her desk, flicks a switch on her retro radio. When it blares out Pussycat Dolls, she turns it down but also lowers her voice. "I don't want Riku to hear this."

"He went off with his latest bundle of parcels," Tegan says. "If he's gone to the post office, he'll be ages."

"That's good." Phoenix exhales. "Listen. I've seen inside the sketchpad that he keeps in his room. He's done a drawing of Amber. It's flattering and looks just like her."

Tegan shrugs. "Maybe he fancied her. A bit creepy, I know. He's not Channing Tatum but Amber might have appreciated the interest."

Phoenix shakes her head. "You don't get it. He's captured the shape of her face, her eyes, her mouth, everything. It's like a photo-graph, like he has spent hours – days – studying her face in detail."

"What are you saying?" Tegan sits forward on the bed, her eyes serious.

"What if he's had more recent … access. He might know where she is."

Imo remembers Riku quickly removing the sketchpad from his desk when they brought Dylan to see the unicycle, but why let them barge into his room if he had something to hide?

251

Tegan, on the other hand, has no doubts. She goes to the door. "I knew he was dodgy. He must be the one warning us off. If he keyed my car, I kill him. Let's see what else he's got in his room."

"We can't just walk in," Phoenix protests.

"You must have done, if you saw Amber's picture, or did he invite you to see all his etchings?"

A flush of colour creeps up Phoenix's neck. "That was an accident. But the door will be locked now if he's gone out."

"Shouldn't be a problem. Come on." Tegan steps into the hallway, but Imo and Phoenix hang back. Tegan rounds on them. "Why is it that you're the ones bleating about Amber, but I'm the one who ends up taking action?"

"But he's our flatmate," Phoenix says.

"And you reckon he's got Amber locked in his wardrobe."

"I thought we could tell Student Services."

"So why didn't you? Why this cloak-and-dagger bollocks? Why tell me if you don't want me to do something?" She turns to Imo. "Are you with me?"

Imo's head's hurting. "I can't. I need to lie down."

"Sod the pair of you." Tegan storms to her room and slams the door.

***

True to her excuse, Imo goes to bed, but doesn't doze off. Who does at noon? Who does, when their head holds ideas so miserable that sleep might bring them back? Who does when their waking hours are numb? How much longer can she meander through each day? She thinks of Sean Hennessy and the look of desolation on his face as he sat in the rain outside the crèche. His meanderings took him to parenthood, but don't seem to have brought happiness. Imo curls up under the duvet. She's no hope of finding Sophia. Couldn't even work out that Lauren does Theatre Studies as well as German, let alone that she has a child.

Imo's skin itches. Amber was studying Theatre Studies. Did Hennessy meet Amber? A thing for drama students? She recalls how, in the first Accountancy lecture, she thought he'd looked familiar and she'd wondered briefly if she'd seen him in a nightclub the previous week. What if he really had been there? It was the day after Amber disappeared. Had he done something to her and gone on the prowl for the next one? That could be the reason he's distracted, making mistakes in lectures and walking out. Guilty conscience. Her heart quickens, remembering the scrap of paper he pulled out of his briefcase: *Death of a Dying Rose*. Is Amber the rose? Poetic perversion compelling him to write about his victims? Lauren could be another victim, held in his thrall by their child. Did she help him lure Amber? That's why she won't admit to knowing her. Could it be? It's no more ludicrous than Phoenix's Riku theory.

Her head burrows under the pillow. Like her suspicions of Hennessey, the idea of Riku's involvement has become a gnawing toothache. Could Riku know where Amber is? Amber was the first one to welcome him when he arrived late at the start of term. Maybe he took a shine, not reciprocated. Imo's stomach knots. Her mind, awash for so long with Sophia, could be playing tricks. But if it isn't? She should have let Tegan get into Riku's room so they could rule him out. Too late now. No way will the girl do anything for her after she hung back and sided with Phoenix. She's going to have to pursue Amber on her own. Maybe Riku hasn't locked his door.

For several more minutes she stays in bed until the nagging grows acute. Heart thumping, she treads across the hallway and presses her hand gently on his door. She jumps out of her skin when another door opens.

But it's Phoenix coming out of her room. "Is it locked?" she whispers, apparently with the same idea.

Tegan, too, sticks her head round her door. "He's still out. Are you two ready to come over to the dark side?"

Imo looks at Phoenix.

Phoenix takes a breath. "Do it. I'll keep watch in case he comes back."

The locked door is no obstacle for Tegan. Imo doesn't see how she manages it but the lock clunks and the door swings open into Riku's room. Tegan and Imo step inside. The fragrance is still sweet, although the tea lights have gone from the window sill. The bed is made, with its silk bedspread hotel-room smooth. The unicycle is back on its hook. Tidy. Immaculate. Imo shudders. Is that normal? She thinks of the carnage of Freddie's room, which their mother says she'll only enter in a fall-out suit. But Imo's own isn't much better. And Sophia's? Her belongings, returned from uni, are piled in boxes, as if her essence has been archived. Maybe Riku's the normal one.

The desk is bare apart from the roll of address labels. Imo spots the sketchpad on the high shelf and reaches up to get it. A newspaper cutting flutters down.

Tegan smooths it out on the desk and reads. "Shit, he's a black belt." She passes it to Imo.

Hertfordshire Taekwondo Association members at their open day (left to right) … Riku Lee (3rd dan) … And there he is, thinner in the face but looking just as bulky in his white training suit. Imo's about to say they should leave when Tegan opens the sketchpad.

"Phoenix was right. Looks at this."

Amber, plump-faced and pretty. Tears prick Imo's eyes and she has to sit on the bed. She has the saddest sense that she'll never see her again.

Tegan flicks to the next page. "No way," she shouts. Her eyes widen and she grows pale. She hurls the pad on the desk and puts her hand over her mouth.

"What is it?" Phoenix asks, leaving her sentry post to come

inside. Gingerly, she picks up the book and folds over Amber's picture to see what's freaked Tegan. Her jaw drops and she turns the page towards Imo. It's a mermaid on a rock in a broderie anglaise off-the-shoulder blouse, combing her thick dark hair. He's captured the hauteur in Tegan's eyes.

"He's a psycho and I'm his next victim," Tegan says. "I've got to find Marlon."

"We don't know that," Imo says, although she can't think of any other reason for him to have sketched Tegan as well as Amber.

"What's in those parcels he keeps getting and posting on?" Tegan swallows. "Good way to get rid of body parts."

When Phoenix turns to the next page of the sketchpad, Imo coughs down bile. From the paper, Imo's own image stares back. Downturned eyes, lank hair falling out of a hood, a tear on a pitted cheek. It's not a caricature, it's not unkind, but Imo wants to weep.

She doesn't get the chance. Riku steps into the room and closes the door behind him.

Chapter 59

Phoenix

Though Riku's face is expressionless, Phoenix sees the fury in his eyes. It pumps in a vein in his reddening neck. Someone told her once that a tenet of martial arts is self-control. She prays Riku knows that too. She hands him the sketchpad. "Sorry."

"He should be the one apologizing," Tegan flares. "What kind of pervert draws pictures of his flatmates?" She rounds on Riku. "Where is she?"

Phoenix has seen people on the receiving end of Tegan's temper before. Some scowl, others blush, all take a step back. But Riku doesn't move. His stillness is chilling and she puts her hands in her pockets to hide their tremor.

Glowering, he slowly folds over the image of Imo and holds the next page out to Phoenix. Her own face grins back with shining eyes. It's a full-length shot that gives movement and energy to her long limbs. If she wasn't terrified, she'd be flattered. Still staring at her, he turns over to the next sketch: Ivor from Flat 7 with a giant lager can in his fist. And the next: a face-only shot of a handsome black man. Phoenix doesn't know him but there's a gasp of recognition from Tegan.

Riku shows them the rest of the pad. The sketches are either exquisite head-and-shoulder drawings, or full-body shots that put the subject into a context: mermaid on a rock, drinking at pre-s, on a motorbike, on a rugby pitch. Phoenix recognizes some of them as people she's seen around campus. All students. No wonder he's always staring at people, committing their faces to memory.

"Why are you admiring this?" Tegan hisses through gritted teeth. "He's got Amber, remember. And he vandalized my car."

Confusion crosses Riku's face and Phoenix grows more uneasy. He's deciphered the word Amber and must know they're on to him. But he stands solidly between them and the door. She trawls her memory for everything her circus family has taught her. There was a hypnosis act based on having the strength of character to get people to do stupid things. Can she coax Riku into letting them go?

Imo's still holding the press cutting about the taekwondo competition. She gets off the bed and waves the paper at him. "Why were you in Hertfordshire three years ago?"

"Save your breath, he won't understand." Tegan folds her arms. She flinches when he puts out his hand but it's to smooth the bed covers where Imo's been sitting. "Great," she mutters, "a psycho with OCD."

Phoenix wills her to shut up. He might not understand the words, but her barbed tone will give him the gist. God knows what he might do if she provokes him.

Another one not taking the danger seriously is Imo. She's put the cutting on his desk and now inspects his bookshelf, pulling off three textbooks and flicking through before replacing them. "These are in English. You're fluent, aren't you?"

Riku's face remains impassive. He folds his arms and casts his eyes slowly over each of them. Phoenix's heart rate rockets.

She can't remember feeling this out of control since Cloud's accident.

His gaze rests on Imo for several seconds, then he lets out a cold laugh. "Of course, I'm fluent; I'm bloody British."

Chapter 60

Phoenix

The shock that cracks through the tiny room has more power than if he'd used a martial arts kick. Tegan sits pale-faced and ramrod straight on the bed. Imo wraps her arms around herself. Phoenix wants to say something but her mouth won't work.

Imo recovers first. "Why did you say you were from Thailand?"

"It was you lot who decided I couldn't speak English." He glares at Tegan. "At least I assume that the sarcasm that came out of your mouth in the taxi was because you thought I wouldn't understand."

Tegan looks away.

"Your friend Amber started it," he goes on. "She met me in the hallway on my first day and started babbling about Thailand. I couldn't get a word in. And, no, I don't know where she is. I didn't know she'd gone until her family came to clear out her room."

No tells, no micro-gestures – that Phoenix can see – nothing to suggest he's lying, but he clutches the sketchpad to his chest.

He notices Phoenix looking at the sketchbook. "My hobby. I do them from memory. No one poses. I wanted to study fine arts but my father said I was throwing away my education. So I'm here doing physics."

"Maybe you don't need to study it," Imo says, her tone conciliatory. "Those sketches look pretty perfect to me."

"True," Phoenix adds. "Your technique is outstanding." The idea of Riku as a serial killer is starting to look unlikely. She doesn't know what to think.

"What's in your parcels?" Tegan asks.

He pauses, narrowing his eyes. "Fingers, thumbs, teeth." He watches the panic rise in her face, then he laughs. "Shoes. Trainers mostly. I pay the duty and ship them out to the Far East. My grandparents still live in South Korea. They have contacts."

"What's the profit margin?" Tegan sits forward on the edge of the bed, thoughts of dismembered bodies apparently forgotten now that there's talk of business.

Imo must also feel the conversation drifting. She takes the sketchpad from him and turns to the picture of Amber. Her fingers hover over Amber's soft cheek and mouth. "She's in trouble. I'm sure of it."

They fall silent. Phoenix can't bring herself to look at Riku, ashamed that she's brought them into his space and at a loss for how she can apologize. She senses his angry stance – arms folded, feet apart, glaring.

"So back to our first suspect," Tegan says eventually. She checks her phone. "Crèche time coming up, we could have another snoop around Victoria Lane while Jane's out."

"I don't think Cheryl Burdett's got anything to do with this," Imo says.

It takes Phoenix a moment to remember that Amber's old neighbour might be on campus. The chances are slim. Even more unlikely when she thinks of the name change to Jane Brown on the NHS database. She flushes, ashamed of the intrusion she made into the woman's health record. Months of treatment. No one's business but her own.

Riku clears his throat and puts his hands on his hips. Phoenix gets the message and moves towards the door, ready to leave him in peace.

But Imo's still shaking her head. "I caught a glimpse inside Jane Brown's flat when I was in the foyer. She's a normal mum. There are kiddies' wellies in the hall for God's sake. If she'd seen what happened to Amber at the Freshers' Fair, she'd have told us, wouldn't she?"

Phoenix nods, encouraging Imo. They jumped to conclusions about Riku and shouldn't make the same mistake with this woman.

"Maybe she's stashed her in the cellar," Tegan says. On her hands and knees, she takes one of the parcels from under the desk and rattles it.

"Make yourselves comfortable, why don't you," Riku says, arms folded, directing his comment to all of them. But, apart from Phoenix, the sarcasm falls on deaf ears.

Imo frowns and stands in front of Tegan. "What did you say?"

"What?" Tegan replaces the parcel and stands up. She hesitates, apparently trying to remember her last comment. "The cellar? I was joking. Maybe your pal Jane Brown has kidnapped Amber. It was a joke."

Phoenix holds her breath, watching Imo. She regrets not telling Tegan what Imo revealed about her sister. Tegan wouldn't use words like kidnap if she knew.

But Imo tips her head to the side, studying Tegan. "What cellar?"

Thinking she needs to intervene, Phoenix touches Imo's arm. "I don't think she meant ... We should go."

Imo steps away.

"Are you okay?" Phoenix asks.

Imo turns round. "What cellar, Tegan? What did you mean?"

Leaning back on Riku's bed, Tegan shakes her head and sighs. "My gob lands me in it every time. Even her family thinks she's holed up in a squat, but just on the off chance that nice little Freshers' Fair mummy has taken Amber for her own sordid pleasure, there are cellars under the flats in Victoria Lane. Some of them anyway. Before I found sleeping beauty on the sofa in the wrong flat, I nosed round his kitchen. There was a door leading down some concrete steps. Maybe Jane's flat is the same." She sits up. "Wait, Imo, where are you going? Wait for us."

But Imo has already run out of the flat, leaving the door wide open.

Chapter 61

Phoenix

The adrenaline pumping around Phoenix's body takes a dip when Tegan doesn't turn off campus but parks outside the geography block. Now that they've caught up with Imo and promised to help, Phoenix thought they would drive together straight to Jane's place. Why the detour? Tegan climbs out of the car, releases the bonnet catch and looks up at the building.

Imo opens her door. "We could get a taxi if you're having engine trouble." She checks the time on her phone. Jane will only be out for so long.

"Shall I call Hamid?" But Imo's question dissolves into a gasp as Tegan's thug, Marlon, parks his Merc alongside. He gets out and leans over the open bonnet of the Mini.

Phoenix's adrenaline rushes again but not in a good way. Last time Phoenix saw him, he took Dylan. She realizes she's raised her knees and wrapped her arms around them, cowering on the passenger seat. Pulling herself together, she opens her door to listen.

"It'll have to be tomorrow," he's saying. "I'm not tooled."

"You won't have to *do* anything," Tegan says. "Just be there if anything kicks off."

"Tomorrow."

Tegan makes a big sigh. "Okay, but don't tell my father."

"The boss likes to be kept informed." Marlon closes the bonnet and returns to his car.

Tegan gets back in the Mini. "Jane Brown will have to keep for an extra day." She looks in the mirror as she reverses.

Phoenix has to sit on her hands to hide the tremor. Tooled? Tegan's hired an armed – *armed* – henchman to break into a young mother's house. Phoenix wants no part of it.

"I can't believe you did that, Tegan." Imo lets out an exasperated breath and Phoenix gives a sigh of relief that she shares her alarm.

From the driving seat, Tegan looks round. "Cheryl Burdett left her home in a hurry and changed her identity. There's an outside chance she's pitched up here. And we've agreed one possibility – however half-baked – is Amber's in her cellar. I'm not going in there like … Hansel and Gretel, ready to get locked up too. Marlon's our backup."

Then Imo adds: "We can't wait until tomorrow; it has to be today."

Phoenix is horrified; Imo's as lawless as Tegan. "We should call the police," she suggests.

Tegan lets out a bitter laugh. "You can't trust them."

Phoenix glances sideways at her. "Is that what your dad told you?"

Tegan's voice darkens. "Leave my father out of this."

"Why? Who else taught you how to plan an armed raid, if it wasn't him?"

Tegan slams on the brakes. The seatbelt locks against Phoenix's breastbone. "You can both walk back."

"I haven't done anything," Imo protests.

"I've been in this craphole for under three weeks and all I've done is wipe your backsides. Computer hacking, talking to crackheads, impersonating a parent – you're happy for me to bend the law when it suits you. I'm the mug you hire so you don't get your hands dirty. Well, you're on your own." Tegan leans across Phoenix and opens her door. "Out, both of you."

She leaves them on the roadside by the geography tower and guns her engine.

Imo reaches her phone out of her jeans. "I'll call a cab. It can't wait till tomorrow, with or without Tegan's help. If Amber's in danger, I need to rule Jane Brown out now."

"I'll come with you." The words escape before Phoenix considers what she's getting into. She knows she's fit, stronger than most women, but if – by the remotest chance – Jane Brown is Amber's captor, they'll be facing a serious psycho. "Maybe we should call the police."

"And tell them what? They'll look me up on their system, see all the stuff about Sophia and not believe a word."

"But we need someone with us, if Jane is a kidnapper and turns nasty."

"What do you suggest? You didn't want anything to do with Tegan's hired help."

An idea tumbles into Phoenix's head. It's a long shot, but it's the only option.

***

"What do you want?" Riku's face takes on an expression, but it's not the one Phoenix hoped to see. His eyes narrow and his mouth sets.

Imo seems oblivious and blurts out: "We need you to help us break into a flat in town. Amber could be there."

Riku steps back from his door, clearly not expecting that, but he shakes his head. "What's the plan: find a sketchpad and accuse the owner of every perversion you can think of?"

Phoenix winces and looks away. Stares at the door jamb. "We're sorry. It was a misunderstanding."

Riku glares at them. "Was it a misunderstanding when you hijacked my cab and bad-mouthed me for the whole journey, because you thought I didn't understand English?"

"I didn't say a word against you," Imo says. "And Phoenix wasn't even in the taxi. Your beef should be with Tegan, not us, and we don't blame you." She waves her hand dismissively. How easily she's thrown Tegan under the bus. She gets back to business. "There isn't much time and we might need you to do your taekwondo stuff. Our taxi will be here any minute."

"Forget it," he says. "Even if I wanted to help – which I don't – I've barely practised taekwondo in the last three years."

"You're better than nothing." Imo moves past him into his room. "Martial arts must be like riding a bike; you never forget." The unicycle is hanging in its usual place. She reaches up to touch the wheel and her eyes take on a new light. As if mulling something over, she hesitates. "Can I have a go?" she says eventually, her fingers caressing the wheel spokes.

Riku looks bewildered and Phoenix stands in the doorway, puzzled too. One minute Imo's clamouring to get into Jane's flat as if her life depends on it, the next she wants to play circus. Phoenix recalls how manic she was when she spoke of her sister. The mania must be back.

But she is forced to think again when Imo says, "If one of us manages to ride this thing, will you help? It's not much of a bet as I can't even ride a two-wheeler, but we'll give it our best shot, won't we, Phoenix?" She flicks a thumbs-up at Phoenix and turns back to Riku. "We need your help."

Riku folds his arms. "Everyone can ride a bike."

"I swear on my life, on my sister's life, I can't ride a bike, and I've never tried a unicycle. Just give us the bet. If one of us manages it for three seconds, you help us. If we can't, we'll never bother you again."

His weight shifts from foot to foot as he considers her challenge and the possibility of them humiliating themselves. He unhooks the unicycle. "Thirty seconds." He opens his desk drawer, gets out his beanbags and drops them into Imo's hands. "Juggling these at the same time." He gives her a smug smile.

Imo responds with a smirk of her own. "You're on." She hands the beanbags to Phoenix. "You go first."

Chapter 62

Imogen

There are hearty laughs from Phoenix and Riku in the back seat. Imo strains to hear what they're saying above Hamid's chatter beside her. Despite the trick she played, Riku's in a good mood, asking Phoenix for tips to improve his unicycle technique. And Phoenix's smile is still as broad as when she completed four lengths of their hallway, juggling fast and pedalling slow.

"I've come home," she said as she handed back the unicycle.

Imo loves the atmosphere. Like an outing that she's organized. Maybe that's her forte. Even if this trip to Jane Brown's is as pointless as she fears, she's brought Phoenix and Riku together.

"Shall I stop at the student place?" Hamid asks when they turn into Victoria Lane.

"No." Phoenix and Imo speak in unison.

"There's a side road further on," Imo explains, glancing in her wing mirror at Phoenix. "We'd like to stop there."

The car slows. Have they made Hamid suspicious?

"The side street's nearer to where we're going," Phoenix adds.

Hamid's forehead knits into a puzzled frown, but he speeds up. Imo's insides jump when they pass Jane's house. Can she really break in? Riku and Phoenix have stopped talking. Are they thinking the same thing?

Applying a touch to the brakes, Hamid makes a left into the side road. When he stops behind a blue Mini Convertible, Phoenix lets out a grunt.

Hamid can't contain his delight. "That's your Welsh lady's car, init? She can drive you back. I've got an airport run."

"Can't you wait?" Phoenix snaps. "We're not with her."

"Money, init? But you call me next time. I'll be there for you. Hamid Cars always there."

They pay him and get out, making a show of playing with their phones until he's turned round and driven off.

"Do you think Tegan's gone in already?" Imo asks.

"Looks like it," Phoenix replies.

"I hope she's okay." Imo's voice wobbles and even Phoenix looks concerned.

Riku eyes her suspiciously but with no inkling of the danger they might be walking into.

They walk round the corner to Jane's student hall. Imo, the only one who's been here before, leads the way despite the fear coursing her limbs and making it hard to walk. When they get to the front door, both girls step aside and look to Riku. He sizes up the door and puts out his hand. But the door creeps open.

Tegan is standing in the foyer. "All we need is a mutt and we're the Famous fecking Five." There's no humour in her voice. No anger either, she sounds disappointed. Betrayed. She heads towards Flat 2.

"Thanks for coming," Imo says.

Tegan shrugs. "I knew you wouldn't wait."

A feeling of shame comes over Imo; she's got Tegan involved again. "I'm sorry …"

"Later." Tegan puts a finger to her lips and wedges a credit card into the door of the flat. After a couple of flicks of her wrist, Jane Brown's door opens.

269

There's an intake of breath, and Phoenix and Riku stiffen.

"I'm not sure about this," Riku says, folding his arms, feet slightly apart.

"Me neither." Phoenix stands beside him. "You've got a good heart, Tegan. I shouldn't have said what I said, but I can't ..." Her voice trails off. She looks down and rocks on the balls of her feet.

"You two stay here then," Tegan says and turns to Imo. "Are you coming?"

Imo realizes there's a pecking order to law-breakers. She resisted yesterday when it was just her and Tegan, but compared to the moral high ground Phoenix and Riku have climbed, she's slipped down the slope.

She follows Tegan into the flat, taking in the strong fragrance of air freshener. Something quivers in her belly, and her legs tremble. It's like getting out of bed after a night of sobbing for Sophia, but more concentrated. Maybe it's the fear of getting caught, but her gut tells her it's something else. It's as if her worst nightmare lies in wait and at any moment will become reality. Sophia trapped in a cellar.

A crowded line of coat hooks and an untidy pile of women's and kiddies' shoes and wellies greet them in a tiny hallway. Imo's breathing races and before she's gathered herself, Tegan opens one of two doors to the left of the coats and pulls on a light switch. An extractor fan clatters into life in a small shower room. Two toothbrushes rest on the clean basin. One has a red dinosaur face on the back of its head. She tugs the string to kill the light. The extractor noise continues after she closes the door.

She goes through the other door and Imo follows, taking a deep breath. A cramped bedroom, twin beds with only a small gap between them. One, lower than the other, with countless teddy bears on top of a Paddington duvet. There's a lit lamp on the bedside locker. It lights what would otherwise be a dark room even at this time of day as there's no window.

The main living area is to the left of the hallway, beyond the bathroom and bedroom doors. A beige, L-shaped sofa against the left wall; a bookcase with a built-in computer desk on the right; a pale pink play table and matching stool on a learn-the-alphabet design rug. An old ice-cream tub on the table contains crayons and a half-dressed Barbie doll. Imo remembers what Tegan said about looking for signs of unexpected wealth, but even she can see this isn't a master criminal's home. Jane Brown is a young mum, making ends meet.

"There's nothing here. Let's go," she whispers.

Tegan takes no notice and carries on nosing around. A breakfast bar separates the compact lounge from the kitchen. She coughs. "Blimey, overgenerous with the air freshener at this end."

A frosted window on the back wall above the sink provides the only natural light in the flat. Nothing like the ketchup-smeared worktops and bottle-filled window sill of their student place, this kitchen is showroom-clean despite the old-fashioned units. The few worktops are clear apart from a box of low-sugar Alpen next to the kettle.

The kitchen drawers contain nothing unexpected: cutlery, bin bags, tea towels. Tidier than Imo's parents' kitchen drawers.

Tegan finds a mobile phone. "Damn, the battery's flat," she says, pressing the keys. She replaces it in the drawer where she found it.

A panicky feeling comes over Imo and gets worse when she opens the drawer for another look at the phone. The shattered screen is a white spider web. Doesn't Amber have this make? But so do a million other teenagers. She shuts the drawer.

Tegan has a poke around the fridge. "Hummus, couscous and carrot sticks. I might have guessed she'd have vomit-healthy fodder." She heads for a rummage in what looks to Imo like a broom cupboard but lets out a grunt when the door won't move. "It's got some kind of double mortice," she says. "What's down there that's so precious?"

Imo's breathing rattles in her throat. She rests her hand on the fridge and makes an effort to focus on the drawings secured by magnets. A stick person with long, yellow hair and outsize red cheeks; a house with a green roof; a flower or is it a butterfly? But it's hard to focus; she feels like she's run a marathon. Her lungs are burning.

"We'll have to work the whole thing up and down on its hinges." Tegan is still tapping around the door. "I'll lift it on the handle if you get on the floor, put your fingers underneath in the gap at the bottom and push upwards."

Imo drops to her knees before she falls. She's sweating and her panic is making her dizzy. As she reaches down to cup her hands under the door, she feels faint. *Sophia.* She's about to discover Sophia, every nightmare coming true. But then she remembers where she is. Heat sweeps round her body and envelops her in stifling sadness. She lets out a whimper. Sophia won't be here.

Phoenix rushes in with Riku and gasps when she sees Imo. "We heard a cry. Are you all right?"

"We might as well take her home," Tegan says, rubbing her hands on her jeans. "We'll have to come back with something to lever this door. It must lead to a cellar, like the other flat I went in."

Cellar. Head swimming, Imo wants to flee, get as far from this pain – this place – as possible. But an urgent, irresistible sense of purpose grips her. Clasping her forehead, she turns to Riku. "Can you get it open?"

Phoenix gives another disapproving intake of breath and, surprisingly, Tegan takes her side. "If he smashes it, Jane will know someone's been in her flat and she'll call the police. My prints are everywhere."

But Imo ignores Tegan's protest. Fighting her grief and the drill in her head, she steps up to Riku. "Kick it down now."

Riku glances at Phoenix, but she walks away, shaking her head.

272

Then she comes back, balls her fists and nods. He taps from the handle to the hinge with his hand, pushes a foot into the floor and stretches his upper body behind his hips in a stance reminiscent of the Tai Chi people Imo sees in the park at home.

His other foot comes up, kicks the door hard and something metallic clunks. Before Imo can react, he lands a second, devastating kick. A crack appears across the door and the lock mechanism bursts through. He crouches down and lifts the door from underneath in the way that Imo was trying to when she grew dizzy. More clunking and the hinge breaks. He grabs the side of the door before it topples and props it against the kitchen wall.

Phoenix sucks in her breath and Imo too has a moment of doubt. What if they get caught? Despite her rapid, jumpy breathing, she listens hard for footsteps outside, but hears only silence. The scent of air freshener is stronger now the door is open. But Imo can smell something else too. Something darker. She looks through the door into the pitch black and takes a deep breath.

Tegan steps forward, switching on the torch in her phone, but Riku holds her shoulder. "I'd better go first," he says.

Chapter 63

Imogen

Without arguing, Tegan falls in behind him. Imo puts on her phone light, the tremor in her hand making it jump around. Another cloud of air freshener hits her and she has to cough.

They descend a short, narrow staircase. Riku's phone flashes light onto the bare wall at the bottom. Tegan's phone illuminates his back and shoulders, and Imo finds it comforting to see his solid shape ahead of them. Fearing that her shaking legs will fail her, she keeps her light trained on the concrete steps. There's a sound at the top of the stairs and she stops. Prickles with sweat. But it's only Phoenix catching up.

Riku reaches the bottom and turns left into the cellar. He stands still and his torch begins a sweep of the space, starting with the wall nearest to them. Imo's heart lurches when the torchlight picks out powdery plasterwork. She's seen it before, whenever her darkest fears for Sophia visit her dreams. Every limb trembles and her clothes are damp with sweat. She can smell it, sour and rotten. Her eyes leave Riku's projected circle of light and scour the dark space beyond. She strains to grow accustomed to the weak light that seeps round a grill at the top of the far wall. It's a narrow strip-window – no more than six inches deep – below ground level that must be barely visible outside at the back of the property.

A swaying shadow appears on the wall and makes her jump.

"Relax, it's a bloody tree outside," Tegan hisses.

Imo shines her phone on the damp, concrete floor and shrieks when a spider scuttles away. She has to shield her eyes as the others point their phones in her direction.

Then, behind her breathless "Sorry" and her hammering heartbeat, she detects another sound. A whimper. Feeble, reedy. It stops before she can place it. Nothing. Her imagination.

It starts again. A rhythmic murmur, ending each emission with *pfff, pfff*.

Light right in her eyes again. "Stop it, Imo." Tegan's voice has a tremor in it. "Stop that noise."

"I'm not …" Imo turns away from Tegan's torch, blinking hard until her pupils recover. Her own light picks out a drape at the back of the room. For a split second she thinks it's a person and gasps.

Riku follows her light. The drape falls away when he tugs it, stirring up a nasty smell of mould and dust.

Pfff, pfff.

Imo stiffens. A boy at her school once went into a diabetic coma. This sound is his sound. *Human.*

"There's another room through here," Riku says, stepping through an opening that the drape had concealed.

The others follow. There's a solid structure in the middle. Her torch shines on a plastic bucket on the floor. Sick rises in her throat. It's not her sweat she can smell; it's stagnant urine. She directs the phone light upwards from the bucket, but Tegan gets there before her. Her torchlight rolls over the frame of a camp bed to a mound on a mattress. Tegan makes a noise – not a grunt, or a gasp – more like the thwack of a ball against a tennis racket. Her throat must be blocked. Imo's is too.

"It's okay," Phoenix croaks. She takes Imo's hand and they approach the bed together. She lifts a blanket, filthy in the light from her phone. It might have been yellow once, or cream. Even beige would have been a proper colour, better than the crusts of matter and blood and stench that infest it now. Her torch picks out short, pale hair, matted into greasy clumps. The face is turned away. They lean over for a better look. It's a face that's haunted Imo's dreams. Eyes closed and sunken into hollows. Cracked lips, a rash of scabs around her chin and upper lip. Loose, grey skin. *Sophia. Dead.*

Imo crouches, hugging her knees. World spinning, ending. Lungs on hold, not knowing how to breathe. Her scream long and silent, and through her shock she keeps her eyes on her sister.

Phoenix gently touches Sophia's shoulder. "Amber, can you hear me?"

Amber.

The spinning room slows. Imo stands up, steadying herself until the dizziness passes and she comes to her senses. Tears prick. Imo's private hell breaks. *Not Sophia.*

But why is Phoenix bothering? The smouldering stench of decay, the unnatural stillness – they've just heard Amber's death throes. Imo looks away.

"Amber?" Phoenix tries again.

Amber starts her murmuring. *Pfff, pfff.*

Imo gasps and realizes she's still holding her breath.

"She needs a drink." Tegan casts her phone-torch over plastic water bottles littered on the floor and gives one to Phoenix. "Some of these are unopened. She must have got too weak to unscrew the lids."

Imo feels like she's been punched in her belly, recalling her mother's instinct to make them carry water bottles. Had her mother seen into this abyss?

"And she's too weak to eat," Riku says. "There's a shallow bowl of soup over here and what look like mouse droppings in it."

Imo retches but makes herself shine the torch so that Phoenix can lift Amber's head and put the bottle to her lips. Her mouth doesn't move and water cascades down her chin. Phoenix lifts her head higher and holds the bottle in place. Amber has a violent coughing fit. Imo's worried she's choking, but the coughing seems to bring her to consciousness and she gulps the water.

"We've got to get her out of here," Tegan says. "It's getting late."

Imo's heart races. At any moment, Jane Brown will be back. If she can lock one girl in a damp cellar and half starve her, what will she do to them? Maybe Riku can protect them, maybe not.

"She must have been in here for days, weeks," Riku says, scanning his phone over Amber's shrivelled body. Her sleeve has slipped back to reveal dirty, fraying friendship bracelets over a wasted arm. "We've got to get her to hospital."

"And call the police," Phoenix says.

Amber coughs again. The dryness sounds caustic in her throat. She tries to sit up but falls back against Phoenix. Her eyes open and fix on Imo. "No," she hacks, and has to close her eyes when the coughing takes over.

Tegan finds another unopened water bottle and Amber glugs it down.

The second bottle restores her briefly. "No police," she chokes. But she falls back onto the bed, slipping away. "Too dangerous for Leo."

Chapter 64

Phoenix

Riku takes Phoenix's place at Amber's head and puts his hands under her shoulders and knees to lift her. He raises her about two feet above the mattress but can't get further. Amber yelps in her sleep and he has to put her down. The same thing happens when he tries again. Amber's tortured cry is hard for them to hear.

"Stop, she's tied down," Imo shouts.

Her phone lights the bottom of the camp bed. Around Amber's ankle there's a bracelet of weeping pus, and, in the wound, blue binder twine ties Amber's leg to the metal bedframe. A wave of revulsion hits Phoenix and she thinks she might be sick. This girl has been secured on a lead long enough to reach her piss bucket and her rank soup, but too short to stretch her limbs, to walk.

Tegan shines her phone into her handbag and brings out a pair of manicure scissors. Her hands shake as she tries to get a purchase on the binding at Amber's ankle, and she lets out a stream of expletives.

"Let me try." Phoenix takes the scissors and slits the length of twine halfway between Amber and the bedframe, in the way she used to open hay bales when the circus had animals. "We can remove it properly when we have more light." And more time. Jane could return any minute.

Riku puts Amber on his shoulder and she flops over him like a ragdoll. Phoenix is close behind, shining the light for Riku as he climbs the steps.

"What about the cellar door?" Tegan asks when they reach the kitchen.

"Leave it." Imo's voice is firm despite her complexion looking almost as wasted as Amber's. She holds open the main door of the building for them.

As Riku hurries along the street with Amber over his shoulder, Phoenix runs behind and gathers Amber's hands into hers to stop her arms from bashing into the wing mirror of a parked car. Amber's fingers are ice.

A middle-aged woman steps out of her house across the road. For a moment, Phoenix feels relieved. The woman will see Amber's unconscious body and phone the emergency services. Then she remembers Amber's strange warning about Leo. Could Jane have someone else locked up? Someone she will hurt if they go to the police. There's no time to run back and search the house again.

As Phoenix stands still in the road, Imo lets out a ridiculous, squealing laugh. "Sorry, missus, we're a bit pissed." She leans against Riku, blocking the woman's view of Amber's lolling head. She breaks into noisy giggles and looks back at Phoenix. Her eyes contain an urgent request to play along.

Taking Amber's hands again, Phoenix skips from side to side and gives a squeal of her own – although it's no match for Imo's. It's too far away to see the woman's expression, but her stance suggests pursed lips and affronted eyes. She gets in her car and drives off in the opposite direction.

When they reach Tegan's car, Phoenix goes in the back with

Imo. Riku moves Amber gently off his shoulder and lays her upper body across them. Phoenix has a close-up view of the swarm of seeping blisters surrounding Amber's mouth. They manage to bend her legs to fit her across the small car. She starts to keen and they worry that they're hurting her. They take off their sweatshirts and tuck them underneath to soften her position.

Amber's dressed in the kimono she was wearing at the Freshers' Fair but it's grimy, torn at a shoulder seam and reeking of sweat and urine. Her teeth are chattering.

"We need to keep her warm." Tegan gets a tartan picnic blanket out of the boot. It smells new and it's doubtful Tegan's ever used it. They arrange it over Amber, but it does nothing to mask her stench.

From the driver's seat, Tegan reaches over with another bottle of water. "Make sure she keeps drinking."

Amber's delirium isn't as deep as Phoenix feared and she opens her mouth to take the drink. Phoenix props up her head so that she's in a better position to swallow. Her drinking gets into an efficient rhythm and Phoenix strokes her hair as if nursing a filthy baby. Her hand touches something crusty on the back of Amber's head in Amber's faded hair. Between the slimy tufts is a black patch of dried blood. The wound should have been stitched days ago. She'll probably be left with an ugly scar where the hair won't regrow. But she's lucky she's still alive; head injuries can be deadly.

When she's finished the water, Amber sinks against Phoenix and, for the first time, Phoenix feels optimistic about her condition. Her sleep is silent as they travel back to the university.

With no other students around, Riku carries her unseen to their flat and onto Imo's bed. He pauses to catch his breath. Colour rises up his neck. Suddenly awkward among the girls.

"If you want, I could run out and buy more drinking water and antiseptic," he suggests.

Tegan thanks him. "And some baby food. It means going to the supermarket off campus, if you don't mind. Wait while I check my cupboard; we might need soup too." They leave the bedroom together.

Imo takes a large pair of scissors from her desk but hesitates at Amber's foot.

"I'll do it," Phoenix says. "Get a bowl of warm water and a clean flannel."

Telling herself it's a good thing that Amber is conscious enough to flinch at the touch of the blade on her ankle, she presses the girl's thin calf into the bed to hold the leg steady. "I'm going to cut this binding off your leg then we can bathe it."

She senses Amber's body relax in response to her voice. Phoenix forces the scissor blade under the tight binding and cuts it clean away. The ankle continues to ooze a mixture of blood and pus. The injury is at its ugliest on the outer ankle bone, but the soreness rings the entire leg. How she must have fought to get free, each struggle cutting deeper into her flesh. After how many days of incarceration did she lose the will and the energy to fight?

Imo returns with warm water, soap and paper towel, and gets clean towels and flannels out of her wardrobe. Phoenix rests Amber's foot over the bowl and splashes water on the wound. There's no reflex reaction when she soaps and scrubs Amber's soles. Alarmed, she asks Imo to take over the bowl so she can check Amber's breathing. To her relief, it still sounds settled.

By the time they've finished, the water is grey and awash with vile dirt from the cellar floor. They move the bowl away to ensure the filth doesn't get into her ankle wound.

Tegan comes in with a glass of water and a mug, just as they are dabbing Amber's feet dry with Imo's towel. "It's French onion soup. No lumps and I haven't heated it. I hope she can get it down."

Amber opens her eyes when they lift her head. Drinks the

glass of water and manages some of the soup. They dab her face clean with paper towel, careful not to press on the blisters.

Tegan takes the bowl to get more clean water and says she'll add some of her shower gel. "It's for sensitive skin and it'll get her clean."

Between them, Phoenix and Imo manage to remove Amber's tattered kimono and underwear.

"I'll chuck them in the bin," Imo says.

"Not yet," Phoenix says. They could be evidence. Even if someone called Leo is in danger, she still plans to tell the police.

"Who did this to you?" she asks, wanting to get her facts right for when she makes the call. It must be Jane Brown, but she wants to be sure.

Amber's eyelids flicker. She snatches a breath but doesn't speak.

"Please tell me," Phoenix says gently, brushing Amber's limp fringe off her forehead. "Who was it?"

Amber's eyes stay closed but she manages a whisper. "Cheryl."

She turns her head into the pillow and doesn't say more, but it's all Phoenix needs. Confirmation that Cheryl Burdett became the Jane Brown who held Amber in her cellar.

"Why did Cheryl do it?" Imo asks, but Amber is dozing again. She tries patting her arm. "Amber? Can you hear me? Tell me about Leo?"

Amber seems to squirm in her sleep when Imo says the name, but doesn't wake. They're no nearer knowing who Leo is and why he's in danger.

When Tegan comes back, they wake Amber and wash her emaciated body. So much grime comes off her neck, they change flannels again. Her underarms still stink but the skin grows red and tender as they scrub and they have to stop. Phoenix remembers Amber as a curvy girl, but her breasts have shrunk to empty pockets and her pelvic bone juts out. Her upper arms have matching, fading grey bruises, as if someone has gripped and shaken her. There's a gash on her knee like the kind of trapeze graze Phoenix used to get, but this is bigger, angrier.

Her heart stops when they turn her over and see the pressure sore at Amber's coccyx. She steps away, trembling. It's like the flash burn of black, weeping skin that ended her mother's career. Who wants a fire-eater with scorched, puckered flesh across her belly? Trying out a new trick, her father's error. The catering van is the constant symbol of how Cloud's life changed forever.

"Let me," Tegan says, taking the flannel from her shaking hands.

"Here." Imo hands her a sheet of paper towel. "I think we're all in shock," she says weakly.

Phoenix realizes she's crying. Blinking away the tears doesn't work and they keep running. She cries for the career that the accident took away, from her as well as Cloud. As her mother shrieked with pain, Phoenix's acceptance of risk spiralled away. From then on, she saw danger in everything she used to do as second nature. She can never be brave enough to be a circus girl again and yet homesickness is crushing her.

There's a knock at the door: Riku back with provisions. He's a welcome distraction. Phoenix dries her eyes and takes him into the kitchen to unpack his bags: milk, soups, baby food jars, yoghurt, instant mash packets, hot chocolate powder, and antiseptic dressings.

"I got this bottle of multi-vitamins," he says. "It's meant to be for kids but I thought, because it's a liquid, she'd be able to swallow it."

Tegan comes into the kitchen waving the soup mug they gave Amber. "She's drunk it all." She puts the plug in the sink and runs the tap. "I'll give her some now," she says, spotting the vitamin bottle. She smiles an acknowledgement at Riku as he leaves the kitchen.

"Do you think a spoonful of that kiddie juice is going to be enough?" Phoenix says. "Amber needs an intravenous drip."

"I don't think she's as starved as we thought," Tegan says, grappling with the child-proof lid on the vitamin bottle. "It's probably just the last few days she's stopped eating and we've already managed to rehydrate her a bit."

"That leg could go septic and there's a bad wound on her head. Only a doctor can deal with that."

"No," Tegan snaps, slamming the bottle onto the worktop. "Hospitals ask questions. You heard her. Someone else is in danger."

"Exactly. The police would help find this Leo."

"The police never help." Tegan narrows her eyes and then looks away for a moment. "My mum called the police sometimes. It only made things worse." She rocks against the sink as she washes the mug. Imo and Phoenix both stare at her. "Once it went as far as having her wrists and shoulder photographed. But my father knew her mental pressure points, as well as the physical. The police weren't enough to protect her."

The words trigger Phoenix's memories again. In the big top, sitting on an audience bench, resting her forehead on the back of the bench in front. The cold wood is rough against her skin. Her eyes are closed but she can't block out the sound. In the ring, her mother moans in agony. Her father, voice frantic with panic and regret, says over and over it was an accident, a rehearsal gone wrong. But the policeman, first on the scene before the ambulance, keeps on with his questions.

Tegan turns around, her eyes red-rimmed. "I'm not like my father despite what you think."

And I'm not like mine. Phoenix loves her dad, but it was a stupid trick. At twelve years old she could see its flaws, hear the nerves in her mother's voice. Her dad couldn't see it. She did. It's why she had to get out. That raw, dangerous need for perfection left her that day.

"I know you're not like your father," she says, wiping her tears. "If Amber improves tomorrow, I'll rethink the hospital. And I understand why you don't want the police involved, but we can't ignore what Jane's done. What else is she capable of?"

Tegan slowly puts the mug on the drainer. She keeps her back to Phoenix. "Marlon's still meeting me tomorrow. We can take another look in Jane's flat."

A shudder runs through Phoenix. She doesn't want to join forces with Tegan's hired thug, but she's torn. They left Jane's flat with a broken door and took away her prisoner. If the psycho woman hasn't already fled, she'll be ready and more than a match for them. Marlon might be their only hope.

"Do you trust him?" she asks.

She expects Tegan to fly at her, accuse her of not understanding the ways of the real world, but Tegan speaks softly, eyes watering. "I don't know how to shake it off, all of it. Marlon's always there. I thought I could turn it around and use him. But it's not the way, not the person, I want to be. What can I do?"

Phoenix studies Tegan's quivering shoulders. So this is her other side. And it's taken Amber's trauma for her to show it. Amber's brought something that was hidden out of all of them. "Where are you meeting him tomorrow?"

Tegan blows her nose. "Geography tower. Why?"

Phoenix has an idea so strong it burns her tongue, but she keeps it in. "I'll come with you," she says instead.

Chapter 65

Friday 14 October

Imogen

"Pressure sores?" Imo's mother sounds sceptical down the phone. "You've called to ask for nursing tips?"

"And to see how you are, catch up." Imo kicks herself; she should have made time for small talk first. Now her mother's suspicious. "It's just that my friend's grandmother has bedsores and her mum's worried, so I said I'd ask."

"Have you got a lecture?"

"Why?"

"I'm surprised you're up this early."

"I thought it was a good time to catch you, before your shift." Assuming it's a good day and her mother will make it into work.

The truth is that Imo hasn't been to bed. She sat with Amber through the night, coaxing plain yoghurt and baby food apple puree into her at midnight and then waking her at intervals to drink water. Phoenix came in at 3 a.m. to take over and offered Imo her room. Imo stayed under Phoenix's shower until her fingertips pruned. The stench of Amber's fragility and her dank basement prison had seeped into every pore. Afterwards overwhelming hunger sent her to the kitchen instead of bed. She ate two cans of baked beans, cold and straight from their tins, as if her own liberal consumption would compensate for Amber's privation. She's been in the kitchen ever since.

"Imogen, are you still there?"

"Sorry, Mum, you're right; it's a bit early for me. I'd better go."

"You'll ring again later, won't you?" A hint of anxiety. How would she cope if Imo disappeared too? A double tragedy would corrode her from the inside out. It reminds Imo that they need to tell Amber's mother what's happened. If anyone's going to aid Amber's recovery, it's her mother. But how can they tell her and expect her not to notify the police?

"Imo?"

"Sorry, bye, Mum. Love you … Wait, how do you treat bedsores?"

***

When Imo goes back to her room, Phoenix is spooning more baby food into Amber, who is propped on a pillow with the Groovy Chick duvet pulled up to her chest. She shifts her glazed expression from the advancing spoon to Imo. "Have you seen Leo?"

Imo and Phoenix exchange a glance. Leo was the soundtrack of Imo's night-time vigil and it was probably the same for Phoenix. The *pfff, pfff* of her delirium in the cellar returned. In moments of lucidity she called the name Leo, over and over. But slipped away whenever Imo asked who Leo was. Imo remembers Verity, the girl at Chadcombe Bridge, mentioning it too, and Amber's sister Jade thought Leo was another junkie. Why would Amber's old neighbour kidnap two people from the bridge crowd? Amber's memory must have become muddled. Yet something nags at Imo.

"Leo," Amber whispers again, slipping down the pillow into another doze.

"Who is it?" Imo asks.

But there's no answer. Amber opens her exhausted eyes and settles them plaintively on Imo.

"We're working on it," Imo says. She knows she's giving Amber false hope, and yet she's been grinding Leo around her head all night. There's a pearl there somewhere, just out of shot. If only Imo could make the connection.

Phoenix puts down the baby food jar and feels Amber's forehead. "You're a bit warm. I think we should bathe you again and I'll fetch you another nightshirt." The Mickey Mouse T-shirt that Imo grabbed out of her drawer last night hangs off Amber's shoulders. The Amber of Freshers' Week wouldn't have got it over her chest.

"Did you ask your mum about ..." Phoenix trails off. Amber's still awake and she probably doesn't want to alarm her.

"Everything's going to be fine," Imo says calmly. "They use specialist dressings at the hospital but the best thing is to get the patient on their feet." She touches Amber's thigh. She can feel the muscle wastage, even through the duvet. "Do you think you could manage to walk?"

The duvet flings back with a determination that Imo doesn't expect and Amber slips her feet out of bed. There's a grimy indent in the pillow where her dirty hair has been. The peroxide crop of her first few days at university has disintegrated into a pale, rusty thatch. Imo wonders if they'll be able to get her in the shower later. Can she cope with standing still for a few minutes? There's a dressing over the gash on her knee but the ankle wound is bare.

Phoenix bends down for a closer look. "Keep it open to the air today."

Amber tries to stand, but needs to rest her weight on Phoenix. With Imo's support on the other side, she gets up. Her pallid skin goes a shade lighter and her eyes lose their focus. They stand still a minute until her dizziness has cleared. She moves forward gingerly and they walk her to the bathroom. Her steps are slow and shuffling, and she favours her undamaged leg, but she keeps going. Sits on the loo and wees. Both Imo and Phoenix inspect the bowl as they help her up. The urine is pale and carries little smell. Good; she's rehydrating.

Amber sits on the bed while they wash and dress her in clean nightclothes and they help her walk to the kitchen for something to eat.

"As long as it's not baby food," Amber says and there's a flicker of a smile.

Phoenix whips up runny mash potato from a packet mix. Tegan comes in and makes everyone a hot chocolate. She cools Amber's with extra milk. Amber drinks it straight down and finishes the potato.

Afterwards they walk her around the flat. When they get to Phoenix's room, Amber points at the poster of her fire-eating parents. "Cool. Where did you get that?" And Imo feels a twinge of regret. Amber hasn't ever been in Phoenix's room and knows nothing of her circus background. She's missed so much.

Tegan looks at Phoenix in her onesie. "You'd best get dressed now."

"Let me help Amber first."

"We'll be late getting to Marlon."

"We still have time."

Tegan and Phoenix face each other in a silent battle of wills. Phoenix blinks first. "Okay, I'll get ready."

Tegan takes over supporting Amber.

Imo, clueless about what has passed between her flatmates, takes Amber's other arm, and she and Tegan walk Amber the length of the hallway.

Riku hears them and comes out of his room.

"I remember you," Amber says. "Parcel boy. From Thailand."

"Things have moved on," Tegan says. "He's from Hemel Hempstead and the parcels are export trainers. He's an entrepreneur." There's admiration in her voice.

"He helped us yesterday to get you out," Imo explains.

Amber thanks him blankly, but clearly has no memory of her rescue. Then her eyes go wide and she grips Imo's arm, pinching the skin. "Yesterday? I've been here a day? I have to see Leo." She looks at Tegan. "You've got a car, haven't you? Can you take me to Cheryl's?"

Behind her back, Imo and Tegan swap an incredulous glance. Why would Amber want to return to that hellhole?

"Who is Leo?" Imo asks.

But Amber ignores her, speaking instead to Tegan. "Can we go now?"

"You're not in a fit state to go anywhere," Tegan says. She leads her towards Imo's room. "Phoenix and I will go back for another look. You stay here with Imo."

"You'll find Leo?"

"Is Leo at the house?" Tegan asks.

Amber lifts a hand to her mouth. "Yes."

"You have to tell us who Leo is." Imo tries again.

But Amber starts to cry. "Go now, get Leo," she sobs.

Tegan sighs. "We'll try." But from the tone of her voice, it's clear she doesn't expect to find anyone at Jane's flat. She probably thinks it's another Amber fantasy. Yet Imo senses there *is* someone else involved. Chances are Jane will have fled, expecting Amber – or whoever broke her out of the cellar – to have called the police. But what if there's another victim in the flat, still locked away, close to death? No way is she letting Tegan and Phoenix carry out a half-hearted search.

"Riku, would you mind staying with Amber for a while? I have to go with Tegan," she says.

Tegan opens her mouth to argue, but Imo shakes her head emphatically. She's going too.

***

A siren sounds somewhere outside. A student's chip pan is probably on fire in another hall. The sound pricks Imo's conscience, imagining that other sirens won't be far away if they get Marlon involved. What if Amber's confused about there being another prisoner? But somewhere in the memories of the last few weeks, Imo is sure she's seen something.

"Hurry up. You'll make us late," Tegan shouts outside Phoenix's door. "You can't be still in the shower."

Eventually Phoenix emerges from her room with damp hair. "Sorry, I dozed off. Shall we go? It's best if we walk. We don't want anyone remembering your car's parked next to Marlon's."

"Don't be daft. There's no CCTV." Tegan checks her phone. "Besides, we'll be late if we walk."

The Mini's parked by the dustbins at the back of their hall, but it isn't going anywhere.

"Sod it," Tegan shouts, bending down to the front tyre. "People need to aim better for the bottle bank. Too much glass round here. I've got a flat." When she has a closer look, she finds a paper taped to the hubcap. "Bastards. When I find out …"

Imo's blood runs cold as she reads the note. *I warned you.* The tyre's been deliberately slashed.

Phoenix takes the piece of paper. "Do you want to call the police? I'm sure Marlon will wait, if we're a few minutes late."

"Marlon can deal with this. No one vandalizes my car and gets away with it," Tegan snarls and sets off at a brisk pace along the path towards the geography tower. She's swapped her usual designer sandals and palazzos for hiking boots and leggings. Clothes for every occasion, even for hiring henchmen and confronting kidnappers.

A police car screeches past, siren blaring, and overtakes a white Fiat with an *Abbey Student Union* sticker in the back.

"Wonder what's happened," Imo says.

"Don't know." Phoenix slows down.

Tegan's ahead of them. "Get a move on. We'll run out of time if we don't hoof it."

Imo catches sight of a blue flashing light through the bushes. A few more paces and the geography tower comes into view. Two police cars and a police van block a car in the disabled bay. A black Mercedes. Students outside the police cordon hold up mobiles and take selfies.

Tegan stops in the middle of the road, staring at the scene. Lights flash across her face as she sees the black car. She strides towards a thin boy with ferrety features at the edge of the crowd, leaving Imo and Phoenix in the street.

"What's happening, Josh?"

He colours and scratches his ear. "My name's John."

"Well … John?" Tegan demands.

"They've arrested a man carrying a firearm. From the look of him I don't reckon he's a student."

Tegan's face becomes so rigid it's as if she's turned to stone.

"Sounds like Marlon won't be able to help at Jane's. We should get out of here," Phoenix says as she and Imo catch her up. "If we belt back, we can put on your spare and still get to Victoria Lane."

Tegan turns slowly to face Phoenix. Her jaw clenched. "*You.* You tipped off the police, didn't you? You had it all planned. Running late in the shower, dawdling." Venom in her eyes.

Phoenix stays calm. "You should be pleased that you've finally shaken him off."

Tegan's face bulges with rage. "Did *you* wreck my tyre?"

"What? You seriously think I'd do that?"

Tegan pauses, has the grace to shake her head. But she isn't done yet. "How dare you interfere? I told you no police."

"That was for Amber, not Marlon."

"No police *ever*."

Some of the students turn their attention from the police vehicles to Tegan's raised voice.

"Marlon won't get within a mile of the campus after this. How likely is your father to replace him?" Phoenix says quietly.

Imo's on alert to stand between them if Tegan explodes, but the angry colour in her face subsides. She stares past Phoenix as if getting something clear in her mind. Suddenly she strides off in the direction they came.

"Are you coming then?" she calls over her shoulder. "Fuck knows how to change a tyre."

***

Phoenix has the wheel jacked up and tyre swapped before Imo's finished scrolling her phone for news of Marlon's arrest. But it's almost one o'clock before they reach Victoria Lane. Tegan's credit card trick gets them into the foyer but isn't needed on Jane's front door. It's unlocked.

Imo's heart thunders in her chest. In their flat, her thoughts of solving the Leo mystery were brave, but in this evil place, her legs are jelly. The line of coat pegs is empty except for a child's pink summer jacket, and the shoes have disappeared. Phoenix pushes open the bathroom door. No toothbrushes. Imo moves through the lounge, while Tegan goes into the bedroom. The tub of crayons is no longer on the child's desk, but the cellar door is still propped open. The scent of air freshener is even stronger.

Tegan comes out of the bedroom. "As expected, she's done a bunk. Wardrobe's empty and the cuddly toys have gone."

Imo lets out a sigh of relief. But her breath catches in her throat. The gaping chasm of the open cellar is in her sightline. She's been down there once, but it still brings her nightmare to mind. Sophia trapped, needing her help.

"What if she's abandoned someone else down there?" she whispers.

"One way to find out." Phoenix steps forward.

In reverse order of their last descent, Phoenix goes first, Imo follows, then Tegan. Imo wishes Riku was here. He's rallied round Amber as much as they have. When they reach the bottom step, the stench is as bad as before. How could Jane have thought a few squirts of air freshener upstairs would hide her crime?

Cold fear creeps through Imo, even worse than last time. Now she knows what might lie ahead. Tegan and Phoenix must feel the same and they huddle close, their torches sweeping the room. No phone lights this time; they're all equipped with the proper torches their mothers made them bring to university.

They scour both rooms twice, slowly, up and down, so as not to miss even a pocket of darkness. Camp bed, rancid blanket, bucket of piss. Toxic soup, water bottles. But no mounds of human life, or death. No second mattress. No Sophia. No Leo.

Chapter 66

Imogen

When Imo and the others return, Amber is sitting up in Imo's bed. Some of her normal colour has returned and she's talking to Riku. Her feet stick out of the duvet to keep her wound exposed. She sees them and tries to get out of bed, but her legs won't take her weight. She sits on the side. "Well?" she breathes. "Leo?"

Imo doesn't want to be the one to tell her and glances at Phoenix and Tegan. Tegan shrugs and Phoenix gives a tight, expectant smile.

Imo takes a breath; it's down to her. "Jane wasn't there."

Amber frowns, not understanding. Imo realizes she doesn't even know the new name of her captor.

"Cheryl, I mean."

Amber looks crestfallen.

"There's no sign that a second person was held there," Phoenix says and takes Riku's place at Amber's shoulder as she starts to cry. "Could you have got it wrong about Leo? Lack of food can play with a person's mind."

"She isn't being held, not like that. She doesn't know." Amber puts her head in her hands. "I'll never see her again. I should have thought it through."

Imo's mind races, knocked off one course and onto a new one. *She*. Leo is female. There's a connection somewhere. A memory. Another student? *Think, think.*

Lauren? Of course, she's the answer. Could it be? That's not possible, is it?

Amber begins to cry. But they seem like tears of resignation. While Amber thought there was a chance of them finding Leo, she'd been anxious and demanding. Now she seems to have given up.

"I'll make some hot chocolate." Tegan squeezes Amber's arm gently. Even though Tegan must have had more sleep than Imo, dark circles are visible under her make-up. She gives a commiserating smile as she leaves the room.

Make-up. Imo's mind is on fire. *Covering freckles.*

Freckles and auburn hair on Jane Brown's Facebook profile. Freckles and auburn hair playing round her legs at the Freshers' Fair. Imo's thoughts leap to the photo of Amber and Jade at the theme park on Mrs Murphy's mantelpiece. Celtic looks. Where Jade had dark hair, Amber's was auburn.

"Who is Leo?" She poses the question she's put to Amber many times since her rescue and every time she hasn't replied. This time Imo asks, already knowing the answer.

Amber looks up. "I can't say."

"Why not? You said yourself you won't see her again. Why hide it?" If she's right, Imo will have Lauren to thank.

Amber wails – high-pitched and long – as if she's deflating, like the life is rushing out of her.

"Imo," Phoenix warns. "She's too fragile."

Riku, perching on the desk, clears his throat and gives Imo a reproving glance. She hesitates, but she's sure she's right.

"Leo?" she prompts. "Tell us. It won't make it worse. It might even help."

The little bit of colour Amber's gained since her rescue fades and her eyes fill with tears.

"Say it, Amber," Imo whispers. "No more secrets, okay?"

Amber nods, taking a breath. "Leonie." Her voice cracks. "My baby."

There is a stunned silence. Nobody moves, as Amber begins to cry.

Imo is the first to respond and steps forward. Sits beside Amber and takes her sobbing weight in her arms. She lets her cry for several moments before pressing on. "Why did Jade lie? She convinced me you made up a story about being pregnant."

Amber quivers against Imo's shoulder. "Jade would never lie. It wasn't her fault, or my mum's. Cheryl made me."

Phoenix fetches a roll of loo paper, hands it to Imo and sits on the end of the bed.

Imo tears off a few sheets for Amber. "Tell us what happened."

"I was fourteen and off the rails with grief for my dad. It's not fair to say I got in with a bad crowd; Danno was a lost soul like me. His stepfather used to beat him, and we kind of found each other." She pauses and there's a flicker of a smile. "We used to hang out at the bridge. It was our safe place away from all the crap. Apart from him and Verity, who was off her head most of the time, my only normal friend was our next-door neighbour." New tears trickle down her cheeks.

"Cheryl?" Imo says, dabbing Amber's eyes with a sheet of the tissue.

"I used to tell her everything: how much I missed Dad, how hard I was finding it at home; about Danno. When I got pregnant, I knew she'd understand. She was a lot older than me. I thought she'd help me get an abortion, but she had another idea. I was so stupid, but somehow it made sense at the time. She said she'd pretend to be pregnant and we'd pass the baby off as hers." Her voice falters. "She was kind, thinking what was best for me. She told me how much she longed for a child of her own and how

297

hard she'd work to be the best ever mum. Told me how difficult it was to get an abortion without my mum finding out, how disappointed my family would be. I remember her talking about the nightmare of adoption, all the paperwork and the hassle. And she knew how much I wanted it all to go away. The perfect solution, my family need never know.

"But my mother saw how much weight I'd gained and realized. Cheryl was amazing with her, said she sympathized with finding out her fourteen-year-old was pregnant and suggested, as she was expecting a baby too, we go to our appointments together. Mum, who was still grieving for Dad, didn't need to get involved."

"Where … how did you give birth on your own?" Phoenix asks.

"We told Mum and Jade the baby was due in late January and Cheryl offered to take me away for New Year. Mum couldn't have been happier to see the back of me for a while. Leonie was born on her real due date in a cottage in Derbyshire. It was snowing outside. I couldn't have made it to a hospital even if Cheryl allowed it. She said we'd manage by ourselves. It hurt like hell – my belly still cramps when I think of Leo – but it was an easy birth." She lets out a laugh. "Nature likes fourteen-year-old mothers."

Tegan comes back with a tray of hot chocolates. She puts them on Imo's desk to cool and props herself on the edge of the desk next to Riku. They fill her in on Amber's revelation.

"But are you sure it's that child?" she asks. "Couldn't Cheryl have had her own in the meantime? They seem close."

To Imo's surprise, it's Phoenix who answers, not Amber. She inhales and shakes her head. "I saw Jane Brown's medical history. I was ashamed for intruding and didn't read it all. I saw she'd had fertility treatment but didn't realize it hadn't been successful."

Tegan's eyes narrow. "And you didn't tell us?"

Imo glares too, but her anger is gone as swiftly as it arrived. If they'd suspected that Cheryl was childless, would they have got on to Amber's abduction sooner? Probably the reverse. They might have dismissed the mother from the Freshers' Fair as the wrong Jane Brown and looked elsewhere for Cheryl. Before she can say anything, their attention switches to Amber as she continues speaking. Her voice is quiet, just above a murmur, as if she's recounting the story to herself.

"I fell in love." A fat tear rolls down her face. "The moment I saw her little bud nose, her downy head, her tiny feet." She wipes her eyes. "But Cheryl said I wasn't thinking straight. It was the hormones talking. I couldn't raise a child given my instability. And she knew all about that; I'd told her the stuff I got up to at the bridge. She said I should go home and tell my family I'd made the whole thing up. She'd bring the baby home as her own in a few weeks. I'd get the best of both worlds: I'd be the teenage auntie next door who could see the baby every day, but Cheryl would get the hassle of sleepless nights and nappies."

Tegan passes a mug to Amber. She takes a sip of the chocolate and hands it back. "So I went home and told my mum I'd lied about being pregnant. Our relationship died that day. The only thing that stopped me running away was knowing Cheryl would be back soon with Leonie. But when she came home, she didn't want me near. I had to pester her to let me visit or hold my baby. And the whole time Jade and my mum were devastated I'd faked a pregnancy."

She takes a breath. The top of her bony chest is visible at the gaping neck of the borrowed nightshirt. Imo sees the rapid rise and fall.

"Then one day I went round." She swallows. "Walked next door and noticed her car was gone. Deep down, at that moment, I just knew that I would never see Leonie again. I ran into the garden, climbed over the fence and banged on the windows. Screamed. But inside the place was empty. Deserted. Cheryl was gone. Cleared out when Leonie was two months old. I had a breakdown. Mum did her best, but I think after everything I'd done, she thought I might be faking again. I know Jade did."

Imo remembers Jade's kindness to the waitress who dropped a glass and decides that was the real Jade. How it must have killed her to sever all bonds of sympathy and trust for her sister. Their shattered relationship is another repercussion of Cheryl's crimes.

"I had no one – not even the bridge crowd. I'd had to tell Danno his baby was born dead. Told him it was a boy, because I couldn't say a girl, couldn't say Leonie. I crushed the last bit of hope out of Danno's empty, nothing life. I hurt him more than his stepfather's punches ever did." She grips her arm and her knuckles turn white. "I tried to end it once because of what I said. If Verity hadn't stopped me, I'd have thrown myself off the bridge." She hunches over and rubs her face as if trying to blot out the memory.

"It took me two years to pull myself together and return to school. I was as back to normal as I was ever likely to be when I came here. And then I saw her, handing out parenting leaflets at the Freshers' Fair. And I saw Leonie." She gasps for breath.

"We saw her too," Imo says quietly. "She's beautiful."

"That's why you froze when we were in that aisle," Phoenix says. "I couldn't work out what you'd seen. No wonder you bolted."

"I thought I'd faint if I stayed there. Or that Leonie would fade away like a mirage. I must have walked round the outside of the Great Hall ten times, trying to work out what to do. Then Cheryl came out. I watched her put Leonie into another mum's car and wave goodbye. I should have gone after Leonie, but I was so angry that I followed Cheryl home to confront her."

"How did you follow her if you were on foot?" Tegan asks.

"I flagged down a taxi that was dropping students off. I paid Hamid, the driver, extra not to tell anyone where he took me."

Imo rubs her forehead. All this time Hamid knew where

Amber went and said nothing, not even when he dropped them in Victoria Lane yesterday. Should she admire his discretion, or wish she'd offered him more money? Could he have been bought twice? They'd never know.

"What happened next is only just coming back to me. I've had blackouts, but I remember it now. Cheryl must have seen us following her. She was waiting on her driveway when I got out. Smiling, friendly. Invited me in for coffee, said Daisy would be back later after a Wacky Warehouse party with a friend. Even though she'd given my baby a different name, I thought it was going to be all right. We sat at her breakfast bar while she told me about Daisy and showed me photos on her phone. It was the happiest I'd felt in years. I was going to see my baby again. We'd make a new start. I knew I couldn't bound into Leonie's life and claim her as my own, but I could see her. Be the jolly friend who takes her to feed the ducks in the park and lets her get a refill at the ice-cream factory." She glances at Imo, a look of expectation in her eyes. Does she want Imo to say that could have worked? A renewed friendship with the woman who stole her baby?

Imo can only respond with a wistful smile. "What happened next?"

"After the coffee I started to feel woozy. Everything became a blur. I thought it must be the excitement. Euphoria at finding Leonie. Only later – when I was down *there* – did it dawn on me. Cheryl had drugged my drink. She asked if I'd like to see Daisy's room and pointed to a door next to her kitchen. I was a bit wobbly on my feet, but she told me to go first. The last thing I remember is falling down a concrete staircase and blacking out."

"That explains your head injury," Phoenix says. "Don't touch," she adds when Amber puts her fingers to her head.

"So she kept you locked in that cellar since, when was it, the first Tuesday in Freshers' Week?" Tegan shakes her head. "Raving psycho."

Amber asks what day it is and Imo says it's Friday.

"I was there more than a week?"

Imo and Phoenix exchange a glance. An unspoken agreement passes between them and they don't tell Amber she was there for sixteen days. Not yet.

"But what did she hope to achieve?" Tegan paces the bedroom floor. "I'm guessing she brought you water and occasional bits of food to keep you alive, so what was her end game?"

"I don't think she had one," Amber says. "She never said a word to me after I came round. She left water, crisps and soup, but wouldn't answer my questions. When I got angry and tried to press her, she stayed away until I ached with thirst. When she came back she had one bottle of water and no food. I kept quiet after that so she'd feed me. I think the gaps between her visits grew longer."

"Psycho," Tegan says again. She goes to the window and looks out, hugging her elbows.

"You have to go to the police," Riku says. He's still leaning on Imo's desk with his arms folded. Everyone looks at him; he's been so quiet they've forgotten he's there. "They can get your baby back. DNA will prove it."

Amber shakes her head. "I've thought about that – I've had time to think of little else. There'd be a court case and Cheryl might lose custody, but it wouldn't mean that they'd give Leonie to me, not with my track record. And I couldn't expect my mother to look after another child after the grief I've caused her. If I go to the police, Leonie will end up in care. That would be worse than leaving her with the only mother she knows."

A gloomy silence descends. Even Imo can see a depressing logic in what she's said.

But Tegan wheels round. "You don't believe that." Her voice is hard. "A criminal for a parent. Is that what you want for her? I know about that, and believe me, it's always bad."

Amber shrinks against Imo, sobbing. "What does it matter? I'll never find her again."

Looking over Amber's shoulder, Imo catches Tegan's eye. She senses they're thinking the same thing. She clears her throat. "Don't get your hopes up, but we might know where she is."

Chapter 67

Tegan

The taxi to the station is not driven by Hamid. Luckily for him, as Tegan intends to kick out his headlights for keeping quiet. No one gets away with lying to Tegan Parry, and Amber could have died thanks to him.

They board the first available intercity to Paddington. Amber is still shaking like an addict in withdrawal. It works in their favour when a middle-aged couple take one look at her and vacate a table for four. Tegan occupies the seat by the window and Imo leads Amber to the two seats opposite. A fat woman claims the fourth seat before Phoenix can get to it. She and Riku remain by the carriage doors.

Tegan presses against the cold train window to disconnect her thigh from the outsized woman glued to her Kindle in the seat and a half beside her. Tegan texts Phoenix: Fifty Shades? Phoenix gives a lacklustre smile. Clearly too wired for humour. Opposite's true for Tegan; a few wisecracks are her only way to stay out of the bricking-it zone.

Amber wakes with a start. Her eyes are pinpricks and her forehead is slick with sweat. Even the fat woman looks up. As

Amber's teeth chatter, Imo strokes her hair and gradually she settles and sleeps again. By the time they pull into the terminus, she's deeply asleep. The carriage empties around them. Imo shakes Amber's shoulder, whispers in her ear, pats her knee, but she doesn't stir.

Tegan claps her hands. "Wake up, sleepy head."

Amber cowers in her seat. "I'm sorry, I'm sorry."

"It's okay. You're safe now." Tegan strokes her arm, ashamed that she's startled her. Amber's eyes resemble Tegan's mother's when her father had one of his moods. For the first time, she's completely convinced that they're doing the right thing. The larger-than-life Amber of Freshers' Week has been reduced to a shrivelled wreck. They have to get Leonie away from Jane Brown.

"We're getting a taxi to Ealing," she tells the others when they reach the concourse. "I'm paying."

A cold wind blows outside the station and several people head for the taxi rank. Tegan manages to elbow their way to a mini-bus taxi. Adopting her Welshest persona, Tegan sits beside the driver and distracts him with inane conversation. Hoping he won't notice Amber's distressed cries in the back as she tosses and turns in her sleep.

They hit traffic. Even though the driver uses taxi lanes and rat runs, it's 5 p.m. before they get to Ealing. He pulls up in the service road in front of Jane's apartment block. Tegan hands over the money as Imo and Riku help Amber out of the back.

"We're here," Imo says gently.

Amber gets out of the car and strides towards the building, but the strong wind stops her in her tracks. She loses her breath and collapses against Imo. Tegan takes her arm and helps Imo get her to the entrance as the wind gets stronger. Dark clouds are beginning to form above them.

Before Tegan can stop her, Imo reaches for the doorbell panel. But instead of ringing Jane's bell and giving her a head start, she presses the buzzer for Flat 416. The pensioner. *Good*, thinks Tegan, *she's learning*.

"State your business," a reedy voice says.

"My name's Imogen. I came the other day to see your neighbour. Do you know if she's back?"

"I heard a kiddie crying this morning."

"Leonie," Amber gasps.

"What's that?" The man sounds suspicious.

Tegan takes charge. "Can you buzz us in so we can surprise her?"

"You're the dog whisperer. How are you, love?"

"If you let me in, we can have a chat."

There's a crackle and then the door clicks open. They bundle inside, sheltering from the wind. The old man is in the hallway when they emerge from the lift onto the fourth floor. He greets Tegan as if she's a long-lost granddaughter.

"Come in, come in. I've put the kettle on." He gestures towards his open front door.

"We're short of time," Tegan says, but feels bad for having to disappoint him.

His face falls, but he turns to Riku, apparently resolved to make the best of his last chance at human contact. "Which one's your girlfriend then? They're all smashers." He chuckles until he has a closer look at Amber, who is leaning heavily against Imo. "Is she ..."

"Jetlag," Tegan says. "Back from a round-the-world trip: India, China, South Korea."

The man's face hardens. "My brother died at Imjin River."

"That must have been awful for your family." Tegan adopts what she hopes is a sympathetic tone as she edges towards Jane's door with her credit card in her hand. Trust her to have said Korea. Phoenix picks up on what she's doing and steps between her and the old man.

"Such a terrible waste of lives," she says, keeping his attention away from Tegan.

306

But before Tegan can use her card, there's a click as a key turns in Jane's lock and a bolt is drawn across.

"Eighteen Chinese to every one of ours," the old man says.

Amber continues to doze on Imo's shoulder, unaware that Jane must have barricaded herself inside. Tegan makes eye contact with Riku and he gets the message. He goes to stand in front of the locked door and leans away from it.

"Only twenty made it back alive." The old man gives a sad shake of his head.

"A tragedy." Phoenix nods in sympathy.

Tegan keeps her eyes on Riku.

There's a thump-thump and a crashing clank as Riku's foot connects with the door. Everyone jumps, except Amber who is still dozing. The door breaks loose of its frame, wood splintering.

The old man stares at Riku for a moment, then starts to wheeze. "What ... what do you want?" he pants.

When Imo and Phoenix attempt to comfort him, he backs away. Distracted by their desire to calm him down, they don't notice when what's left of Jane's front door scrapes against the floor and opens. Riku suddenly doubles over, yelping in pain. For one terrifying moment Tegan thinks he's been stabbed. But it's a knee to the groin. Jane Brown appears in the doorway, her eyes blazing. She darts past them with the child in her arms. Runs down the hall and clatters through the fire escape at the end.

"Leonie!" Amber is wide awake now and lumbers after them. Imo goes with her, still holding onto Amber's arm.

"Let's go down in the lift. We can head them off," Phoenix shouts and presses the elevator call button.

Tegan pauses, turning to the old man. "This is not what it looks like," she tells him, but he hastens into his flat and bolts the door.

Tegan sees the lift descend with Phoenix and Riku inside. Too late. She'll have to take the fire escape. But when she reaches the stairwell, a sound makes her stop. A metal door clanks shut above her and a realization settles in her gut. Jane hasn't run downstairs; she's gone up to the roof garden. Tegan stares up the steps. If Imo and Amber have chased her there, they'll be facing her on their own. Riku and Phoenix have gone the wrong way.

Chapter 68

Tegan

Heart pounding, Tegan mounts the fire escape. The steps are
steep – designed for rushing down, not up. She struggles up to
the top and wrestles with the heavy door. Through the grubby
window she can see the roof garden, plants blowing around in
the wind. She forces the handle down hard and hears a click.
Pulls the door open and, when the gap's wide enough, she slips
through and the door slams behind her.

A blast of cold air knocks her back and she has to catch
her breath. She must have got it wrong. They're not here. All
she can see is a wooden trellis, the size of a football net, fixed
into a raised flowerbed, built up with railway sleepers. A
magnificent yellow climbing rose fills the trellis. This must be
the old man's pride and joy. He mentioned his roof garden on
their last visit.

She's about to go down again, when the wind changes direction
and carries a woman's voice. Tegan creeps along the flowerbed
until she can see four figures on the far side of the vast, open
roof space. Imo and Amber huddle together against the wind
with their backs to her.

Beyond them, in the corner, where two sides of the perimeter wall meet, is Jane. With the child on her hip, she uses her free hand to push a garden table to the wall on her right. When she's positioned it, she strokes the child's back, but keeps her eyes on Amber and speaks. Tegan edges closer to hear her above traffic sounds.

"You should have stayed away," she says. "We were doing fine. Three years fine. This isn't helping anyone. Least of all yourself." She spots Tegan. "Perhaps you can make your friends see sense," she calls. "Get them off here. It's dangerous."

As she talks, she comes forward to a wooden picnic bench that's been knocked over. Taking hold of a leg, she drags it awkwardly back to her corner. She swaps the child to her left side to get a better hold on the bench.

Tegan raises her palms submissively and joins Imo and Amber. The three watch as Jane rights the bench and pushes it lengthways to the end of the table, creating a barricade for her and the child between the garden furniture and the back wall. The wind howls across the concrete roof and Tegan folds her arms against the cold.

Jane speaks again. "What will your mother think of you, Amber, if she finds out you lied again?" She sounds like a middle-class mummy reprimanding a naughty child. She even looks the part: swinging ponytail, cropped trousers, moccasins, blue and white striped sailor sweater.

Amber's breathing is heavy and she rests her weight against Imo. Despite Jane's barricade, Amber seems to be the one cornered. The perimeter wall is six-foot high, bottom half brick, top half railings. You couldn't topple by accident, but a humiliated, half-starved Amber might find the determination to climb and jump. Didn't she tell them she nearly went off the Chadcombe Bridge?

Jane presses the child against her chest. "It's too cold for Daisy. You need to go, so I can bring her down." She looks behind her, at the darkening sky. "Before it starts to rain."

The child's eyes are wide. She seems to be trying to pull away but Jane holds her still.

The wind stings Tegan's ears and her hair swirls in front of her face. Her phone vibrates with a text from Phoenix: Lost them. Where are you? She keeps the phone out, unsure. Tell her what's happening? And Riku – if he's recovered from Jane's attack – might come thundering up. There'd be no telling what would happen. But say nothing, and she's alone with only Imo to help end this nightmare. All colour has drained from Imo's face and she keeps her eyes dead ahead, away from the perimeter wall, her hand trembling. Tegan remembers Imo's fear of heights.

"I saved you, Amber," Jane says. "Why couldn't you *stay* saved? Why throw away everything I gave you? Go home. There are other universities. Forget this ever happened."

Amber sinks deeper into Imo's shoulder. Stiffly – as if trying to avoid sudden movements – Imo wipes her friend's tears with the sleeve of her hoodie.

A gust of wind buffets them and Jane has to take half a step backwards. "Go now, Amber, there's a good girl," she says, her voice soothing. "You have to leave, before anyone gets hurt."

Amber hesitates, shivering. Tegan's finding the cold hard to take, but the emaciated girl must be risking hypothermia. She holds her breath, willing Amber to accept Jane's words, so they can all get back in the warm building.

After an age, Amber nods weakly and turns towards the rose trellis, still leaning against Imo. Amber's shoulders are hunched – the stance of a beaten puppy. Tegan feels outraged, but she'll wait to tell Jane Brown as much when they're back at ground level. She senses Jane still believes she's behaving like a normal mum and will bring her daughter safely down once Amber is out of the way.

The wind brings the first spots of rain, hard and icy on Tegan's face. She turns, mentally shooing Amber and Imo past the trellis. With any luck they can be off the roof before it buckets down.

"Mummy, can we go now?" says a small voice.

Suddenly everything changes.

Chapter 69

Tegan

They spin round to the little sound and see the child's anxious face gazing up at Jane.

Whether it's the word Mummy or just hearing the child, something triggers Amber. She stands up straight. "Who's she speaking to, Cheryl? She'll always know it's not you."

Jane gives a shrug and a smile, probably meant to show Amber's words don't hurt, but she holds the child closer. A damp strand of hair has come loose from her ponytail. She brushes it out of her eyes as the rain gets stronger. Her tone rational, she turns to Tegan with a smile. "Bring her home. She needs rest."

Tegan takes Amber's arm and prepares to steer her to the exit, but a wave of anger hits her. All she thinks is: how can she let this woman tell her what to do? After everything she has done, after the lives she's ruined. She's a psycho not an earth mother.

"Whose fault is it that she needs rest?" she snaps. "We're only up here because of you." Her grip on Amber loosens and Amber lunges for Jane. Tegan's insides churn. What the hell has she done?

Thank God Imo clings on, anchoring Amber by her side as she struggles across the roof towards Jane.

"Why did you do it?" Amber yells. "Why steal my baby?"

For a second, Jane's face twists with fury. She covers the child's ears between her hand and her chest.

"You came to me. A snivelling, doped-up little tart. Scared of what Mummy would say. You jumped at the chance I offered you. We had an agreement. You were all for it."

"I was fourteen." Amber is still resisting Imo's grip and edging closer to the bench. She raises an arm to shield her eyes from the icy rain.

"Exactly. I'd longed for a child for years. What did an idiot teenager like you know about motherhood?"

"You knew I'd changed my mind. But you dumped me, three days after giving birth, at the train station in Derbyshire and made me travel home without her. *Three days.*"

"You're remembering it all wrong." Her composure restored, Jane stands the child on her bench. "I'm the one who's suffered. Always looking over my shoulder. Always having to move on. You've been all right for three years, haven't you? You'll get over it again." She says something else, but the fierce wind whips it away and all Tegan can hear are Amber's sobs. The sounds of the streets below – a siren wailing, a barking dog – and the drumming of rain against the roof.

It comes down harder. Imo adjusts the hood of her sweatshirt and pulls the hoodie she's lent Amber over her friend's head, even though she now seems oblivious to the deteriorating weather. Tegan turns up her collar, but it's useless. The rain pelts the roof garden and bounces up like daggers, sharp and wet against her ankles.

"You can run as many times as you like," Amber shouts. "But I'll always find you. I'm the living proof of the lie you live every day of your life. Of her life." She points at the child. The little girl's body is shaking and her face is hidden in Jane's sweater. It looks like she's sobbing.

"You want proof?" Jane shakes her head dismissively. "Who

does she snuggle up to for a bedtime story? Who does she run to when she comes out of crèche? Who does she cry for when her tummy hurts?" She gently turns the child to face them and rests her hands on her shoulders. "This is *my* daughter, Daisy." The child's eyes look red and swollen against her chalk-white skin.

Tegan swallows and texts a reply to Phoenix: Roof.

The dog is still barking. Traffic noise fades behind more sirens and the relentless rain.

"*Hush, little baby, don't you cry.*" Jane climbs on the bench beside the child. She starts to murmur a lullaby, stroking her wet hair. Her voice remains calm but her eyes are knives aimed straight at Tegan. "This is your fault. I warned you. Twice. But you didn't listen."

The damage to her car. It wasn't Marlon, or Riku or Phoenix. "You're deranged," she shouts, her voice battling against the deluge.

Without warning, Amber throws her weight forward, causing Imo to stagger after her. Tegan grabs Amber's other arm. Her heart booms, loud-pounding in her ears. She's not sure she can hold her. Despite her weakened physical state, Amber has the strength of a lioness protecting her young.

Another text comes in. Still clinging onto Amber, Tegan twists her hand to see it, wiping the wet screen with her thumb. Police here. Old man called them. Tegan's breathing increases. It's doubtful the police will get up here in time. Amber's rage will blow at any second.

"What about when Leonie's older and disobeys you?" Amber shouts. "What then? Lock her in a cellar?"

Jane shakes her head, tone still reasonable, patronizing. "I helped you. For your own good."

"You helped yourself," Amber shouts. The sodden shoulders of the sweatshirt press on her fragile frame. "You turned my mother and sister against me. You made me destroy their trust."

The child stands on the bench and stares down at them blankly. Shivering. Her hair sticks to her scalp in coils and her lips are blue with cold. *Stay blank, kid, blank.* Tegan wills her not to make another sound. If Leonie speaks again, there's no knowing what Amber will do.

Behind them, the fire exit door clangs open and a moment later a policewoman appears around the rose trellis. Middle-aged, bulky in her stab vest, sensible eyes. Tegan gives a sigh of relief. The first time she's been pleased to see a cop.

Still balancing on the bench, Jane picks up the child. "We're fine. Stay where you are. I've got this covered," she says, like one colleague to another. She takes a step towards the table.

"No!" Amber shouts.

Chapter 70

Tegan

Tegan tightens her grip on Amber's shoulder. Or at least she tries; numb with cold, she can no longer feel her fingers. How high up are they? Fourth floor, no fifth … a thirty-five-foot drop at least. Her throat clogs with fear.

"On the roof," the policewoman speaks into her crackling radio. She raises her hands in a calming gesture and calls out: "What's the little girl's name?"

"Leonie," Imo says.

"Daisy," Jane corrects her.

The child bursts into fresh tears.

At a loss, the policewoman looks at Tegan.

"Call her Daisy. The woman is Jane or Cheryl." The police officer looks more bewildered. "Try both," Tegan suggests, helping the police with their enquiries. Another first.

"Jane, love, can you come down for me?" The officer edges forward. A solid presence, apparently unmoved by the driving rain and wind. "Daisy's crying."

How far is it to the wall? Maybe six feet, Tegan thinks. Could they make it to her in time to stop her from jumping?

Jane lifts the child to her face, as if examining her for signs of distress. She parts her soaking fringe to kiss her forehead.

"Please, Jane ... Cheryl?" The officer keeps up eye contact – steady, composed, conflict-trained.

Jane's hold on the child loosens and it looks as if she's going to let her slip from her arms onto the bench. Amber sees it too and relaxes under Tegan's grip.

But at the last second, Jane's eyes drift to Amber. Her calm demeanour vanishes. She hauls the child onto her hip and steps from the bench onto the table.

Tegan and Imo wrestle with Amber, struggling to keep their footing on the slippery painted concrete.

"Don't come near me," Jane shouts. She takes three steps along the table to reach the wall. Behind her is nothing but the blackened heavens and pouring rain. Tegan's stomach clenches.

Jane's free hand grabs the railings on the upper half of the wall and she steps onto the lower, brick half. She lifts the child but she slips. Her weight continues forward and the child slams into the metal rails. She yells in pain and begins to cry again.

"My baby." Amber breaks free of Imo and Tegan, dashes forward and clambers onto the bench. The policewoman shouts and runs towards Amber.

With her back towards them, Jane places her right foot further along the rail. Turns to face them, mascara streaking her cheeks. "You're not getting her."

The policewoman stops a few metres from the bench and speaks into her radio. Her voice is drowned by the rain drumming on the surface of the table.

"Amber," Imo shouts. "Don't."

Amber's tuned out. Her eyes locked on the crying child. She gulps for air, her physical frailty catching up with her. Tegan approaches the bench cautiously and holds out a hand. But Amber recovers and moves closer to the table.

Balancing with her feet apart, Jane sits Leonie on the top of the railing. The child stares down through the falling rain to the street below and screams. She turns and buries her head into Jane's chest.

"Please, God," Tegan whispers. Panic rising and then free-falling inside her. Panic on top of panic. If Jane lets go, the child will …

The policewoman stares open-mouthed, arms raised. Why doesn't she *do* something? Tegan would, if she could for the life of her think what. But making a grab for Amber won't help. Dominos. Toppling. Is this how it's going to end? Tegan braces herself and looks away.

"Amber, come down," Imo pleads again, her teeth chattering. "You're making things worse."

But Amber's in a different space, everything a vacuum between her and the child. She climbs onto the table.

Tegan clutches her chest. Another two, three steps and Amber's fingertips will reach the railing. What then?

Jane kisses the child, muttering into her hair, "Mummy loves you, Mummy loves you." A farewell? Tegan feels sick.

Amber's feet have stopped advancing but her upper body is lolling, veering. Any loss of balance could send her careering into Jane. Like an archer pulling back a bow, she leans away, ready to fly forward. Tegan can't watch.

"This isn't right," Imo yells suddenly. "Amber, think."

Amber hesitates. "Shut up, Imogen."

"Let me tell you about *my* family." Imo runs forward and screams, her voice hoarse with the effort. "You have to listen."

Amber inches closer to the wall. "Don't come near me."

Imo takes a shaky breath and climbs onto the bench. Her face is marble, the fear of heights plain to see. "You're better than this, Amber. Let me explain."

"Fuck off, Imogen. Get away from me."

Amber stumbles. Tegan stands below the table, holding out her hands.

On the bench, Imo moves towards them, arms out like a novice tightrope walker. "Listen, Amber," she says. "You've found her. Come down, or lose her forever."

A gust of wind rattles the trellis behind them, ripping off petals and leaves. Something hits Imo's face and she wobbles. The drop off the bench is less than two feet, but Tegan can see the terror in her eyes.

Imo regains her balance and wraps her arms around herself. "Do you want to go back? To the constant pain that greets you every morning?"

"Don't you dare," Amber shrieks and takes another step closer to the wall. The child screams again and tries to wriggle free, but Jane's grip is firm.

"Don't come any closer," Jane shouts. "I'm warning you."

Tegan wills Imo to shut it, but in a calm voice she carries on. "Pain that stays with you all day, follows you to the canteen. Whispers in your ear during lectures, shadows you at nightclubs. Taunts you when you go to bed and invades every dream."

Clutching her ears, Amber rocks from side to side, as if trying to dislodge a thought. "Stop," she whispers.

"My sister went missing in February. She might never be found. But your precious girl is right here." Imo climbs onto the table. Two feet away from Amber.

Amber stops moving. She turns to Imo. So does Tegan. What the hell is this? Tears stream down Imo's frightened face. What sister? Suddenly Imo's erratic behaviour makes sense. It's one thing to mourn the dead, but the lost? For a moment no one moves. The only sound Tegan can hear is her own heartbeat.

A change comes over Amber's face. A light behind her eyes flickers with a clarity that's been missing since they found her in the cellar. Maybe since Tegan has known her. She takes the three steps towards Imo and hugs her. They stand for a moment, sobbing into each other's arms, as the rain pours down.

Tegan helps them onto the bench and then the ground. The

320

policewoman produces a foil blanket and places it around Amber's shaking shoulders.

"This is my fault," Amber tells her. "Please take care of the child."

Imo, putty-faced and unsteady on her feet, leads Amber towards the fire exit. "Good girl. Keep moving," she whispers, her voice sounding old. "Don't look back."

More police file past them onto the roof. They fan out around the edge and surround Jane, moving quickly through the rain. Jane pauses for a long moment and stares down at them. She looks into the street below at the moving traffic and Tegan holds her breath. But the fight dies in her eyes at the sight of the officers. She lifts the child off the railing and passes her down to the female officer. She holds her gently against her padded clothing and reassures her in a quiet voice. Two policemen guide Jane firmly along the table and bench. They keep hold of her arms when she's back on the ground, and one of them takes out a pair of handcuffs.

Tegan is shivering uncontrollably now and she turns to catch up with Imo and Amber on the fire escape. They meet another police officer on the stairs.

"All yours," Tegan tells him, though she's not sure what the hell's just happened. He says he'll take their statements on the ground floor.

"This is Amber Murphy," Imo slurs, sounding dazed. "Leonie's mother."

Chapter 71

Friday 18 November (Five Weeks Later)

Phoenix

Weighed down by a bin bag of juggling props, Phoenix walks beside Riku. They've pooled quite a collection between them: balls, beanbags, hoops. With his unicycle over one shoulder, Riku carries a new sketchpad under the other arm.

Pitch dark, no streetlamps on the shortcut to the student union building. They don't want to use the main road in case someone sees them in their full make-up and it spoils the effect.

Riku adjusts the weight of the unicycle and ploughs on.

It's been icy drizzle for days. She'd have still practised outside though, like her parents always did, but Riku's a light-weight. They've rehearsed in the long hallway of their flat every night, banning Tegan and Imo from watching. And they've developed quite an act: juggling, unicycling, acrobatics, taekwondo. Not good enough for the circus – minimal risk – but fun. At least that's what Keren reckons. It's her idea to have them entertaining the partying students. Phoenix feels a prickle of nerves. She doesn't want to let Keren down; a lot's happened since she first met her at the LGBTQ stand at the Freshers' Fair.

When they reach the student union entrance, Riku halts and grips her arm. "What if they find out I'm straight?"

"It might be Pride Night but it's not compulsory," Phoenix replies, trying to keep her tone civil. Has she spent the last month practising with someone she hardly knows at all? Then she sees the grin on his face. She play-slaps him. "Wind-up merchant."

He holds up his hand and they high-five.

Keren greets them. She hugs Riku. "Thanks for coming. They're going to love it. I'll show you where to put your stuff." She turns to Phoenix. Her eyes sparkle their usual beautiful blue.

They hold hands as Keren leads the way to the stage door.

Tegan

Tegan comes off the phone to Kanya and stays on her bed. Another snatched call. Although the nanny was only there for the journey with Marlon, her father's been home a lot. Keeping an eye on Dylan since Tegan borrowed him. Kanya's paying the price – and Tegan flinches at what that cost might be – but she always seems thrilled to hear Tegan's voice and to let Dylan speak to his sister.

Jane Brown is currently on remand on charges of kidnap and false imprisonment. If Tegan, Imo and Phoenix can find a missing student and reunite her with her lost child, maybe they can do something to help Kanya. Especially now that Marlon has skipped bail and the country, but her father hasn't replaced him. Tegan's still looking over her shoulder – it's an ingrained habit she may never kick – but there's never one of her dad's lackeys in view.

Kanya mentioned the postcard from Montreux tonight and Tegan lied that it was pinned on her noticeboard. Does Ivor in

Flat 7 still have it? She takes a breath and heads downstairs, mentally preparing for a nerd overdose.

But it's not nerdy Ivor who answers the door. It's no one nerdy at all. It's the black guy from the parents' barbecue. Still beautiful. Her heart flutters, but he's also still a dad. Her mood plummets.

"Can you get Ivor for me?" she says, haughty, dismissive. "He has my postcard."

He cocks his head on one side. "Greetings from Montreux? Are you Tegan?"

"You've read it?" How dare he?

"It's been on our fridge for weeks."

"*Your* fridge. You live here?" How could she have missed that?

He nods. "I'm a third year, away on placements mostly. And you must live upstairs. With your son."

"That wasn't my son. I'm single." Why is she telling him that, offering herself up to a sleazy married man? She switches to snooty cow. "If you could get my card, I'll be on my way."

His eyes linger on her chiffon blouse, tucked in at the waist. "Big night out?"

"Pride Night," she says defiantly.

"Me too."

That's thrown her. A gay dad. Didn't see that one coming. "Is Ivor babysitting your kids?"

"I'm not a parent. I was working at the bar that day." He throws back his head and laughs. The sound is rich and throaty. Sexy. "That's why I'm going to Pride Night. I do the odd bar shift at the Abbi."

"Me too," Tegan says again. She clears her throat. "I mean: I'm there to support the circus act. I'm not ..."

"Shall we walk down together?" he asks.

She shrugs and nods, her best effort at nonchalance. She was going to drive, but, hey, the exercise ...

He smiles. "I'll get your postcard."

Imogen

Imo's acne is as bad as it's ever been. Pits and peaks across her cheeks and chin. Vesuvius. Going make-up free hasn't worked so far but the skin website she's found says to allow six weeks. That's all very well if you're a hermit but she has lectures and she's promised Phoenix and Riku she'll go tonight. Maybe she can shift a few of the *Jesus Christ Superstar* tickets that Doris talked her into selling.

Bone-weary she lies down on her bed. The leaflet Jane Brown gave her is on the pillow. Step 5 to beating the blues: *Make one effort every day.* Step 6: *Avoid isolation; spend time with others.* She's got close to throwing it in the bin many times, telling herself it's disloyal to Amber to keep it. But Jane didn't write the leaflet. Whoever did, talks sense. Even on the days when the advice is too hard to take, Imo knows it's right.

True loyalty to Amber means getting well enough to face the train journey to Chadcombe to visit her. Even though Jane was arrested and Leonie taken into temporary foster care, finding Amber hasn't been the happy ever after Imo hoped for. What-if dreams of Sophia still haunt her and her mood has stayed down, sinking so low for a few days that she missed lectures. Thank the lord for David and Lauren who kept her up to date with notes from Dr Wyatt. Tegan covered Business. They've got a new Accountancy lecturer as Hennessey is on long-term sick leave.

At least her depression is out in the open now. Step 1: *Tell a friend how you feel.* David was great, said his mother had bouts. He played it down: he and his dad have learnt to deal with it. His mum always comes through, lives her life. Lauren said she couldn't see how anyone as hot and clever as Imo could get depressed. She didn't get it at all, even when Imo told her about Sophia, but her words gave Imo a tiny flicker of light in a dark week. That and letting her hold her baby girl, Sophie. Not quite Sophia. Not Sophia at all, but still …

Lauren finally admitted to meeting Amber at the start of term. Amber had seen her with her baby and made a beeline for them, trying to be friends. The mother's instinct in Lauren sensed something not right about the stranger. Amber's interest in the baby seemed somehow desperate. She spent the next two days, until Amber disappeared, trying to shake her off. That was why she denied knowing her when Imo mentioned her at the audition.

But the desperation in Amber that unnerved Lauren made her understand Imo better than anyone. When they spoke on the phone, Amber recounted Imo's symptoms right back at her. She had much to be depressed about: her father's death, her drug abuse, falling out with her family, loss of her baby.

Yet Amber is nearer to a happy end than Imo will ever be. A shadow crosses her thoughts. What chance has she got of learning to live with her loss, when she can't even grow out of acne? Maybe it's time to try the counsellor Phoenix suggested.

Amber's back at home, taking a BTEC drama course. There's talk of drama school next year but Leonie comes first. Despite Amber's fears, her family welcomed her home, begging forgiveness for not seeing what she was going through. Their lawyer thinks Amber's mother will get the custody they've applied for, as the courts have already agreed to Mrs Murphy, Amber and Jade visiting Leonie at the foster carer's.

Imo gives a big sigh. If Amber can come through all that, she can go to a Pride Night. She gets off the bed and puts on her leopard print platform boots.

The phone goes. *Not now.* She looks at the screen. Freddie? Odd, twice in two months. She wasn't expecting him to call again after the audition. *Unless …*

Barely able to get her breath, she answers. "Hello?"

Silence, then Freddie's voice: "There's been another sighting."

Acknowledgements

Thank you for reading *The Roommates*. I hope you enjoyed it.

I'd like to thank my editor Finn Cotton at HarperCollins for helping me knock the original draft into shape (a lot of knocking was needed, believe me), my agent Marilia Savvides and all at PFD for the continued support for my writing, and my copy editor Rhian McKay for her attention to detail.

Once again I'm indebted to the book bloggers and authors who've blogged, reviewed, tweeted and hosted me on their websites. Thank you to everyone who has taken the trouble to write a post about my books.

As with my previous novels, fellow writers Fergus Smith, Peter Garrett and Gillian Walker gave valuable advice on my early drafts and I thank them for their support.

Many thanks to the younger members of my family who stopped my student characters from being thirty years out of date, and to my husband Nigel for his enthusiasm, PR skills and proofreading.

If you'd like to know more about my writing and reading, please visit my website at:

https://www.rachelsargeant.co.uk/

I'm also on Twitter:
https://twitter.com/RachelSargeant3
And you can follow me on Bookbub: bit.ly/RachelSargeant
BookBubFollow
If you'd be willing to write a short review of *The Roommates*, I would love to read it.